Run AWAY

LAURA SALTERS

WITNESS
IMPULSE

An Imprint of HarperCollins*Publishers*

EPub Edition MAY 2015 ISBN: 9780062403582

Print Edition ISBN: 9780062403575

10 9 8 7 6 5 4 3 2 1

To Mum and Dad, for being great parents—
and even better friends

Acknowledgments

PERHAPS THE MOST surreal moment of this whole book-writing thing is sitting down to write these acknowledgments. And if I can get to the end without tearing up or having an emotional breakdown, I'll be downright amazed. So here goes!

First and foremost, I have to say thank you to my mum, dad, and brother. You may all tease me relentlessly about my bookish habits and strange imagination, but I know deep down you're all buzzing about the whole book deal thing. And thank you to my gran, for not really understanding what an e-book is but cheering me on anyway, and to the rest of my crazy family, for always being on hand with champagne to toast every success.

Thank you to my best friend on the planet, Victoria Chandler, and my beautiful goddaughter, Amelia. You two never fail to put a smile on my face, and I'm so grateful to have you in my life (even though every time I told you I had good news, you wished I was bearing a best friend for Millie, not signing with a superstar literary agent. But I forgive you). You're my favorites.

To the loveliest girls I could ever wish for: Nic, Hannah, and

Lauren. You've been my rocks since we could talk, and there aren't enough words for how great you are! And to Geoff, for not breaking up with me no matter how deep in my writing cave I go. You're a trooper.

To Ajita, for always supporting me, even from the other side of the world, and to Amy Leigh, for encouraging me to follow my dreams (and stop slamming my door). To Roz, for kitchen dances, Tumblr hysteria, and thinking I'm cool when I'm really, really not, and to Spike, for not laughing in my face (much) when I told you I was writing a book.

Speaking of writing a book, I've had some amazing writing support over the last couple of years, from Chloe and Nancy, the poor souls who read my first draft, to my awesome NAC friends— Sribindu, Meredith, Amanda, Ara, Kate, Jessica, Marie, and Sophia—who are there for every victory and defeat, both of which usually result in alcoholic behavior (and Nutella). I'm so excited for all of our books to be out in the world. And going back even further, a big fat thank you to Paul Brooke, for making me fall in love with English literature, even in my teen years (when it really wasn't cool to do so), and to Barbara Henderson, for making me believe that writing a book was actually something I could do.

A very special mention has to go to Kelly, for digging me out of too many plot holes to count, and to Karen, for digging me out of just as many life holes. You're both wonderful, and neither I nor *Run Away* would be where we are without you.

Then there's the incredible team of professionals I've had behind me at HarperCollins— they've helped *Run Away* become what it is today. My wonderful editor, Emily Krump, has made me more enthusiastic about my own story than I ever thought I could be, and her amazing eye has transformed it beyond my wildest expectations. Emily Homonoff, my brilliant publicist, believes my relentless enthusiasm makes me a "firecracker" (which I love!), and the fantastic design team at HarperCollins created a cover I couldn't possibly love any more.

And now we have the amazing team at New Leaf Literary & Media Inc. There's Joanna Volpe, who's been so kind in welcoming me to the New Leaf family; Dave Caccavo, who helped me navigate the minefield that is the IRS and HMRC (and managed not to tear his hair out at my incessant questions, so kudos); Kathleen Ortiz, who handled UK submissions beautifully; and the super-talented assistants—Danielle, Jaida, and Jackie—who are incredibly helpful and so lovely to work with. A special shout-out goes to Jess Dallow, who's become a great friend over the last few months. You're all wonderful.

I've saved the best for the last. Suzie Townsend. Where would I be without you? You took a chance on a manuscript that was so far from perfect, because you saw something in my writing that even I didn't see. You stuck with me through deep, dark revisions and brought the very best out of a story we both loved but knew needed a lot of work. You're the ultimate cheerleader, an insanely talented agent and a wonderful friend, and I'm grateful every day to have you on my side. Thank you.

I hope to have you all on my side for many years to come. But for now, it's time to hand this baby over to the readers. Enjoy!

Chapter 1

June 17, Thailand

THERE WAS ONLY *one other time in my life I'd seen this much blood.*

Or, at least, this breed of blood—not the poppy red hue of a shaving cut swirling into bathwater, or the stale maroon of a drying scab begging to be scratched. This was angry. A deep crimson syrup whose quantity betrayed its origins. This blood was a consequence of pain.

My mind whirled, stuck on a waltzer of panic.

The worst part was knowing who the blood belonged to. It belonged to the man I cared about most in the world.

Why is it always the ones I loved the most?

Like my brother. My late brother, whose own blood I'd found seeping into his bedroom carpet only four months earlier. It had squelched beneath my feet like a soggy sponge. The sound still haunts my dreams.

My stomach lurched. This couldn't be happening. Not again. Someone had to be playing some sort of practical joke, albeit a sensationally cruel one. He was gone. How could he be gone? How could there possibly be this much blood? I'd only seen him thirty minutes earlier, when I told him exactly how I felt. When he gazed at me through his sad brown eyes and uttered the last words I'd ever hear him say: "I'm sorry."

I stepped back from the crimson pools. The bedroom started spinning. My thoughts were bleeding into each other. Splotches of red seeped into my vision. Think, Kayla. Focus. This cannot really be happening. Not again.

There was no body and no indicators of foul play. No smashed windows, no screaming, no sirens wailing in the distance to tend to the crime scene. Just blood. Lots and lots of blood.

But somewhere deep within my gut I knew the truth. My body knew. My knees buckled. I fell to the floor, causing a ripple in the red lagoon rapidly forming on the tiled floor. Sam's blood. The sticky air was difficult to inhale, and I could feel myself losing consciousness. Good. Maybe I'd wake up and realize none of this had ever happened.

But it had happened.

Sam was gone. And somehow, it was all my fault.

DETECTIVE NIRAN SAOWALUK handed Kayla a damp cloth.

She leaned back in the hard plastic chair, laying the washcloth across her forehead and closing her eyes. One of the worst things about being a murder suspect, it seemed, was being made to remain in a sundress soaked in your best friend's blood. The fabric was beginning to stiffen as the blood dried rapidly in the heat. But judging by the look on the detective's face, the damp cloth had already pushed the limits of his patience. A cold shower and a change of clothes were out of the question.

Not that it would make a difference anyway. Not that it would bring him back.

So much blood.

Sitting in the stuffy interview room of the Phuket police station, Kayla struggled to remember the exact events of the previous three hours, let alone the past three months. She couldn't focus—everything was foggy, like her memories were shrouded in a haze of fear. Her brain performed a maypole dance around each strand of thought, not truly making contact with any in particular.

It was hot. Too hot. Kayla's mouth was dry and her throat scratchy with intense thirst. The two men staring intensely at her from the other side of the table seemed agitated—after over an hour of questioning, she still hadn't spoken. She wasn't trying to be difficult, but debilitating terror had her body in a viselike grip, paralyzing her voice box and freezing her blood. *Why is this happening again?*

Despite the muggy temperature, the hairs on the nape of her neck stood on end. Goose bumps covered her tanned forearms. Everything seemed amplified. The heat, the strip lighting, the sounds of the city in the distance. Like all her senses were on high alert, anticipating danger.

She licked a bead of sweat off her upper lip. She wasn't worried about appearing suspicious through her silence. She had an alibi. Instead, she focused all of her attention on one thing: not vomiting.

So much blood.

"Fuck!" Seni, the ferret-faced interpreter, cursed. He swiveled on his heel and started pacing.

The detective didn't seem to mirror his colleague's urgency. He leaned back in his chair and dabbed at his moist forehead with a handkerchief he produced from deep within his khaki trouser pocket. He glanced at the wall clock behind him, ticking aggressively at what seemed like eight hundred decibels: it was 10:22 P.M. His stomach growled loudly, reminding Kayla that she hadn't eaten for well over twelve hours. The memory of sitting around the table eating breakfast seemed completely alien, like it didn't belong to her. She eaten overflowing bowls of chocolatey cereal and weird foreign milk with her friends, cackling hysterically at something one of them said, with absolutely no sense of premonition or dread. Weren't you meant to know instinctively when tragedy was about to strike? For the second time this year she'd been caught completely and utterly off guard. Now it felt like she'd never experience hunger again.

The lethargic ceiling fan ground clumsily to a halt, quashing any hope of cool relief once and for all. Kayla's skin prickled from the heat and the stares. Niran muttered something inaudible in Thai before rolling his eyes and rearranging his gargantuan frame in his too-small chair.

He spoke again, more clearly this time, in a staccato burst of aggressive Thai. Seni translated. "So you saw no one coming or going from your residence? No one at all?"

Kayla swallowed. "No."

"And you didn't hear anything? No sign of a struggle?"

She shook her head.

"There were droplets of blood dripped along the corridor leading to Mr. Kingfisher's bedroom. Did you not notice as you walked through the house?"

Kayla thought hard. "N-No . . . I don't think—" She trailed off as Niran cocked his eyebrow at Seni, who frowned. "I mustn't have been paying attention." She wished her cheeks would stop blushing so furiously. Her body was determined to make her look guilty.

Niran muttered something else that Seni didn't translate. Then he said, "Okay. Let's assume, for argument's sake, that you are innocent. Can you think of any other explanation for Mr. Kingfisher's . . . disappearance?"

Kayla sat up, allowing the soggy cloth to slap to the floor. Her sweaty thighs squelched against the plastic. "N-No. I can't think at all. None of this makes any sense." *What if I never get to see his dopey smile again?* She swallowed hard. *What if nobody does?* She gripped the arms of the chair, trying to steady herself. The room was swirling. Her mouth was claggy, like she'd just eaten a spoonful of peanut butter.

Seni relayed Kayla's message to Niran. It only served to anger him. His bottom lip quivered and his bulbous face reddened with rage. He thumped the table with his balled-up fist. Seni flinched. "You'll have to at least *try* to think. If you aren't guilty, and your friend is still alive, you could be wasting precious time. Time that could be spent finding him."

His sharp tone jolted the proactive part of Kayla's brain that, until now, had been overridden by dread. *This is really happening. Sam is really gone.* A fresh wave of nausea struck. The room smelled of grease and day-old bleach. *There was so much blood . . .* "Okay. Okay. I'm sorry. I'm really trying. What do you want to know?" She wrung her clammy hands together.

"Had Mr. Kingfisher been acting strangely?" Niran's voice was getting louder, more urgent.

Kayla didn't know whether to look him or Seni. She settled for the ceiling. *Don't vomit.* "In what way?"

"In any way that could be relevant to the case."

"I—I guess so," Kayla mumbled. "He hasn't been himself, really."

Seni didn't even wait for Niran to react. He used his own initiative to ask, "Why?"

Kayla closed her eyes. A fat tear slid out, despite her best efforts to hold it in. "That's the problem. I don't know."

Ignorance is bliss until there's blood involved.

After another hour of questioning, Niran granted Kayla ten minutes of fresh air. Despite his initial hostility toward her, she sensed him beginning to soften. Beginning to believe the genuine pain in her eyes belonged to a heartbroken friend, not a cold-hearted killer. Who could believe a normal young woman could do this to her best friend?

Plus she had an alibi.

Once outside, Kayla gazed up into the dark sky, the pulsating sounds of Phuket Town serving as a painful reminder of the millions of people blissfully continuing with their lives. Their mundane, boring, delightfully average lives that would never know the kind of tragedy that had struck her not once, but twice.

Why was this happening again?

And why was she not more surprised?

There was a pit forming in her stomach—a tight knot of anxiety and fear that felt all too familiar.

In fact, she wasn't sure it had ever really left.

Chapter 2

June 17, Thailand

"YOU ARE THE island and the traffic is the stream. Let it move around you."

Kayla rubbed her eyes, partly to remove any traces of sleep that might be nestled in the corners, and partly in an attempt to relieve the stinging sensation caused by the cloud of smog hovering over Bangkok. There seemed to be more cars, scooters, and motorbikes than there were people, weaving through the nonexistent lanes in a manic frenzy. Noting the bashed-up hoods and dented doors, she wasn't sure she trusted Chanarong, their native tour guide, and his advice on road safety.

Angry car horns blared in Kayla's ears. The swarms of pedestrians spilled off the packed pavements and onto the roads like ants, with no regard for the havoc they were causing the flow of traffic. But the buzz was infectious. The air was alive with the jovial sounds of old friends greeting each other, authentic Thai music jingling from stallholders' radios, and street carts flogging their spicy, fragrant-smelling fare to passersby.

Their English rep, Oliver, was still asleep at the front of the coach. He'd spent the entire journey in silence, hiding behind mirrored aviators with the pained expression of someone who was trying desperately hard not to be sick in their own mouth. Nursing a hangover, Kayla suspected. She'd heard that Khao San Road, the location of their first hostel, was a notorious party street, bustling with backpackers from around the globe. She couldn't wait.

If I can cope with partying in this heat, that is. She twirled her long, chocolate-brown hair deftly in her fingertips and fixed it in a messy bun on the top of her head. The whisper of a breeze on the back of her neck provided some relief, however subtle. She nudged the petite Asian girl next to her. She had a delicate face, caterpillar eyebrows, and skin like a porcelain doll. "I can't believe we're finally here. Are you as excited as I am?"

Zhang Qiang—a name Chanarong had clumsily mispronounced when taking the school-style register outside Bangkok International Airport—looked unfamiliar with the concept of communication. "Oh, erm, yes, very excited." She quickly buried her bespectacled face into a guidebook. *Charming.*

Someone behind Kayla tapped her right shoulder. She swiveled around to see a broad, towering figure—the lagger who'd held them up at the airport. He'd taken over an hour to get through customs. When he'd finally clambered onto the bus, he'd been met with countless sighs of impatience from his fellow ravelers. She'd almost felt sorry for him, with his bashful demeanor and apologetic half smile. Almost. "Yes?"

"On a scale of one to Saddam Hussein," he asked, "how much does everyone hate me?"

She stifled a laugh, fixing an expression of deep consideration on her face. "I'd say Osama Bin Laden. At least."

"Crikey. How do you think I can swing the trial for heinous hate crime in my favor? Reckon a round of Jägerbombs would do it?"

"Possibly. You'd have a better shot if you threw in some pizza. We might've had time to eat by now if you hadn't taken three decades to navigate airport security."

"Oops, sorry about that. I'm Sam." He extended a tennis-racket-sized hand to shake.

"Kayla. A handshake? Very formal." She shook his hand, cringing about how sweaty hers was.

"What can I say? I'm a true gentleman. I give blood and tell my mother I love her on a daily basis." Sam smiled. The papery skin around his eyes crinkled and a slight dimple appeared in his right cheek.

Praise the Lord, this one has a sense of humor. He wasn't bad-looking either, though not conventionally handsome. He was extremely tall, possibly around six-foot-five, and very broad. She'd overheard two posh guys on the bus ask him if he was a fellow rugby player. He must be, with his huge frame and crooked nose. "Nah," Sam had replied. "I have the athletic capacity of a concussed slug."

"So wh—" Sam was cut off as Chanarong began announcing who'd be sharing rooms with who. "I bet I'm with those private schoolboys. I bet you anything."

Chanarong was mid-flow, and Kayla had missed who she'd be sharing with. She struggled to hear him over the noise on the street. "All of the boys will be together, so that's Ralph, Thomas,

Daivat, Sam, Evan, and your English rep, Oliver." An eye-roll from Sam. "I'll be making some occasional appearances, usually on your day trips, and in the meantime, you'll be left in the, erm . . . capable hands of Oliver. If he ever wakes up." He laughed.

"I feel like we're on a school trip," Kayla said, turning to Sam, who was fiddling with the straps on his backpack. Despite his size, he looked awkward and uncomfortable with the huge contraption on his back. "Have you ever done anything like this before? Or even, I don't know, left the house?"

"Nope. First time. The sun is quite amazing," Sam retorted. Kayla grinned. Some people thought sarcasm was the lowest form of wit, but she was not one of them. Laughter, or something similar, fluttered in her belly. "Kidding, obviously. No, I'm not exactly the outdoorsy type. More of a textbooks sort of guy. Have you?"

"Nah, but I've always loved the idea of traveling. Before I booked this trip, I used to spend my days almost booking flights, reading travel blogs, researching the best hostels, that kind of thing. It's a bit surreal that I'm actually doing it." She stopped talking as a short, bosomy blonde sauntered up to them. A flash of frustration caught her off-guard—she wanted to keep chatting to Sam.

"Hi! I'm Minya. Looks like we're roomies. You're Kayla, right?" Minya was, Kayla had to admit, insanely attractive, with full cheeks, a big smile, and even bigger eyes. They were characteristics that, however jealousy-inducing, were completely unintimidating. You knew instinctively you'd like her.

"Yep, that's me," Kayla replied.

Minya sighed. "Cool. God, I can't wait for a vodka." Almost as means of explanation, she continued, "I'm Russian, what can I say?"

I like her already, Kayla thought.

"SHALL WE MEET up with the others in that bar next door? I think we should all buy outfits to wear from one of those little stalls on the street. Just for a laugh?" Minya hadn't stopped talking since they'd reached the sweltering cell of a bedroom. If awkward silence had ever been a fear of Kayla's, it wasn't now.

A girl named Ai Ling was delicately sifting through the meticulously folded contents of her backpack. She hadn't said a word to any of them, and was visibly disgusted by her surroundings.

Meanwhile, Francesca, a posh brunette whose hair was so glossy it belonged on a shampoo commercial, seemed to be embracing the grubby mattresses, cardboard walls, and completely alien vibe more wholeheartedly than any of them. "Hey Russia—can I call you Russia?—may I borrow some of that deodorant?" she said. "Mine was confiscated at airport security. I smell like a badger's ass."

"Of course. You do smell awful." The newly dubbed Russia threw the roll-on across the room, narrowing missing Ai Ling's head.

"Oh, you bitch!" Francesca cackled a deep, throaty laugh. "Thanks babe, you're a doll. Bling, do you want some? You aren't smelling too fresh either."

"My name is Ai Ling. And no, thank you."

"Oh come on, I was kidding! You smell like a bed of daisies. Or roses. Whatever. Are you coming out tonight?"

"I'm not sure. I'm pretty tired. I might just get some sleep."

"Some *sleep*?" Francesca seemed personally offended, smearing the mascara she was lathering onto her eyelashes all over her eyelids. She gaped at Ai Ling. "No! It's our first night, you have to come out. Do some bonding and all that jazz. Please, Bling!"

"It's Ai Ling. I might come out for a bit." Ai Ling was very pretty, and obviously of mixed ethnicity. Her small nose and cheeks were dusted with freckles, and her almond-shaped eyes were dark and framed with immaculately groomed eyebrows. She was perched on the edge of her bed, trying to connect to the hostel's ropey WiFi. Kayla shook her head. *Who comes away on the trip of a lifetime just to stay in the hostel and browse Facebook?*

"Leave her alone, guys," Kayla said. "She doesn't have to come out if she doesn't want to." Russia pulled a face and disappeared into the bathroom.

"No, I mean, no, it's fine, I will come out. It's fine." Ai Ling feigned bravery and plastered an unconvincing smile on her face.

Francesca had already lost interest in the Bling saga and was hastily stuffing her cosmetics case back into her rucksack. "Fuck it, I can't be bothered with makeup. It's just going to sweat off me anyway. Might as well accept that I'll be spending this whole trip ugly. Right, I need a cigarette and some booze. When Russia's finished shitting, shall we go?"

THE SUN HAD only just set, but Khao San Road was already thriving. Backpackers and travelers, locals and workers, bustled around the suspiciously discounted "designer" clothing stalls, the pavement bars and cafés pouring onto the road, and the myriad markets and minimalls. A part of Rattanakosin, one of Bangkok's oldest districts, Khao San was dotted with old shop houses and intricate temples, though exploring the region's heritage wasn't at the top of the evening's agenda.

An interesting assortment of the Escaping Grey party were sitting around a table in the aptly named Streetside Bar. The other girls had decided, as Ai Ling almost did, to sleep off their jet lag. Oliver, the utterly useless guide, was nowhere to be seen. The rest were all thirstily drinking cool pints of Chang beer. Well, all except Francesca, who had announced, "I only drink water and wine. I'm like Jesus."

They'd all laughed, and Ralph countered, "I'm the opposite. I'll put anything in my mouth."

"I'd be careful about shouting that in the middle of the street, mate," Sam said.

"Ha! Yes! People might think you mean penis!" said a scrawny Indian guy whose eyes were already glossed over after half a pint of beer.

"Sorry, I didn't catch your name?" Russia asked him.

"Daivat. Daivat Singh." He picked up her hand and planted a slobbery kiss right in the center. Russia looked baffled, but not as disgusted as one might expect.

"Basically, he's called David Smith. We've taken to calling him Dave," Ralph's wingman Thomas added, as if "Dave" wasn't sitting right next to him. Ralph and Thomas might as well have been twins, only with different hair colors. They both had tans, deliberately messy hair—Ralph's dirty blond, Thomas's vivid ginger— and were wearing Abercrombie & Fitch polo shirts and chino shorts.

"Dave! I love being Dave. I should probably be angry that you're trying to Westernize me or something. I can't work out if it's racist or not. But I love it. Dave!" He raised his glass skyward, toasting his new name, and downed the rest of his pint in one go. "Who wants another drink?"

"Yeah, all right, then. This could get messy," Russia said, following Dave's lead and polishing off her beverage. "I'll come with you to the bar."

Two hours later Russia's prophecy had been fulfilled. They had relocated to Gazebo, a bustling rooftop bar just down the road, and were borderline hysterical when a man in a fez greeted them at the door. Several of them had dropped off—Bling left in search of some food, while Ralph, Thomas and Francesca all drank themselves into oblivion and staggered back to the hostel. Russia was grinding against Dave on the packed dance floor as he clutched a bottle of beer in each hand, alternating sips from the two straws in time to the gangsteresque music.

Sam and Kayla were slumped in one of the black leather booths, pretending to be able to hear each other over the pounding bass.

"I can't feel my face," Kayla giggled.

"What?"

"I can't feel my face!"

"What?"

"I SAID, I CAN'T FEEL MY FACE!"

"All right, no need to shout." Sam grinned. "It's a very nice face, if that's any consolation. Congratulations on that."

"What?"

"CONGRATULATIONS ON YOUR FACE!"

And so the stilted conversation continued, until Bling came storming across to them, donning a much more stained dress than she had when she left. The skintight, red number was now adorned with a chow mein collage. "Some wanker threw noodles at me!"

Kayla couldn't help but laugh. "What? Why? Where? You have a chunk of vegetable on your left boob."

"At the flipping noodle stand, where do you think? It's not funny. Ugh, I didn't even get anything to eat. I hate Thailand. I hate Bangkok. I hate drunk people."

"Just suck on your dress if you're hungry, it'll taste like soy sauce," Sam suggested helpfully.

"What, just because I'm Asian you think I'm bound to like soy-fucking-sauce?"

"Well, no, but you do have it spilt over ninety-eight percent of your dress. Which is lovely by the way. Very pretty." Sam tried to fix a concerned expression on his face, but his alcohol-slackened muscles failed to cooperate.

Bling scoffed and turned on her heel, storming away toward the hostel.

"And the events we have just witnessed shall henceforth be known as the Noodlegate Scandal," Sam said earnestly.

"Are we sure what just happened was actually about noodles? The music is insanely loud. We must have misheard. Who gets that worked up over *noodles*?"

"WHAT?"

"Never mind," Kayla said, holding Sam's gaze for a fraction of a second too long.

She smiled without even realizing she had, and looked away quickly.

This wasn't part of the plan.

Chapter 3

June 24, England

WALKING OUT OF Newcastle International Airport's revolving doors, the rain soaked through Kayla's T-shirt in an instant. Everywhere she looked it was gray: gray skies, gray cars, gray roads.

What was that literary device her old English teacher used to bang on about? Pathetic fallacy? Appropriate. The headlights of cars were blurry round the edges as the drizzle-mist hybrid enveloped the car parks. The air was warm and wet—if she closed her eyes, she could easily still be in Thailand, embracing the upcoming monsoon season. But she'd never be able to return to Thailand. Not now.

After much investigation, the police had concluded that Sam's disappearance was linked to the drug debt he'd accumulated. Kayla had insisted this didn't make sense. Sam hated drugs.

But the police had found fairly damning evidence to suggest otherwise. In Sam's backpack, they uncovered a small bag of MDMA, traces of marijuana, and his wallet, which contained several tightly rolled banknotes and a credit card laced with particles of impure cocaine. A search of his mobile phone showed that Sam had been in contact with several well-known drug dealers in Phuket.

Whenever Kayla tried to make sense of any of it, her head spun. She'd never seen Sam completely out of it. He always stopped drinking early for fear of losing control. Why would he seek out drug dealers in a new city, acquire a range of illegal substances without paying for them, then snort, smoke, and swallow them in private? It didn't fit, but there was fairly conclusive evidence to the contrary.

Once the Thais had labeled it as "Self-entitled Westerner goes on a bender and gets himself in a spot of bother," they'd rapidly lost interest, and let Kayla catch the next plane back to England. They said the British police would be in touch if they needed anything more from her, but because she wasn't being charged with anything, she was free to go. She was too shell-shocked to be relieved.

She spotted her parents' Range Rover parked in the drop-off zone. She stopped and took a deep breath, mentally preparing for the onslaught of concern from her mother and up-by-the-bootstraps bravado from her dad. God, she'd love a cigarette right now. But her parents didn't know she smoked—that was just one of the many secrets she'd kept from them over the last six months. Sam, by contrast, had known everything. Both good and otherwise.

"Sweetheart! Oh Kay, come here." Martha Finch sprinted across the zebra crossing to embrace her only living child, enveloping her in a cloud of musky perfume and the vague scent of last night's whiskey. Straight, no ice.

"Hi, Mum."

"Are you okay? Oh, what am I saying, of course you're not. Gosh, you look awful. Have you slept since—you know . . ." Martha's eyebrows were tilted upward in the center like a sad-face emoticon. The damp fur on her coat felt like a dead animal against Kayla's face.

"Yes, Mum. I've been sleeping like a baby. Not a care in the world!" Kayla tried to bite back the sarcasm, but it spilled out before she could stop it. Even when she was on the verge of tears, she couldn't help but make jokes. She sniffed like a toddler, wiping her nose on her soggy sleeve.

"Of course you haven't. I am so sorry, my love, I really am. Come on, let's get you home. I'll make you a nice mug of hot cocoa. I'll even put marshmallows and whipped cream on, just how you like it. I went to Sainsbury's especially."

Martha had been a beautiful woman not too long ago. But gone were the weekly blow-dries, shiny manicures, and immaculate clothes—a long battle with alcoholism and the death of her young son had taken its toll on her appearance. Now, standing in the middle of a road and trying to comfort her bereaved daughter, she looked twenty years older. "We're just grateful it wasn't you, sweetheart. What would we do without you?"

Kayla wanted to chastise her mother for being so inconsiderate, for wishing that kind of pain on another family, but she was too exhausted. It had been a long flight. Well, a long six months. She dragged her feet along the pavement and slung her rucksack into the trunk of the car.

"All right, kiddo. Nice to see you back on home turf," Kayla's dad, Mark, greeted her on the pavement. He also looked older, more world-weary, than the last time she'd seen him. "How you holding up?"

"I've been better." She hugged him quickly—and awkwardly—then climbed into the backseat of the car, her wet hair dripping onto the leather seats. It took three attempts to shut the door behind her. She felt weak with exhaustion.

"I get that, Kayls. I do. I'm just glad you're home in one piece. What happened to Sam . . . it's a tragedy. To be honest, when you left, we were terrified something similar was going to happen to you. You were in a fragile place, emotionally, and in a dangerous country. Frankly, we're just glad—"

"Yes, Dad. I get it." Kayla turned to face the window, dodging the concerned stares in her direction through the rearview mirror. "Glad it wasn't me."

I wish I could say the same.

BERRY HILL HOUSE seemed bigger than when she'd left. Perhaps it was because she'd become used to mattress-in-a-box style hostel rooms, or maybe because everything seemed distorted and alien to her. Like she was in a House of Mirrors, except it wasn't her own reflection that was warped beyond recognition—it was everything else. One thing remained the same, though. The door to her brother's room was still locked. It always would be.

God, I miss Gabe. Her little brother, wise beyond his years, would know exactly what to say. He'd know it hurt her to hear her family so relieved that someone else's child had violently vanished. He'd talk to her for as long as she needed, and leave her alone when she needed space. He'd bring her hot cocoa just the way she liked it, but not in the patronizing, this-will-solve-everything way that her mum would. God, she missed him.

She peeked into the guest bedroom next to hers. Her nan, Iris (though Kayla had never called her that), was towel-drying her permed, silvery hair, humming a tune Kayla had never heard before. She longed to burst through the door and cuddle her. Kayla loved Nan's hugs—she wasn't spidery and frail like a lot of old ladies, who felt like they'd shatter if you squeezed too hard. She baked cakes and drank sugary tea and served up hearty servings of mince and dumplings with complete disregard to the fat content. If Kayla cuddled her now, Nan would smell the same as she always had: burnt toast and lavender. The homeliest smell Kayla could imagine. Her nan's scratchy jumper would tickle her nose as she rested her head on her shoulder.

She kept walking to her own room.

The conversation over dinner that night was among the most uncomfortable of Kayla's life. Everyone was at a loss—they knew they had to eat, and they knew they had to make an effort to stay together as a family, but all of them wished they were elsewhere. Kayla? Checking the news, trawling the Web, doing anything she could to keep Sam alive in her mind. Mark? Drinking in the golf clubhouse with his business partners. Martha? Just drinking, period.

Iris was their only conversational hope. "Was the weather nice on your holidays, Kayla?"

"It was boiling. I wouldn't say nice, though. It felt like I was in a sauna most of the time."

"I know what you mean," Iris nodded. "It was like that when I went to Portugal last year."

More silence.

"Did you make lots of nice friends?" Iris persevered.

"Well, yeah. We had a group of five of us that were really close. But then, you know . . ."

"Oh goodness, it's so sad isn't it. So sad." Her Nan removed a congealed chunk of steak pie from her mouth—her dentures couldn't chew it adequately. They sounded loose when she chewed. "What was the food like over there? Spicy, I'd imagine. I can't handle any of that Chinese food, personally. Far too hot. Give me a roast dinner any day."

"I wasn't in China, Nan. I was in Thailand."

"Oh, it's all the same to me, love. Can you pass the potatoes?"

Kayla wondered how she would survive the night, let alone the next few weeks. *I don't even know how I'm going to survive tonight*, Kayla thought. *Let alone the next few weeks.* The tension was thick, like the cloud of smog hanging over Bangkok on that very first day. It seemed liked a lifetime ago that she'd stepped off that bus. That Sam had tapped on her shoulder . . . *No.* She forced the memory to the back of her mind, locking it away in a box marked "Sam." She'd reopen it later, when she was alone.

"Kayla, honey, your father and I have been thinking," Martha started, glancing at Mark for approval. He nodded. "We think you should see someone. You know, professionally."

"But—"

"No, please listen to what I have to say. Your father and I, well . . . we'd love to talk to you about all of this, and of course we will, sweetheart, whatever you need. But I know you often get frustrated when we aren't on the same wavelength. It's hard for us, love. We're still grieving for your brother." Martha's eyes filled with tears, and she gulped down a large mouthful of sauvignon blanc. "It's difficult for us to imagine coping with two deaths at once, like you are."

In the movies when parents suggested therapy, it was standard procedure for the child to kick up a fuss, insist they were fine, run up to the bedroom and slam the door in protest. But it made sense to Kayla, as much as she hated to admit it. She felt a little relieved that she wouldn't be spending all of her days in her bedroom, allowing toxic thoughts to manifest into rage, depression, or paranoia inside her head. She needed to let it out. She knew that. She wasn't so blinded by grief that she could convince herself, or anyone else, otherwise. "Okay."

Martha's shoulders, which she hadn't even realized were hunched in tension, visibly dropped. "Oh honey, thank you. Thank you for understanding. You're such a great kid, you know . . ." More tears slid down her face, forming a river with the trickles of watery snot escaping from her nostrils. "W-We're going to get through this. As a family, and with a little outside help. I know a great lady called Cassie. Cassandra Myers. She helped me immensely, but it's not just addiction she specializes in. She's a wonderful grief counselor."

"Thanks, Mum. And Dad. Is it okay if I finish my dinner in my room? I think I need to be alone for a while."

Mark smiled gently. "Of course, sweetheart, whatever you need. You know where we are if you need anything."

No sooner had she closed the bedroom door behind her, perching heavily on the edge of her four-poster bed, did Kayla realize that needing to be "alone" was another one of those clichés that she was simply expected to spout. And, in reality, it wasn't at all what she wanted or needed. She hadn't been properly alone for months.

Alone wasn't good.

Alone was absolutely terrifying.

Chapter 4

March 30, Thailand

"I THINK SOMEBODY slipped a hangover in my drink last night."

The girls groaned in unison. Bling, mourning the irreparable damage of her favorite dress on the first night. Francesca, voicing her dismay at the dried vomit in her hair. Russia? Well, it was perfectly possible that Russia might not have survived the night.

"Urgh, I'm sorry I was such a bitch last night, Kayla," Bling groaned. "If it helps, I think I'm hung over by osmosis."

"It's fine. As long as you're suffering today, we're good," Kayla joked.

"What happened?" Russia, it seemed, was alive, if not particularly well.

"The Noodlegate Scandal."

"The . . . the what?" Bling couldn't help but laugh.

"Someone threw Singapore noodles at Bling, and she came after Sam and I like we'd pissed on her birthday cake."

Everyone laughed, and Bling buried her face in her pillow. "Oh God, I'm such a twat." She looked up, sheepish. "I'll buy you breakfast to make up for it? I think we all need something in our stomachs besides beer, anyway."

Kayla hungrily imagined bacon sandwiches dripping in ketchup, or even a full English fry-up with juicy sausages . . . her stomach cramped with hunger. She leapt out of bed, instantly regretting the sudden movement as an invisible man attacked her skull with a hammer. She picked up the beer and sweat-stained T-shirt she'd worn the night before. She pulled it on despite the fact that it failed the sniff test, and shook Russia's shoulders.

"It's food time. Food!" No response. She'd fallen back into a comalike state. "Wake up, woman."

"Leave my hangover and I alone," Russia grumbled.

RICE SOUP. *SINCE when were either rice or soup acceptable breakfast options?* While Kayla knew she was in no danger of fading away—she had an Olympic swimmer's appetite and the curves to prove it—she feared she might be emaciated by the end of the first week if this was what they'd be living off. The soup looked like the vomit Francesca still had cemented in her hair. Russia turned her nose up at the greasy waiter.

"I think I'll stick to the coffee, thanks. Triple shot, plenty of cream."

"Make that two," Kayla agreed. "Today is a hard day."

The rest of the Escaping Grey crew piled into the tiny, low-ceilinged café, making it completely inaccessible to any other customers. The windows had obviously been cleaned rather haphazardly, still streaked with spirals of soap suds, and exhaust fumes from the road leaked in every time the door opened.

Dave slumped dramatically into a spare seat. "Wow." Kayla caught him exchanging a sly glance with Russia, who blushed and turned away. "What the bloody hell happened last night?"

"Beats me. Do they sell sausage and egg McMuffins in here, do you reckon?" Sam looked around for something, anything, he could realistically eat for breakfast without throwing up.

"There's no Ronald McDonald to be seen, sadly. You're welcome to sample some of this horse semen soup, though."

"Russia! That's disgusting," Bling said, without looking up from the smartphone she was deeply absorbed in.

"Hey Sam, where'd you get a British newspaper?" Kayla asked. Sam was flicking through the same broadsheet Kayla's dad bought every Sunday morning. CYBERTERRORISTS LEAK INTELLIGENCE AGENCY INFO was the headline.

"Little newsagent round the corner. Cost me more baht than the average house deposit. Won't be doing that again." Sam took a sip of the lukewarm coffee the tiny Thai waiter had just plonked in front of him, which Kayla had now discovered was more akin to dishwater. He grimaced slightly as it slid past his taste buds and down his throat. "Cheers!"

BUS POLITICS: FUELING adolescent insecurity since the invention of the wheel.

For some reason, deciding who sits where and next to whom causes an uproar regardless of age. Ralph, Thomas, and Francesca commanded the back row. Zhang Qiang sat at the very front next to Oliver, who had livened up after sleeping off his life-threatening hangover. He was now faced with the daunting task of making conversation with a young Chinese girl who suffered from a crippling case of shyness. Which left Kayla, Russia, Bling, Sam, and Dave in the exact same position they'd all been in during high school: the middle of the bus, neither cool nor uncool.

Apart from Dave. Dave was desperately uncool. But such was his appeal.

Kayla grabbed a window seat. It was going to be a long journey, and she wanted to absorb as much scenery as she could before returning to smog central. Sam swung into the aisle seat next to her, landing on her left leg in a clumsy fashion that gave telling context to his wonky nose. She laughed. "Oh hello, you useless twat." She instantly blushed. *Is it too soon to take the piss out of him?*

"Excuse me, my name is Sam, if you don't mind. I don't know who this Useless Twat fellow is." Kayla thumped his arm, too tired to construct a witty response. Sam popped the foil circle on his carton of orange juice with the sharp end of a straw and slurped thirstily. Smacking his lips, he said, "I think we should spend this bus journey really getting to know each other, since you don't even know my name. And after we shared such a tender moment together last night." He faked a sob.

"What tender moment?" Kayla laughed, trying to jog her memory. The bus whirred into life.

"You know, when I congratulated you on your face. It really was heartfelt. I don't take these matters lightly."

"Oh yes, that. What a truly heartwarming compliment. I shall treasure it forever. Now how do you suppose we get to know each other?"

"First things first, let's start with the basics." He nodded, stroking his chin and miming a reporter jotting down information in a notepad. "Age?"

"Twenty."

"Snap! Occupation?"

"Former intern for Greyfinch International, now unemployed beach bum."

"Hobbies?"

"Running, drinking tequila, talking to strange men on buses."

"Hilarious. Favorite food?"

"Cheesecake, without question."

"Any brothers or sisters?"

A pause.

"Erm, yeah. I had a brother."

Sam went pale. "Had? Shit. I'm sorry. I had no idea. I'm an idiot."

"It's fine. How could you know?" He bit his bottom lip. She touched his arm. His skin was warm and already a little pink from the sun. "Really, Sam, it's fine."

"Was it . . . was it a long time ago?"

"Not really. About three weeks"

"*Three weeks?* What the . . . holy shit. Kayla, are you okay? I'm so sorry . . ."

"Yeah. It's kind of why I'm here, if I'm honest. I couldn't bear to be at home."

"I can imagine. How . . . how old was he?"

"Seventeen. Can we talk about something else now?"

"Of course, sure. Sorry."

"Stop apologizing! You didn't know," Kayla said.

"No. Right. Sorry. Erm, so you interned for Greyfinch? I didn't know they took on interns."

"Yeah," Kayla said, only partly thankful for the change of subject. "My dad partially owns it."

"Whoa. Wait. Is he the 'Finch' part of Greyfinch International?"

"The one and only."

"Crikey. What's that like?"

"I don't really think about it. It's just my dad's job, you know?"

"So you're like . . . loaded?" Sam tried to act nonchalant.

"Yeah, I guess." Kayla blushed. Her family's wealth always made her feel uncomfortable.

Sam seemed genuinely interested, angling himself to face Kayla. "So what exactly does he do?"

"The company owns all of the CCTV cameras in the country. The department my dad runs uses the cameras as kind of a marketing tool."

"How do you mean?"

Ugh. Her hangover wasn't in the mood to explain. She missed her bed already. "So my grandpa Elijah founded Finch Marketing Limited about thirty years ago. Before the Internet and all that. It started really small. They had a few marketing operatives who would stand outside coffee shops, and they'd record foot traffic at certain times of the day, taking note of the kind of clientele who were buying coffee, what order they tended to place, that kind of thing. Then the experts—like my grandpa—would analyze the data coming in, write up really detailed reports, and sell the information to the companies they'd analyzed, who would then know how best to target consumers, what their spending patterns were like, all of that. They got big pretty fast."

"Bloody hell. I had no idea that kind of thing even happened."

"I know. It's little creepy. So when the government announced that they wanted to privatize national surveillance, my dad jumped at the chance, 'cause imagine what that would do for his marketing? Nobody would need to stand outside anywhere. So they contacted one of the other bidders, Greyhawk Financial. They joined forces, hence Greyfinch. Now, instead of selling reports to a single coffee shop, they'll sell huge quantities of data to international chains like Starbucks."

"Jesus." Sam leaned back in his seat, taking it all in. Kayla could almost hear the hungover cogs in his brain clunking. "I can't decide whether it's some sort of Orwellian nightmare or a genius money-making business plan. So when you interned there, you were a spy? Did you ever catch me doing something embarrassing?"

Kayla laughed. "They aren't spies! No, I was strictly a telephone answerer and tea maker. Anyway, enough about my dad's empire. What about you? What do you do? Or did you do, before you started gallivanting across the world?"

"Well, okay. Promise you won't think less of me?"

"Probably not, unless you're about to tell me you rob banks or exploit old people."

"No! Okay, well I got into one of the best universities in the country to study medicine. It was all going well, I aced the first semester exams, then it all went down the toilet. My parents announced they were getting a divorce, I stopped going to lectures and fell behind pretty quickly. I couldn't catch up at all—the course was so intense that once you fall off the wagon a little bit, you're screwed. So I've dropped out and reapplied to start again next year."

"Makes sense if your heart isn't in it. Medicine is pretty hard-core, so I don't suppose you can half-ass it. Did you reapply at the same university?"

"Yeah, and few others. I'm still not sure I'll go back at all, though. I did enjoy it, despite the fact it was bloody hard, but I'm just not sure it's what I want to do with my life."

"Yeah, I get that. I have no idea who I am outside of Greyfinch. It's kind of expected of me that I'll take over the business, now that my brother . . . can't. But I don't know. Part of me wants to go to university. I originally didn't even apply because there was already a career waiting for me at Greyfinch, so what would have been the point? But now . . . now, escaping reality at school for another three years is hugely appealing."

Sam leaned back in his seat. "Hopefully we'll both make sense of a few things while we're out here."

"Maybe." Kayla turned her attention to the scenery—a lot of fields, mainly—flashing past the window. She'd been in Bangkok less than a day and she was already missing the countryside. She leaned her head against the glass until the vibrations from the bus's inferior suspension made her feel sick.

"Hey," Sam said, slurping the dregs of his orange juice. "Want to know something weird about Dave?"

"Always. How weird we talking? Stalker weird? Foot fetish weird? Quite frankly, I wouldn't be surprised."

Sam chuckled. "No. Weird as in he's really sick. He told me last night when I brought him a glass of water to the bathroom, where he was throwing up pretty spectacularly. You wouldn't think it, would you? He seems so . . . enthusiastic. About everything."

"Sick how?"

"Ever heard of ALS?"

"Isn't that where sufferers become slowly paralyzed?" Kayla mused aloud. Her eyes widened as she realized the implications for her new friend.

"Yeah. Dave," Sam sighed. "Amyotrophic Lateral Sclerosis. Degenerative motor neuron disease. Your brain and your thoughts aren't usually affected at all, at least not until the very end. Nor is your eyesight. But it essentially causes your muscles to progressively weaken and atrophy. It's so scary. Eventually he won't be able to walk, or move his arms. But he'll be aware of it all. He'll still be able to think like Dave, but he'll be trapped inside his own body."

"Are you kidding? No way." A head shake. "Puts everything in perspective, doesn't it? Tragedy has a way of doing that. Ugh. He's such a sweet guy. How quickly—I mean—when will it happen? Is that still years away? Or you know . . . soon?"

"I was trying to work that out myself. It's hard to estimate without quizzing him on when his symptoms began. Basically, there's this scale doctors use where forty-eight is normal bodily function and zero is severely disabled. Most ALS patients lose around one point per month." Sam looked across at Dave, who was chatting animatedly to Russia in the seats next to them, gesturing rudely with his hands. She was laughing. Sam and Kayla were both silent for a moment as they watched their hyperactive friend during a moment of candid happiness.

"That sucks," said Kayla. "Well . . . it more than sucks."

"Yeah. It does. Don't tell him I told you, though. I don't think he'd appreciate pity." Sam did a funny kind of half smile, his lips curling upward only on one side, and reached into his backpack to produce a small hip flask. "Hair of the dog? Forget all the shit in the world?"

"Good God, no. Are you mental? We're about to go and stroke tigers. Actual tigers. You could get us all killed."

Chapter 5

June 27, England

Kayla hadn't even started her sessions with Cassandra Myers but already regretted agreeing to it. Sitting in the waiting room of the private practice, with its oak-paneled walls and antique furniture, she couldn't help but think that despite everything that had happened, she still wasn't quite nuts enough to need therapy.

Glancing around the room, she took care not to make direct eye contact with her fellow patients. Was she really as crazy as the man who shook erratically and swore in a methodic rhythm? "Shit, bollock, cock. Arse, twat, fuck. Shit, bollock, cock. Arse, twat, fuck." Or the girl who looked so thin her bones threatened to poke through her skin, her arms shredded with angry red and purple crisscrosses? Oh come on, she can't possibly be as messed up as the middle-aged woman she'd just seen swallow half a bottle of painkillers without even a sip of water; a seasoned professional.

She really tried not to judge people. Everyone had their problems, she knew that better than anyone. But she'd never felt like the most sane person in a room before. And that was worrying.

"Kayla Finch?" A pretty assistant summoned her to Dr. Myers's office. Kayla flinched at the sound of her full name. Weren't they meant to protect a patient's identity at this kind of place? She didn't really know—it was her first time being certifiably mental.

Cassandra Myers sat behind her imposing mahogany desk, surrounded by all sorts of psychology paraphernalia: a wall of bookcases lined with medical journals and case studies, a series of awards and diplomas in proud gold frames, a model of a human skeleton in a cylindrical glass case. *Why do they even have those? They're doctors of the mind—it's unlikely they'll ever have to point out to a patient where the fibula is.*

There were no personal accents in the room, besides the diplomas. No photographs of her family adorning the desk, no jacket hung up on the old-fashioned coat rack. The only sign she really worked here at all was the tiny gray dictaphone perched on the side of the desk, a red light flashing on its surface: paused between patients. *That's all I am to this woman,* she thought. *Another recording to discuss tonight as she enjoys a civilized dinner and bottle of wine with her partner. He probably worked in finance.*

Dr. Myers had a dramatic black bob haircut that skimmed her sharp jawline, and some severely framed spectacles resting on her petite ski-slope nose. She was dressed in a tailored gray suit and purple blouse. "Kayla, take a seat. Nice to meet you. I'm Dr. Myers."

"Hi," Kayla said, feeling suddenly shy.

"I understand this is your first visit to a psychiatrist." Dr. Myers rested her elbows on the desk, pressed the record button on the dictaphone, and steepled her fingers in front of her.

"What gave it away? I'm not really sure how to act," Kayla smiled.

"Just relax, and tell me a little bit about why you're here."

A deep breath. "Okay. Why I'm here. A little over three months ago, on March seventh, my younger brother died unexpectedly. And ten days ago, I was traveling in Thailand when I walked into my best friend's bedroom and discovered that it was drenched in his blood. He disappeared with no explanation and more than one sign of violence. Please don't ask me how I feel about that."

"Of course. So what would you like to achieve while you're here?"

Kayla shrugged. "If I knew what answers I was looking for, I wouldn't be here in the first place. I'm not even sure there is an answer. I just figured it was better than sitting alone in my bedroom with nobody to talk to." She stared into her hands, using her thumb to remove a stubborn fleck of dirt from beneath her index fingernail. "In a way, I guess it hasn't sunk in yet. I'm just at a loss over what to think or do with myself. I can't start to deal with it yet, because I still feel like I'm in a bad dream that I'm going to snap out of at any second."

"I see. Well, that's perfectly normal at this stage in the grieving process—to be in denial. But that's why I'm here. To help you work through the process. To help you understand your feelings and find a way to deal with them. Why don't we talk a little about your brother?"

Silence. Dr. Myers waited for Kayla to fill it. She didn't.

"Have you talked about your brother much since his death?"

"Not really. I guess it still doesn't even feel real. I wouldn't even know where to start."

"Wherever you like, Kayla." Dr. Myers smiled. Her hands were folded neatly in front of her as she peered over her glasses. *She has the mannerisms of a scary headmistress and the looks of a beautician.* "Perhaps you could begin by telling me his name?"

"Gabriel. We all called him Gabe."

"Okay. And do you mind me asking what happened? It's fine if you'd rather not discuss it. We'll work at your own pace. There's no rush."

Kayla exhaled and leaned back in the seat. Her voice box felt paralyzed. She willed herself to start speaking, knowing that once she began, the worst part would be over. But the words didn't come. The red light on the dictaphone was no longer flashing—it was steady, catching the corner of her eye repeatedly.

She cleared her throat and forced the words out.

"Gabe killed himself. I found his body."

Chapter 6

March 30, Thailand

KAYLA HAD NEVER seen anyone as petrified as Sam was at Tiger Temple.

They'd all been a little spooked when they were informed of a recent attack on a tourist, which had occurred at the temple the previous season. Sam apparently hadn't thought the killer cats would be strolling around the Theravada Buddhist Forest Temple quite so casually. They traversed the sunbaked ground lazily, several resting in the patchy shade beneath the sparse trees.

"Jesus Christ," he said, "can you imagine what the British health and safety police would have to say about this? There are tigers. Chilling. In plain air. I could practically reach out and stroke them. I mean, they could literally rip my face off, right now. What if the scent of tequila drives them wild? I'm a goner. A dead man. Tell my mum I love her."

Kayla laughed, pointedly blowing a kiss at a passing feline. They were down by the quarry, observing the tigers on their daily wander from a mere ten meters away. "They're perfectly tame, you idiot. Do you really think they'd let us in here if they weren't? Last year was a freaky one-off. Look at them, they're properly chilled out. I can almost imagine them cracking open a cold beer and smoking a Cuban cigar. Plus, it'd be a pretty cool thing to have on your gravestone: mauled to death by a Bengal tiger. What on earth are you doing?"

Sam was standing stock-still, unblinking. "That one is staring at me. Look. Look! I'm trying not to make any sudden movements. That's what you're meant to avoid, right? Sudden movements?"

"If I agreed with you, we'd both be wrong. See you back in this exact spot in about four hours, then?"

The tigers were becoming drowsier as the temple got hotter and the sun higher. Kayla knew how they felt. The girls had been made to wear ankle-length jeans and sleeved T-shirts so as not to offend the celibate monks who lived at the Buddhist sanctuary on site. Russia hadn't been allowed in due to her denim hot pants, and was still in the middle of a feminist outburst toward the ticket vendor, who had long since stopped listening. Feminism apparently wasn't a pressing issue in Thai monasteries.

An elderly member of the staff approached them. "Would you like to pet them?" He grinned at them, exposing a row of teeth that vaguely resembled a rotting picket fence: brown, gappy, and in danger of collapsing at any second. His tiny eyes almost disappeared when he smiled, turning into miniature pinpricks that couldn't possibly have provided him with adequate peripheral vision to keep tabs on ferocious wildcats. Sam's eyes were drawn to a deep purple scar traversing the man's wrinkled upper arm.

Kayla wondered if it had been a claw or a tooth that tore clean through his bicep.

"Erm . . . I think I'll pass, mate. I mean, sir. Mister. I mean . . . is that even safe?" Sam stumbled over his words much in the same way he did inanimate objects—clumsily.

"Oh come on, Sam!" Kayla said. "You'll regret it if you don't. You know you will."

"No, Kayla, I'd regret having my face mauled. I'll watch you, though, and try not to say I told you so when Tigger over there is chewing your eyeball like a stuffed olive appetizer."

"Suit yourself," Kayla replied, following the monk-slash-zookeeper toward an especially docile tiger. It was lying on the dusty ground, which was probably lush with grass during monsoon season, licking its paw. It looked remarkably similar to her beloved old Labrador, Max, whom she'd had to have put down last year. Max would lie by the French patio doors all day and alternate between licking his paws, his balls, and his arse. He was vulgar, but she loved him dearly. A tiger licking its own testicles? Now *that* she'd like to see.

She knelt down next to the beautiful Bengal tiger. She was more apprehensive than she'd expected, and glanced up at Tiny Eyes for guidance.

"It's okay, you can stroke him. He's friendly. His name is Mek."

Mek's fur was both soft and dense. He barely glanced up when her fingers glided through his coat, and Kayla couldn't help but wonder whether he'd been drugged. Surely it wasn't natural for wild animals to be so tame? *Stop overthinking, Kayla. Just enjoy the experience.* He gazed up at her, his eyes glossy and deep. She grinned, almost as a reflex. It was magical.

She turned back to the group and caught Sam's eye, subtly jerking her head backward to summon him across. Even from a distance she saw his eyes widen, but he cautiously started to tiptoe across to her and her new friend.

"See? He doesn't bite."

"I'm still not convinced. Look into his eyes. Pure, unfiltered malice."

"Don't be ridiculous! He's beautiful."

"They can smell fear, can't they? If they can, I'm screwed."

Tiny Eyes smelt fear, even if Mek didn't. And whether he was a cheeky rascal or just plain bored, he turned to Sam with a miniature sparkle in his eye and said, "Would you like to feed him, sir?"

"F-Feed him?" Sam backed away a fraction of an inch.

"Here, take the bottle."

"No, no thanks. Sorry." But he didn't have a choice. The bottle of formula was thrust into his hands. "I said no, I can't do it!"

"Hey, Sam," Kayla said. "Carpe diem, and all that. You can do it, you know you can. I know you can."

He held her gaze. For a moment the quarry behind them disappeared, Mek vanished. Tiny Eyes evaporated in a puff of magician's smoke. It was just the two of them, for a fraction of a second. It was all the convincing Sam would need; the first of many times that Kayla's mosaic eyes, flecked with green, blue, and hazel, would give him a surge of adrenaline that made him feel like he could do anything.

He took a deep breath. "Okay. Okay. What do I do?"

Chapter 7

June 28, England

PERCHED ON A bar stool at the marble breakfast bar in her family kitchen, Kayla pushed her soggy cereal around in the bowl. Her earlier bravado in thinking she could handle a regular portion of food had vanished around the same time she'd flicked on the morning news to see a picture of Sam. His big, brown, doelike eyes and tufty dark hair had caught her off guard. The delay had irrevocably compromised the structural integrity of her Cheerios.

Today was the day she was to go and meet the police officer who was handling the case in the UK. DCI Mason Shepherd. The Thais had originally wanted her to talk to him as soon as she landed in Newcastle, but he seemed conscientious enough to allow her to sleep off her jet lag and gather her thoughts before their debrief.

There had been no progress in the search for Sam, or what was left of him. None whatsoever. The manhunt team had quickly lost interest when they followed the trail of blood, which stopped abruptly halfway down the road outside the villa, and searched the obvious places to no avail. They'd received no tips, other than some obviously fake ones—including a man who'd insisted that Alex Garland's *The Beach* was real and that's where Sam was— and no new leads.

Nothing had come of talking undercover to the drug dealers Sam had supposedly been in contact with, or following them with Phuket's patchy and fuzzy CCTV footage. Maybe if Greyfinch had been in charge of Thailand's surveillance, finding a broad, six-foot-five twenty-year-old might have been a little easier.

Kayla pushed the bowl aside and slumped onto the counter, her head nestled in the crook of her elbow. It had been a long week. Now that they'd offloaded her onto Dr. Myers, her parents were largely attempting to continue their lives as if nothing had happened. As if there had never been a Gabe, or a Sam. Her dad was working fourteen-hour days, and her mum, ever the good Samaritan, was dividing her time between charity ball committees, volunteering at an animal shelter, and teaching kids French at a series of free community night classes. Keeping busy, for them, meant avoiding what awaited them at home: a grieving daughter and an empty bedroom where their son used to sleep.

Kayla heaved herself off the stool, which was just a bit too far from the ground for her five-foot-four frame to maneuver with a single ounce of grace, and made her way across to the white French doors. The sun was peering lazily through the steely gray clouds, and the blustery chill of the wind bit her skin with unusual aggression for this time of year. She lit a cigarette with the oversized candle lighter her mother was forever misplacing and wrapped her spare arm around her waist, shivering involuntarily.

Still, she rather liked the sensation of feeling cold after months of sweaty, sleepless nights and muggy air so thick you could practically chew it. The climate had been one of the few things she'd missed about her family home in north Northumberland. Some, she'd forgotten about, but loved nonetheless, like the powerful, fragrant scent of the vivid yellow oilseed rape fields that scattered the countryside like a patchwork quilt. Oh, and the unrivaled taste of a good old mug of English breakfast tea—none of that aromatic bathwater the Thais paraded as a substitute.

From inside she could still hear the chirpy northern economics journalist on the morning news questioning whether the Bank of England's interest rates would remain low this month. Kayla frankly couldn't think of anything more repetitious than inflation or gross domestic product. Politics, perhaps.

What bothered her most about the UK's reaction to Sam's disappearance was the utter disinterest from the mainstream media. For whatever reason, it just wasn't one of those stories the major channels latched onto. Perhaps they had no emotional connection to it, or perhaps they had no element of mystery to use as a hook to attract viewers. He wasn't young enough to tug at heartstrings, or middle class enough for the incident to be considered as scandalous as some of the higher profile cases.

"A twenty-year-old British man, who was traveling in Thailand on a gap year scheme, is still missing after disappearing in Phuket Town last week. Police believe the incident to be drug-related, and are currently appealing for any witnesses to come forward with any information that may aid them in their search." That was the ten seconds usually allocated to his story. The problem was that as soon as most people heard the word drugs, their compassion evaporated.

Kayla wondered what impression somebody would have of Sam who knew nothing other than what the news reader told them. Sam was a university dropout (nobody would care that he had planned to return the following fall) and a supposed drug addict. It was so frustrating to her that television, radio, and print had such immense power over public opinion, and yet only poured their efforts into the stories that really interested them. Like how many boob jobs the latest gormless glamour model had denied having, or how much a premiership football club planned to bid for an overrated striker before the transfer deadline arrived.

She buried her cigarette butt in a plant pot, pulled the doors shut again, and punched the off button on the TV remote.

Any hope she'd had of Sam being found was vanishing almost as quickly as he had.

THE RECEPTION KAYLA received at the police station in Northumberland was much warmer (figuratively, at least—they had functional air-conditioning) than Niran and Seni's in Phuket. Although she had been taken to the interview room, Kayla didn't have that suffocating feeling that came with being interrogated. With being a suspect.

Gladly accepting the glass of water DCI Shepherd handed to her, she shuffled in her seat. She tried not to look at her reflection in the mirror on the other side of the room, which she knew, from watching crime dramas, was one-sided. Whether or not there was anyone watching from the other side, she didn't know. Probably.

The man standing in front of her was around her father's age, but looked more frayed around the edges than Mark Finch. A bulging paunch spilled over his belted trousers, and his graying moustache had flecks of ginger and black sliced through it. His hairline was receding dangerously, his skin was pale from too much time spent indoors, and his blue-gray eyes were weak and weary, fronted with frameless glasses. He looked like he desperately needed a green smoothie and an early night.

"How are you today, Miss Finch?" he asked, distractedly flicking through the file in his hands. She could smell the sour, stale coffee on his breath from across the table. He stopped on a page and frowned before moving on.

"I'm fine, thank you," she answered. A reflexive platitude she instantly regretted. *Fine?* she chastised herself. *What kind of psychopath collapses in her best friend's blood and admits she's fine nine days later?*

Shepherd didn't seem to notice. "Good, good." He dragged the chair opposite Kayla backward, the metal feet grating along the floor, and sunk into it with a sigh. "Now, although this meeting is largely a formality, and I don't want to keep you here all day, we do have some things to discuss. Namely, your friend Mr. Kingfisher's, ah . . . disappearance."

Kayla nodded, unsure what to say. She pressed her lips together to prevent any more silly responses from spilling out, then realized it made her look slightly insane and quickly slackened them again.

"It looks like the Thais have done a fairly good job of covering all the bases, but let's start from the beginning, shall we?" He looked up at her for the first time. There was no intensity behind his eyes.

"Okay," said Kayla meekly. *Stop looking so bloody guilty, Finch. You didn't do it. Stop acting like you did.*

A strange silence. Kayla waited for him to ask a question. He seemed off, like half his brain was in another room, another police station. Another country.

"So," he said, coughing into the back of his hand. "Talk me

through the events of the afternoon of June seventeenth." He removed his glasses and rubbed his eyes, as though trying to rub some life back into them.

It seemed like a decade ago. Kayla strained to remember how the day had started. "Well, we woke up at around eleven-thirty A.M. We'd had a lot to drink the night before—"

Shepherd started gesturing vaguely. Kayla thought he might flag up the fact they'd been drinking—could that mean anything?—but instead he said, "We can skip the morning. Mr. Kingfisher was reported missing at, uh, just before seven in the evening? Let's start at six."

She frowned. Wouldn't he want to know about their exact movements that day? Wouldn't it help them to retrace Sam's footsteps? "Okay . . . if you like. So at around six, I was with Sam down by the lake. We had a lake near our villa," she added.

"So you were the last person to see Sam alive?" Shepherd asked.

"Uh, yeah. I was." Kayla paused, waiting for him to comment on the way that looked: bad. He didn't. "So we were by the lake. We were talking about . . ." She gulped. She couldn't tell the truth, but she certainly couldn't lie. Not to a police officer. " . . . about the last few months," she finished vaguely.

He nodded. No further questions. He gestured to continue.

Wouldn't he want to know if Sam seemed on edge? If he had mentioned the drugs? If there was a sense of fear?

Kayla cleared her throat. "Sam went inside at around twenty past six, and my friend Russia—I mean, Minya—came out to join me by the lake."

"And that's your alibi."

"Yes," Kayla replied, caught off guard by his bluntness. "That's my alibi. I was with Minya when Sam went missing."

He nodded again. "Ms. Pavlova corroborated this statement. Okay. Carry on."

"We smoked and chatted for a while. Mainly about how strange Sam had been acting . . ." She paused, but Shepherd didn't visibly react. " . . . until I headed inside to find him. That's when I discovered all the blood."

"So you were the last person to see him alive, and the person who realized he was missing?"

"Right." *Jeez, when you say it like that . . . it's a wonder I'm not locked up.*

Shepherd stared at another page in his file. *A file all about Sam.* Kayla wondered what it'd be like to read it. To see all the cold, hard facts laid out before her. Images of blood splatters, DNA, footprints. Timelines. Evidence. The thought made her stomach turn, but a small part of her wanted to see it.

"Were you aware that Mr. Kingfisher was in debt?"

Kayla flinched, not anticipating the change of conversational pace. "No. But like I mentioned, he had been acting strangely."

"Strangely in the way that a person in a lot of drug debt would?" He seemed to emphasize the word *drug*.

Kayla shrugged. "It's hard to identify what kind of strange until you look back in hindsight."

"You have hindsight now. Would you say that's what it was?" he pressed.

Uneasiness crept over her. Was he trying to put words in her mouth? "Maybe . . ."

"Right, right." Something about Shepherd's tone didn't sit right with her. Was it boredom? Apathy?

She pushed on. "It was more like . . . anger. Like he was angry with all of us. With the world."

"With you?"

"With me."

With everything.

WHEN KAYLA GOT back to the house, she felt a little deflated. Empty. Even Shepherd, the guy who was meant to be leading the investigation on UK soil, hadn't seemed all that invested in Sam's case. After and twenty minutes of lackluster debriefing, he'd let her go. His questions had seemed vague and disjointed. His eyes betrayed his exhaustion—his desire to be anywhere but in that room, talking to her.

She'd expected—hoped, maybe—to meet someone as desperate to find Sam as she was. Okay, so maybe he already had all the detailed notes he needed from her interviews in Phuket. Or maybe he thought finding Sam wasn't possible. Maybe he thought finding him would just mean finding a beaten body. The Thais could do that.

Maybe he just didn't care.

She slung her handbag—a knitted, rainbow-colored hobo bag she'd bought in Bangkok—onto the breakfast bar. It clashed horribly with everything in the sleek kitchen, which made her love it even more.

She looked around the room. In the middle of the oversized oak dining table stood a big glass vase holding cream-colored lilies, which had bloomed a couple of days ago and were now a little droopy. The chrome tap dripped water every few seconds, the sound of fat droplets hitting the sink echoing around the silent kitchen. Her breakfast bowl was still abandoned on the counter above the dishwasher—opening the door and putting it in had seemed like too much effort—and the TV remotes were strewn across the breakfast bar from when she'd angrily punched the off buttons that morning.

Nobody had been here since she'd left. Kayla swallowed down the lump rising in her throat—the hard knot of loneliness and grief she'd been desperately trying to bury—and grabbed the kettle, filling it too full with water from the dripping tap. She plonked it on the stove. Coffee would help. Coffee always helps.

On autopilot, she clattered around with expensive mugs and the secret stash of instant coffee she'd hidden in the back of the cupboard. Her dad abhorred her preference for cheap coffee ("We have a thousand-pound espresso machine and you choose that crap every time!"), which, again, made her like it even more. Some teenagers rebelled with drugs and tattoos—she chain-drank Nescafé Gold Blend.

After spooning granules into the biggest mug she could find, she leaned back against the counter, the ridge digging into the bottom of her spine. The water in the kettle was just starting to whir and bubble, wisps of steam pouring from the spout. The scent of freshly cut grass and lawn-mower fuel drifted through the open window, and a few patches of sunlight were beginning to break through the fleecy clouds. It was an ordinary June day.

And yet the normality of the day felt suffocating. *How dare I live through these blissfully average days when my brother is dead and my best friend is gone?* The sheer absurdity of the idea pierced her chest. *How can the world keep turning as if nothing has happened when everything, everything, has changed? How can I be making coffee and smelling freshly cut grass and feeling the warmth of the early summer sun when so much blood has been shed?*

Time kept ticking relentlessly forward.

Her throat felt thick and her lungs tight. She cranked the

window open even farther, struggling to gulp in enough fresh air. Her limbs were heavy and her stomach was hollow, hollowed out by grief and longing, longing for everything to be back to normal. There was a ringing in her ears—or was it the kettle whistling?—and she was being crushed, crushed by the weight of a depression so dense there was no way to escape. She slid to the floor.

With her legs twisted awkwardly and her head tilted backward and resting on the cupboard, Kayla breathed deeply, laboriously, trying to escape the helplessness enveloping her. *They're gone. They're never coming back. I'll never see them again. Never.* Her shoulders crumpled and she writhed with gasping sobs.

When can I wake up? When can I wake up from this nightmare? When can I go back to my real life?

The kettle kept whistling. The tap kept dripping. The world kept spinning.

The room stayed empty.

Chapter 8

April 15, Thailand

IT WAS HOT.

Though not an especially deep or descriptive sentiment, it was the only one Kayla could focus on: it was hot. There was nothing else. The heat seeped into every orifice, every pore in her body. If ever there was an apt time to use the adjective "stifling," it was now. It stifled movement, it stifled thoughts, it stifled feelings. Which, in all fairness, was rather nice. If only temporary.

"Jesus. What is this? What actually is this heat?" Even Dave's usual shrieks and splutters had been dulled to a murmur by the oppressive temperature. Every sentence was half yawn, half incoherent muttering.

"I feel like I'm trapped under a hot air vent," Russia mumbled. "You know when you walk into the supermarket and just outside there's a vent that hurls baking hot air at your face, but it's all right cause it only lasts a second? Yeah. That. Except I can't escape it." With as much energy as she could muster, she fanned her face with the intricately painted fan she'd bought from a stall on Khao San Road. Two of the flimsy wooden toothpicks holding it together had already snapped. Like most of the group, it was on its last legs. She discarded it with a sigh, letting it drop onto the patchy grass next to her.

It was mid-April, and two weeks of intense partying and adventuring in the hottest time of the year had started to take its toll. They'd soaked up the dynamic party scene of Bangkok—Ralph and Thomas had enjoyed the "massage parlors" in particular—explored Lampang's enchanted ruins by bike, eaten fried bugs at the Sukhothai night market, and taken a canal boat trip that resulted in most of its hungover passengers hurling over the side into the water. Kayla could hardly believe they'd only been here two weeks. It felt like these people, these near strangers, were the only friends she'd ever had. It was relentless, sure, with no alone time. But that's exactly what she'd been looking for when she booked the trip. No time to think meant no time to sink into the deep depression that was looming on her horizon.

Today was the last day of the Songkran Festival and, incidentally, their last night staying on Khao San Road before traveling to Kanchanaburi for the next leg of their trip. Songkran marked the Thai new year, and their adopted home street had been transformed into a flurry of flags and festivities.

One of her favorite Songkran traditions—in no small part due to the climate—was the mammoth water fight that took place, with officials and visitors alike roaming the streets and drenching each other with full containers, water pistols, and water bombs. Khao San Road sang with a chorus of unfaltering laughter, almost like birdsong in perfect harmony. There was no time for sadness here.

The practical problems? The sheer volume of water had rinsed their skin of sun cream, leaving the group burnt, uncomfortable, and irritable. Sam, Kayla, Russia, Dave, and Bling were currently seeking respite in Lumphini Park. They were laying on a small grassy bank next to a green-tinted lake, a grand old tree providing them with some delicious shade. The intoxicating scent of pink lotus flowers clung to the air. The faint sound of traffic was distant.

Bling lay with her eyes closed, her hands behind her head and her eyelids twitching as she succumbed to the wave of fatigue enveloping her. Sunstroke, really, though she'd insisted otherwise. Bling did not show weakness. Russia had her head in Dave's lap, grabbing clusters of grass with her hands and wrenching them out of the soil to throw over Bling's face like confetti. Sam sat with his feet on the ground and his arms resting on his upright knees, running his hands through his fluffy brown hair and facing the ground.

Kayla kept trying to catch his eye, then wondering why she did.

"So are we going out tonight?" Russia asked.

"Nah, Russia, I thought we'd just stay in," Kayla replied. "Catch up on some sleep. It's not like it's our last night in Bangkok, or anything."

Russia laughed. "You know, sarcasm is the lowest form of wit."

"Well, I try to cater for my audience."

Russia threw a handful of grass at her, though it didn't even come close to reaching Kayla. Instead it blew back into Dave's face, who shook violently and sent Russia rolling down the bank. Sam snorted with laughter and said, "You two are so woefully idiotic that I sort of admire you."

Dave nodded sincerely. "Thanks, mate. 'Preciate it."

FAST FORWARD EIGHT hours and it'd just be Kayla and Sam in the park. They'd left the others in the bar. Dave and Russia were sucking face in one of the booths, Ralph was hitting on an unimpressed Bling, and everyone else was in the middle of the dance floor. Sam had turned to her and said, "I miss the park. Want to go back one last time before we leave?" He didn't quite have a twinkle in his eye—the alcohol had stolen off with such sharpness. But his eyes were definitely glazed over with something more than intoxication.

After one more shot of tequila for luck, they'd hailed a cab to the park entrance and returned to the exact same spot they'd been earlier that day. Just as they'd sat down and gazed awkwardly at each other, not knowing quite what to say, Kayla's phone rang in her pocket. She picked it up.

"Hello?"

"Kayla? Kaaaay-la?"

"Yes, hello?"

"Kayla! It's your nan! Can you hear me? I don't think my phone works abroad."

"But you aren't abroad, Nan. I am." Kayla turned to shoot a disapproving glare at Sam, who was sniggering drunkenly. She was the only one who was allowed to laugh at her nan.

"Right you are, poppet. Are you having a nice time on your holidays?"

Kayla concentrated very hard on not slurring. "Yes. Wonderful. Hot. Nice."

"Good, that's good. I've not been up to much. Today I went for afternoon tea with Muriel. You know Muriel, she was married to your great-uncle Bill before the nasty business with his secretary. Anyway, I had a really lovely scone. A fruit one, it was lovely, and a pot of tea. One of those new flavors—peppermint, I think it was—then I went for a walk with your mother." A pause. She waited for Kayla to ask the question. She didn't. "She's not doing well, Kayla love. She misses your brother, and now that you're not here . . ."

Kayla looked away from Sam. The park was so quiet, she knew he could hear exactly what her nan was saying, though whether he was sober enough to make sense of it was another matter. "Now isn't a great time, actually, Nan, we're about to go out, erm, volunteering. Building schools and that. Can we talk another time?" A little white lie wouldn't hurt. Her eighty-five-year-old grandmother had no concept of time zones, after all. Plus she really wasn't in the mood for another guilt trip. She'd been subjected to enough of those before she left. Her family couldn't believe how selfish she was being, jetting off during such a tumultuous time.

"All right love. Well I hope you're looking after yourself out there?"

"I am." *Don't cry.*

"I'm glad. I love you, sweetheart. I can't wait for you to come home!"

"Bye, Nan. Love you too." Kayla hung up and peered upward through her eyelids to stop the tears prickling behind her pupils. She worried that Sam would ask her what was wrong, then realized he was on the phone too. He was having significantly more trouble forming full words than whoever was on the other end.

"Okay . . . but mate . . . th'park . . . wha . . . ?" The recipient lost patience and seemed to hang up, leaving Sam frowning at the mobile in his hand. "That was Bling. She's mad."

"What? Why is she mad?"

"I dunno. Probably something to do with noodles." Sam rolled over onto his front and smiled dopily. "You're all right, you."

"Not bad yourself."

Sam rested his head on the grass. A few moments of silence passed, but it wasn't awkward. Just peaceful. "Kayla?"

"Sam?"

He paused, as if uncertain whether to continue. "What happened to your brother?"

She considered getting angry and defensive, but decided against it. She felt too sad after talking to her nan. Besides, she'd have to tell Sam eventually, if they were ever to— She stopped the thought before it ended. She reached into the patchwork bum bag she'd taken to using every day and pulled out a squashed packet of cigarettes. Russia had gotten her into the bad habit. She lit it slowly.

Blowing the smoke away from Sam's face—as a sort-of med student, he deplored the very concept—she tapped the cigarette free of its loose ash and sighed. "He killed himself."

Sam didn't say anything. He closed his eyes and pressed his lips together, only peeling them open when he'd processed the information. He looked up at her, though had difficulty meeting her eyes. "I'm so sorry. That must . . . that must have sucked. It must still suck."

"Yeah."

They sat in silence for a few moments. Kayla finished her cigarette, and once she flicked it away into the pond—*Sorry, fish*—Sam began tracing infinity signs on the palm of her hand with his fingertip. It was more absentminded comfort than anything of metaphorical significance, but the touch of his skin felt nice.

"His name was Gabe. He . . . he was my best friend. I know it's probably really generic to say that in retrospect. I can hardly say I hated him, can I? But it's true. We weren't like siblings who tolerated each other's existence just because we had to. We just . . . liked each other. He was hilarious, so funny. And so sweet." Kayla bit down hard on her bottom lip. "I miss him, you know?"

Sam propped himself up so he was sitting parallel to Kayla, and she rested her head on his football-sized shoulder. In a soft voice, he asked, "Why did he . . . do it?"

"He was bullied. Threatened. He was gay, and someone took a disliking to him. Just like that, no rhyme or reason."

A contemplative pause. "How are you doing? You know . . . it must be so hard . . ."

She shrugged. "I'm trying not to think about it. I know that's bad. I know I should be crippled with grief. But . . . it's too hard. It's too hard to think about. So I don't."

A hand stroked her hair, even though it was matted and tangled from a day of water fighting, sweating, and dancing. "But Kayla . . . numbing the pain for a while will only make it worse when you finally feel it."

She spluttered with laughter.

Sam looked shocked at her outburst—comedy hadn't been what he was going for. "What? Why are you laughing?"

She could hardly catch her breath. "Isn't that from Harry Potter? That numbing the pain line?"

Sam's cheeks went pink. "Oh, shut up. I was trying to be insightful . . ." He trailed off. Another hand traced down her jawline, from her ear to her chin, then gently nudged her head upward so she was nose-to-nose with him. His breath tickled her sun-chapped lips, and he leaned in, tenderly brushing them with his.

Kayla pulled away. It didn't feel right. "No, Sam."

His eyes betrayed his hurt. "Sorry, I thought . . . I don't know what I thought."

"No, I mean . . . I don't mean no. I mean not like this. Not while we're talking about my brother. It feels . . . cheap. I don't want to cheapen his memory."

"What? That's not what I—"

"Yeah, but it's what it felt like." Kayla pushed herself up off the bank, losing her balance a little at the top. Sam didn't follow. "I think we should go back and meet the others."

"Okay. I'll see you there in a bit."

"Are you not coming with me? I don't really want to walk back through the park by myself in the dark. Bangkok is . . . well, it's Bangkok."

Sam rubbed his eyes. "Okay, Kayla. Let's go back."

Her stomach twisted. Not an excited flutter of expectation, like only moments ago, but the sensation of reaching for a top step that doesn't exist.

It was a feeling she would come to know all too well.

KAYLA AND SAM walked back through the park in silence. Her mind kept racing with things she wanted to say—*I'm sorry. I'm not angry. I'm not sad. Kiss me again. I promise I'll kiss you back*—but her tongue felt too big for her mouth, and the words wouldn't come. Sam walked two steps in front of her, scuffing the bottom of his dirty Converses along the dusty path.

A branch cracked somewhere southwest of where they walked. Sam didn't hear, but Kayla stopped abruptly and swung around. There was a silhouetted figure standing next to a thick tree trunk.

She rubbed her eyes but couldn't bring the shadowy person into focus. It was too dark.

Her skin prickled. Why were they just standing there? "Sam, wait." He stopped, bemused. "Who's there?" Kayla called, lifting her voice.

The figure jerked slightly. Cicadas rattled and hissed in the trees. The air was still humid.

Sam muttered, "Leave it, Kayla. Why do you care who's there? We're in Bangkok, it's not like—"

"I said, who's there?" she called. Her voice trembled. *Why am I getting so worked up about the fact there's someone else in the park?*

The person started toward them, and as he walked under the ornate streetlamp, his face came into view.

"O-Oliver?" Kayla stammered. "What are y-you doing here?"

He grinned clumsily. He was slouching. Drunk. Drunker than them.

"Just shh-checking up on my favorite traveler . . . and her mate," he slurred.

Was he . . . winking? It was hard to tell in the dark.

Sam rolled his eyes and turned on his heel. "Now you have another chaperone, I'm off. See ya."

"W-Wait up, Sam," Kayla said, running after him.

"What the hell's his problem?" Sam almost spat when she caught up. "Who lurks in the shadows like that? S'creepy."

"Yeah." Kayla shuddered. Sam was walking too fast, and she was almost jogging to keep up.

"The way he looks at you . . . it's gross. I mean, I don't blame him, but . . ."

Kayla smiled despite the queasiness building in her belly. Was Sam jealous?

They kept walking in silence. After a couple of minutes, she looked back over her shoulder to see if they were being followed. But Oliver was gone. There were only shadows in his place.

Chapter 9

July 5, England

AN UNBLINKING RED light. More uncomfortable silence. A ticking wall clock. The bitter smell of Dr. Myers's coffee.

It was their second meeting, a week after the first, which already felt like a lifetime ago. Kayla clenched her fists, watching her knuckles turn white. Her fingernails, which hadn't been cut for weeks, dug into the palm of her hand. She found the painful sensation strangely relieving. She decided not to think any further into that.

"Take all the time you need," Dr. Myers said.

More silence. Tick, tick, tick. The sound of the persistent clock was like a cheese grater on Kayla's nerve endings.

The only option, she thought, was to talk over it. "Gabe was gay."

Dr. Myers looked up. "I see. And how—"

"We all fully supported him," Kayla interrupted. She'd started now, and to stem the flow of her monologue would be counter-productive. "He came out last year, and it just kind of . . . fit. My mum cried, at first, then gave him a hug. My dad slapped him on the back and told him he was bloody brave for telling them. My nan was a little off about it, but she's old-fashioned like that. She soon got used to it."

"How did *you* feel about it?"

"Honestly? It never really bothered me. I was proud of him for coming out, obviously, but I just never understood what the big deal was. And like I said, it just kind of fit. It wasn't unexpected."

"I see."

Kayla stared into her hands, examining the crescent-shaped in-dents her nails had left behind. They still stung a little. "We were all so supportive. We loved him to bits. He brought a boy around, once, before they went on a date. My dad gave the guy a stern talking to, like he would if I was seeing someone, and said stuff like, 'You take care of my son, now,' just like it was normal. Which it was. My mum quizzed him all about it when he got home. She put the kettle on, and despite his bashful grin, she insisted he told her everything over a cuppa. What Zack's parents did, did Zack offer to pay for the meal, did he smell nice. It didn't work out with Zack—he didn't smell that nice at all—but we just knew everything would be fine.

"Everyone loved him. He did well in his exams, and he helped his friends study by sharing his notes. He played rugby for the town, and he went to parties and gigs too. He loved music. Not as a performer, though—everyone in our family is rhythmically challenged. And he'd recently told my parents he wanted to go traveling after school, and he was so excited for that. He was just a normal seventeen-year-old. Liking the same sex was nothing but . . . a side note.

"But then he started getting these messages. On Facebook, Twitter, Tumblr. At first, they were nasty, but not threatening. 'You make me sick, you fucking faggot.'" Dr. Myers flinched at the profanity, though she tried her best to disguise it. Kayla swallowed the bile rising in her throat and continued. "'You disgust me. You're sick.' That kind of thing. Disgusting, disgusting abuse. Then . . . then they got worse. Much worse. They said they were going to . . . They threatened to anally rape him, because 'that's the way you like it,' and then they said . . ." Kayla cleared her throat. "Then they said they were going to rape me in front of him, to show him how it should be done."

A pause. Dr. Myers was initially lost for words, but she recovered quickly. "I'm so sorry to hear that, Kayla. Really, I am." She blew out through her lips, causing them to vibrate. "Was there a police investigation? They can be difficult to deal with when you're grieving."

Kayla shook her head. "No. Not an extensive one anyway. Once they'd ruled it as suicide, what was the point? Online bullying is, sadly, very common. That's what they told my bereaved parents, anyway. As if Gabe was just another statistic."

"I understand that must have been difficult, Kay—"

"You don't, though. Nobody does, and nobody ever will. I desperately need somebody to blame, somebody other than myself, but there's *no one*. The social media accounts were anonymous, all under different names. Whoever it was—if it was only one person—used different e-mail addresses to set up each one. And we never found the messages on Gabe's laptop until after . . . you know. So it's not like we can just ask him who had it in for him."

Dr. Myers considered this for a moment. She mused, "Maybe that's for the best, as unlikely as it may seem. You'll never get closure if you're constantly seeking answers that don't exist. And having someone to blame, to channel all your anger toward, can hinder the healing process. Some people find themselves constantly dreaming about exacting revenge, and if you have a face to attach to that, it can quickly become an obsession. An obsession that ultimately will destroy you, without ever soothing your heartache."

GABE HAD A birthmark on his forearm. It was shaped like nothing, really, not a perfect heart or five-point star like in songs or poems. Just a splodge of pigment that she had tried to lick off when she was tiny, thinking it was melted chocolate. She'd always had a rampant sweet tooth.

For some reason, she couldn't get that birthmark out of her head. Would it still exist? Would it still be a quirk of nature, a sign of life, imperfectly printed on his skin? Or was the death long enough ago now that it had started to melt away into the earth?

Kayla had once voiced a similar thought to Sam. He'd found it strange, even morbid, that she was so concerned with the physical details, not the emotional implications. She didn't know why, really. Thinking about it from an scientific perspective seemed to hurt less than the alternative. She could deal with the fact that Gabe's body would eventually become a part of the earth—a simple shift in energy that'd ultimately claim us all. But what she couldn't grasp was the fact that he'd never pop his head around her door again to ask if she'd like a cup of tea (strong, with milk and two sugars, just how she liked it) or flop down onto her bed, sinking into the memory-foam mattress and insisting that she *had* to listen to this new band he'd discovered on YouTube.

More than just simple grief, the unbearable boredom of being pent up in her parents' enormous house all day was suffocating Kayla. Nobody told you how dull it was to be in mourning. Did it make her a monster to admit that?

It had been nearly four weeks with no clues, no new developments. No reason for hope. The police hadn't contacted her with any further questions since her meeting with Shepherd. Even though she hadn't been a suspect for a while, she'd still expected them to be in touch again. She shook off the uneasy feeling that had settled on her shoulders. Shepherd's strangely disengaged demeanor had left her cold.

With nothing else to do, she'd read every magazine imaginable, devoured every book on her parents' bookshelf, given the cleaner a hand with the housework, and even honed her baking skills to perfection with a rather impressive Victoria sponge cake, which her nan had crowned the finest in all of England.

She hadn't been out running yet. She used to love it, pounding the English countryside with her beat-up, muddy trainers. She was never very fast, or particularly graceful, but there was something therapeutic about the rhythm of her thudding feet and deep breathing. Her mum had bought her pair after pair of shiny new Nikes, in vivid shades of neon pink and girly turquoise, but she still loved her old school PE trainers, molded to her feet with hundreds and hundreds of miles built into their worn-down soles and fraying toes.

Running gave her time to think, to plug in her headphones and put one foot in front of the other until she'd left every bad grade, traumatic breakup, and argument with her drunken mother behind her on the grassy fields, muddy trails, and potholed roads. But she had a feeling that now, her issues were too great to be cured by the simplest of remedies, and that terrified her. She was too scared to confirm her fears—to be stranded in a field, miles from home, with only her own thoughts for company.

No, she didn't feel ready to run yet. Instead she did something she hadn't done in a long time: opened the shiny laptop her parents had bought her for passing her A levels. It was wafer thin and ultra-professional, and all Kayla had ever done on it was read pop culture blogs. Until now.

Forget what Dr. Myers had said. She needed someone to blame, and she was going to find them.

Aran Peters. The sum total of Kayla's communication with the wiry-haired, pointy-faced Aran had been his attempts to fondle her blossoming bosom at their end-of-school dance, age thirteen and a quarter. Kayla had told her friends she batted him away in disgust. She'd actually granted him an overdress graze and a slobbery kiss, resulting in the tangling together of their clunky braces. But she was far too concerned with her reputation to admit that.

After that incident, she and Aran went their separate ways, to different schools in different counties. Now it was time for a reconciliation.

Aran Peters was an IT whiz, and not just in the quite-good-at-making-spreadsheets way that most school-taught kids were. He was ruthless when it came to learning everything he could possibly know about computers. He'd mastered the basics by the end of primary school, and had a solid grasp of the most sophisticated systems in the country by the time most teenagers were discovering Bacardi. Once, he'd hacked into the school's server and awarded everyone in their year a 100 percent grade in all of their mid-semester exams. He was twelve then. Afterward he had bigger fish to fry. He compromised a national exam board and swapped what were meant to be AS level essay questions with replacements that a particularly slow Labradoodle would find easy.

Kayla had no idea where Aran was now. He could be at university, possibly studying for his Ph.D. already, or he could be working in a top secret government facility specializing in homeland security, or something equally heroic. Either that or he'd gone down the route of digital mafia boss and currently had control over ninety-nine percent of Western civilization. Knowing Aran, both were equally plausible scenarios.

Eventually she found his school's alumni website, where she came across an article on his resounding success at one of the best universities in the country. He'd completed a four-year curriculum in eighteen months, achieving the highest marks ever recorded by an undergraduate Information Technology student. He'd be attending the same university again in September, to complete his Ph.D. at the ripe old age of twenty. Perfect.

She clicked on the university's website and browsed the list of staff, identifying the way in which their e-mail addresses were composed: joe.bloggs@ldmuniversity.ac.uk. Assuming the students would have similar accounts, she started typing a message to the address aran.peters@ldmuniversity.ac.uk.

It was worth a try. Especially considering what was at stake.

Chapter 10

July 6, England

KAYLA CHECKED HER e-mails as soon as she woke up, one eye peeled opened as she stared at the glaring screen of her laptop. Nothing.

She dropped her head back onto her pillow, allowing the laptop to slide into bed next to her. She'd been hoping for a faint glimmer of hope before midday—she wasn't exactly looking forward to meeting Kathy Kingfisher, Sam's mother, for the first time. These things were awkward enough when the love interest was still alive.

Realizing it was already ten-thirty, Kayla rolled reluctantly out of bed, wrapping a fluffy white dressing gown around her and slipping her unsightly feet into a pair of matching slippers. Both garments had been stolen from a hotel in Dubai by her out-raged mother, who was convinced the maid was stealing from the minibar and leaving them to foot the bill. To exact revenge, she'd pilfered not only the complimentary miniature cosmetics—standard behavior in hotels—but also the dressing gowns, slippers, and bath towels. The hotel had charged her through the teeth, and the excess baggage charges at the airport amounted to more than the original cost of the flights, but her mother had insisted that was beside the point.

Kayla glanced into the mirror. Weren't the bereaved meant to gaze upon their own reflections and declare that they no longer recognized themselves? Everything still looked to her as it always had. Her deep tan was fading, her waist-length dark hair was as unruly as ever, and her generous breasts and rounded hips hadn't shrunk in the slightest.

Her interest in her appearance had almost completely evaporated. Still, she wanted to make a good impression with Kathy, and so forced herself to brush her hair, apply some dried-up mascara she'd found at the back of a bedroom drawer, and pick out the nicest day dress she owned: a floaty, buttercup-yellow affair with a delicate daisy print. Why was she so worried what Sam's mum would think of her? She spritzed some floral, overly sugary perfume onto her neck—in case Kathy hugged her—and borrowed a dainty black leather watch from her mother's impeccably organized jewelry box. Her heart twitched as her fingertips grazed the woven bracelet that sat next to it on her wrist. She pressed her eyes firmly together until the moment of intense grief had subsided.

It wasn't even eleven yet.

Time to check my e-mails once more.

Still nothing.

KATHY KINGFISHER WAS quite obviously grieving. Kayla tried not to feel embarrassed that the middle-aged woman sitting opposite her in a busy coffee shop was sobbing loudly into a sodden handkerchief, drowning out the clattering noise of the cappuccino maker grinding coffee beans and ferociously frothing milk. She tentatively handed Kathy the paper napkin that had been placed underneath her lemon and poppy seed muffin.

Am I grieving wrong? It hasn't even been a month yet. Why am I not this publicly distraught? Shouldn't I be weeping into whatever nearby material I can find, crying Sam's name repeatedly through a dry and sticky mouth? Or dabbing at my haggard face to try and soak up some of my never-ending tears?

Dr. Myers insisted everyone dealt with loss differently, and Kayla understood that. But she couldn't help but feel guilty that she wasn't as overtly upset as she should be. It wasn't that she didn't love or miss the people she'd lost. It was more that she couldn't connect with the deaths, couldn't make enough sense of them to even begin to feel that kind of sadness.

She found herself looking at her mum's watch. Eight minutes. Kathy Kingfisher hadn't spoken a word since saying, "Hello hi Kayla nice to meet you I'm Kathy would you like a coffee or maybe some cake," all in one sentence, as if trying to get the words out before she had a breakdown. Which she did, three-point-five seconds later. Kayla had bought the coffee and the cake, and sat in an uncomfortable wooden chair in equally uncomfortable silence ever since. For eight minutes.

Kayla looked around and saw a queue, as there always was at a busy chain like this, waiting to order, a generic soundtrack of inoffensive, devoid-of-personality music playing in the background. The controlled temperature was on the cooler end of the thermostat—lower temperatures made you feel hungrier and more likely to overindulge in cake, her coffee shop expert of a father had taught her. The air smelled of espresso and the warm rain clinging to customers as they traipsed in from outside.

They were in Newcastle city center, as Kathy had driven up from Yorkshire that morning to chat with Kayla about what Sam had been like in his final days and weeks. She'd initiated contact with Kayla by asking Escaping Grey for her number, and considering the circumstances, they'd waived their confidentiality rules. Kayla was glad they had. She felt less alone, knowing she wasn't the only one suffering in the aftermath.

Through a line of mothers with prams and a group of teenagers with vibrant hair colors, Kayla caught the tattooed male barista staring at her. She looked away quickly, guiltily, before remembering she actually wasn't in a relationship and flirtatious eye contact was by no means off-limits. She also realized the poor guy was probably just concerned for her companion's mental well-being. She shot him an apologetic glance, but he'd turned his back to her.

Kayla cleared her throat. No reaction. "Kathy? Would you like me to get you anything? Some water or some fresh tissues?"

Kathy looked up, as if noticing her for the first time, and sniffed deeply. "Oh Kayla, I'm so sorry," she said, her words lulling with a gentle Yorkshire accent. Just like Sam's. "This is so pathetic of me. I've never been such an emotional person but . . . losing your son . . . it just—it ruins you." Her eyes were bloodshot and puffy, with grape-sized dark bags underneath that betrayed her lack of sleep over the past ten days.

"We don't know that you've lost him for sure," Kayla argued, albeit gently.

"Oh, I know, love, but you know what they say about Thailand. Once you've disappeared there, you're never coming back. Especially when there was so much blood, just from one boy . . ."

"But I still think—"

"Come on, Kayla. There's no use clutching at straws. You can't lose that much blood and survive. Sam's dad . . . I've never seen him like this before. He's usually so hard. Steely faced. But not now. I'm the strong one of the pair of us these days." A feeble laugh. "Sam took after me, you know. Always had his feelings on show." Kayla winced at the past tense. It sounded like a fresh wave of tears had erupted behind Kathy's eyes, but her face was dry. She had cried for so long that her body had abandoned all hope of trying to keep up.

"That's weird," Kayla said. "In the past month, he never really . . ." She didn't know how to approach the subject. She had no idea how much Kathy knew about her and Sam's relationship. "I mean, he didn't really talk about what was going on in his head. Kept his distance. Did he . . . did he talk to you about anything strange?"

Kathy shook her head slowly, and not very convincingly. "Not really. He did seem a bit distant in the last six weeks, which wasn't like him. The phone calls got a bit more abrupt, whereas usually he'd tell me every little detail. He spoke a lot about you, especially for the first month or so," Kathy forced a smile. "But that's why I didn't think anything was wrong, Kayla, because I thought that if there was, he'd surely tell me."

Kayla nodded. "Yeah, I know what you mean. I keep feeling angry at myself for not trying harder to make sure he was okay. But then I think that if anything were really wrong, like . . . like what the police are saying, he would have told me. We were pretty close." As she talked, she was systematically destroying a discarded sugar wrapper in her fingertips. "I should have . . . I *would* have known."

"So you'd think. But one thing was a bit weird." Kathy was

staring out of the window, not focusing on anything in particular. "Sam was always good with money—always. As a little kid, he would meticulously save every single copper he could in his piggy bank, until you physically couldn't squeeze another penny in. He cried when I smashed it, so I bought him another, much bigger one. He just put all of the money from the first into that and kept saving. I don't know why I'm telling you this." She sighed, taking a sip of what must have now been a rather tepid latte. "I guess it just took me by surprise when he phoned me a few weeks ago and said he needed to borrow some cash."

"He did?" This was news to Kayla. Sam hadn't seemed particularly tight for money. Though he was rarely extravagant in his purchases, he would never turn down a meal out or a day trip for frugality's sake.

"Yes. He said he'd run out of funds quicker than he'd thought, and needed more if he was to follow the four of you to Cambodia after Phuket. I thought it was odd too, you know? He'd budgeted the trip so carefully. But I knew it must have been genuine for him to ask me. He knows I'm not exactly Richard Branson. I live in my overdraft most of the time. And considering how much he was asking for . . ."

"How much?"

Kathy pursed her lips and cradled her coffee cup between her hands. "Three thousand."

There it was again. That sudden sinking feeling in Kayla's stomach that felt like she'd reached for a top step that wasn't there. *Drug money. It has to be. But three grand?*

Kathy was oblivious to Kayla's shock. "I couldn't give it to him, though. I did want my boy to have an amazing trip, see the world like I never did. But I just couldn't afford it, so I told him he would have to come home. I had no idea he might have needed it for something else."

"You couldn't have known, Kathy."

More tears. "I should have tried harder to get the money together, then none of this would have . . ."

A knot was starting to form in Kayla's stomach. If she'd pushed Sam for an explanation, she might have been able to help. It was common knowledge that her family wasn't exactly strapped for cash. Three thousand pounds would have been pocket change for her dad, who'd spend a similar amount on a suit without a second thought. To think Sam might have lost his life over something as vulgar as money was unthinkable. No wonder Kathy was so distraught. She would forever carry around the knowledge that if she'd had some savings behind her, she might still have a son.

Kayla asked the question she'd been dying to know the answer to. "Do you really think, though, that Sam would have got himself into so much trouble over *drugs*? I mean, he was so careful and thoughtful. He's the kind of guy who would never cheat on a test. If he found a wallet on the street, he'd take it to the police station, or if he saw somebody fall over, he'd rush over to help them up while the rest of us laughed uncontrollably. He was—or still is—a good person. You must know that more than anyone. I mean . . . *cocaine*? Debt? Drug deals gone wrong?" The room seemed to have suddenly quieted a few decibels, and Kayla lowered her voice in case anyone was listening. "I just can't see it. I really can't. Those theories do not fit that boy."

"That was my initial reaction, too," Kathy said, nodding. "I thought they had the wrong person. Then when they told me it was definitely my Sam who was missing, something inside me still wouldn't believe it. I thought the DNA tests would show it was somebody else's blood, or he'd pop up somewhere in a couple of hours having cut his foot on a rock, or something equally clumsy and Samlike." Kayla couldn't help but smile. Sam's ungraceful mannerisms were like a shared secret between the two grieving women. "But the hours turned into days, and the days into weeks. Still no Sam. I don't know what else to think, Kayla. There's no other explanation. I keep trying to think about what would drive him to that."

The knot in Kayla's stomach tightened.

Chapter 11

April 16, Thailand

"SAM'S STILL IN bed, marinating in shame and tequila sweat," Dave practically sang, the café's air-conditioning allowing his voice to resume normal, ear-piercing service.

"Delightful." Russia shot Kayla a sideways look. Kayla hadn't fully divulged what had happened between her and Sam in the park the night before. That would mean explaining about her brother. But Russia had a well-trained radar for these things. Two people disappearing together for two hours, then returning to the hostel in mutual silence, spelled gossip.

Sam, it transpired, did not share the same sense of discretion.

"So, Kayla. I hear you shot old Sammy boy down last night. Brutal—I like it!" Dave offered his hand to Kayla, demanding a high five.

Kayla declined. "He told you?"

"Well, yes," Dave said, dropping his arm and looking hurt at the rejection. "But he would have told me anything last night. He told me all of the passwords and security questions I'd need to commit serious fraud on his Internet banking, but I'm a top friend and just pinched a tenner."

"That was noble of you."

Russia chimed in, "I think I deserve a cut, Dave. I did buy him that shot rack of black Sambuca, so I'm to thank for getting him in such a state to begin with." She winked at him.

"All right then, missus, I'll buy you breakfast. Full English?"

"Please." Russia smiled, pecking him on the lips with a delicate, entirely romantic kiss. They both froze, realizing that their public display of affection meant they could no longer deny that things between them were going a little beyond a drunken hookup. They'd been nearly inseparable in the three weeks since they first met. Kayla and Bling exchanged a smirk, but decided not to humiliate the happy couple with the dramatic scene the moment warranted. Kayla couldn't help but wonder when Dave, the eternally loose-lipped chatterbox, would bother telling Russia about his ALS.

Bling turned to face her. "So, uh, Sam tried to kiss you?" She couldn't meet Kayla's eye, instead making miniature mountains of salt on the table they were huddled around. The café's booths were dirty, the smell of grease clung to the air, the laminated, handwritten menus were peeling, and the owner was a lecherous old man with a hunchback. But when you need bacon, you need bacon.

"Yeah," Kayla admitted, unsure why she felt guilty for telling Bling. Maybe because she'd seen her friend's eyes linger on Sam for a moment longer than usual, or because Bling often made excuses to initiate skin-to-skin contact. Nobody was quicker to take up Sam's request for sunscreen to be rubbed into his back than her. "It was a weird moment. We were both pretty drunk. But it was nothing."

"Oh my God, do you think he likes you?" A girly giggle an octave too high and a failed attempt at a casual tone. Subtle, Bling was not.

"Nah, we're just friends." Kayla found herself wondering what Sam had told Dave in answer to that inevitable question. Or whether boys even discussed that kind of thing beyond the obligatory, "She's hot."

"Really?" Bling tucked a lock of hair behind her ears and sipped the watery apple juice in front of her. As a strict vegan, it was the only thing she could really order. "Do you like him as more than a friend? You guys do spend a lot of time together."

Before she could reply, Sam entered the café, scanning the room for some familiar faces. Kayla's stomach fluttered. She wondered how he'd act today, uncertain which of them was actually in the wrong. Was he the kind of stubbornly proud man her father was, who'd pretend that nothing had happened and treat her with even more aloofness than he had before?

"Hi guys! Would anyone like a coffee? Kayla? Let me guess . . . triple shot espresso with cream?"

Kayla smiled to herself.

THE BUS JOURNEY to Kanchanaburi took almost three hours. Instead of sitting next to Sam as she'd have liked to, Kayla decided to make him sweat a little longer and chose Bling as her travel partner. It took all of the willpower in her arsenal not to make eye contact with him throughout the whole journey, even though she knew already that she forgave him for being overly forward.

Whether she forgave herself for rejecting him was an entirely different matter.

Their new accommodation was the height of luxury in comparison with the last, though still squalor to anyone in possession of nostrils or, well, retinas. Kayla felt a little grateful that she'd been too hung over to insert her contact lenses that morning. When it came to hostel decor, ignorance really was bliss, though there was no disguising the intrinsic scent of mildew. It gave her a strange little thrill to imagine her snobby parents' faces if they could see where she was staying.

Oliver had shown them to their room. After last night in the park, Kayla had started to notice the way he looked at her—like he was hungry. Sam was right. It was gross. Over the past few weeks, he'd taken quite the liking to her, staring intensely and making derogatory comments whenever she was in the vicinity. It was almost as if he believed that referencing the "slutty blond chick" he'd "nailed" the previous evening would convince Kayla of his sensational lovemaking skills. It didn't.

Still, whether he remembered the events of the previous night or not, Oliver resumed his usual disgusting ways. As he was eventually leaving Kayla, Russia, and Bling's bedroom, he'd offered to show them around the finest drinking establishments in the area. He'd said this while twiddling his spiky, overly gelled hair and smoothing down his groomed eyebrows in their murky mirror, and so hadn't noticed Russia's stifled laughter from the farthest bed. With a final, delightful parting comment ("If your bed is too gross, you're welcome to share mine"), he strutted back into the hallway.

Kayla let out a breath she hadn't realized she was holding. His presence made her uneasy.

As the girls were unpacking, there was another knock on the cardboardlike door, which was folded pathetically against the wall at an extreme angle. Sam stood in the doorway. He looked proud of himself, despite his disheveled mane, which hadn't seen a hairdresser's scissors since they'd arrived in Thailand. "Ladies, I come bearing snacks," he said triumphantly, tossing a family pack of tortilla chips onto the nearest bed. He knew the way to a hungry girl's heart. "Kayla, can we chat quickly?"

Kayla grumbled. "All right, but not for too long. The Doritos will be demolished by the time I get back." Russia had already torn into the packet like there was gold dust at the bottom.

"I love where your priorities lie," Sam laughed as he followed Kayla out into the narrow hallway. Then, glancing in both directions to make sure they didn't have company, he shuffled his feet awkwardly and said, "Look, Kayla, I'm sorry—"

"It's fine," she interrupted. "We were both drunk. Let's just forget about it."

"Yeah, we were, but . . . do you really want to just forget about it?" Sam pretended to examine his flip-flops.

"Seems like the right thing to do."

"Okay. If that's what you want." He tried, and failed, not to look too put out.

"Yeah."

Uncomfortable silence filled the corridor. Sam started to dig around in his pocket. "I got you something. I was going to give it to you last night, but . . . well, I forgot."

"You forgot?" She laughed. "Must be a special gift."

"Hey, I forgot my own name last night. I forgot what country we were in. I forgot what year it is. Give me a break, I'm a useless drunk. Anyway, it's really stupid. Totally daft, really. But, um, here you go." He opened his palm to display a friendship brace-let. It was a delicate, woven creation in blue, green, and turquoise threads, with a single silver bead in the center. "It's so cheesy, I know. I got it off some random woman at Songkran. She wouldn't leave me alone till I bought it. Honestly, I swear I only looked at her for a fraction of a second, but she pounced on me . . ."

Kayla grinned. She almost didn't want to smile. She wanted to act cool, not like a schoolgirl being presented with her very first Valentine's Day card. But Sam's ridiculous cuteness did some-thing funny to her facial muscles. They no longer behaved as she told them to. "That's so sweet, Sam!"

"Oh, I mean, it's not really. It's just because she, uh, made me buy it. And I thought I might as well give it to someone, 'cause I'd bought it, obviously. And it sort of made sense to give it to you." He bashfully rubbed the back of his head, tilting his head and allowing his lips to twist into a semismile. Kayla imagined what it'd be like if he tried to kiss her again. Probably salty, from the heat-induced sweat on his upper lip, but gentle and tender. She'd have to reach up on her tiptoes, as he was so tall, and he'd wrap his thick, muscular arms around her waist to support her. Her skin tingled at the prospect.

"Will you put it on for me?"

It wasn't a romantic moment. Sam's huge hands weren't built for dainty work, fumbling with the ends of the bracelet and trying numerous times to maneuver the strands into something vaguely resembling a knot. But Kayla didn't mind the delay. It meant that Sam's hands lightly tickled the inside of her wrists, which felt, at that moment, like the most intimate touch in the world.

"There you go." He stood back, admiring his shoddy handi-work. He laughed at the clumsy knot, bigger than the bead itself. "You'll never be able to get that off now. I'm going to be with you wherever you are in the world."

Kayla looked up at him and smiled. "I hope so."

Chapter 12

May 4, Thailand

KIDS, AS A general rule, were good judges of character. They sensed an aura about a person that most adults had lost the ability to recognize. And they flocked around Sam like he was a shiny new toy, clinging onto his legs and giggling manically for no obvious reason.

After Kayla was presented with the friendship bracelet, the group spent just over two weeks in Kanchanaburi. They visited Erawan National Park, exploring the grounds through the metropolis of wooden footbridges and swimming in the freshwater pools, which were fed by seven tiers of tumbling waterfalls. They attended an open air Thai cooking lesson, which saw them peruse the aromatic food markets for fresh ingredients to use in their dishes. Russia and Dave got rather carried away and held a competition to see who could use the most varied range of herbs and spices in their menu. Russia won, but the chef wasn't too impressed.

They also went on a temple tour, where they learned all about Buddhism, and practiced their own meditations at Daen Maha Mongkol Meditation Center. When Kayla originally read the itinerary, she'd expected to find the whole day awkward and embarrassing, and already planned to mock the entire ordeal with the group afterward. She'd never been a religious person, but was strangely moved by the experience.

They entered the center by crossing the teak bridge over Mae Nam Khwae Noi, changed into the plain white shirts and trousers provided to them, and paid their respects to the wooden Buddha image in the meditation pavilion. This, Kayla had found cringeworthy. But the overwhelming tranquility of the whole sanctuary was intoxicating; the more she was exposed to it, the more peace-drunk she felt. She found herself experiencing pangs of jealousy toward the three hundred residents who lived there all year round. It was basic, sure. Nothing extravagant. There were no smart phones, social media, or reality TV. Perhaps that was why she had never witnessed those serene smiles in the Western world. The relaxed, tension-free expressions would make the Botox industry redundant, if the movement was to catch on.

After an afternoon of guided meditations, she had turned to Sam and smiled. She whispered, "I feel so . . . you know?"

"I know," he replied. He took hold of her hand and squeezed it gently. Every inch of her body tingled.

It hadn't lasted, of course. As soon as she'd heard deep house music again and spoken at a higher volume than a murmur and smelled exhaust fumes, the illusion was shattered.

They had arrived in Sangkhlaburi, close to the Burmese border, five days ago to begin their planned volunteer fortnight. Most of the Escaping Grey group had opted to aid the local children in a holistic community center, where their sole job was to ensure that the kids had fun. Kayla was just grateful for the chance to escape Oliver's sleazy gaze and slimy comments, and spend time with some adorable little people with tiny feet and absolutely no concept of the evil in the world.

"This language barrier is doing wonders for my creativity." Sam laughed as a swarm of Thai kids ran around his feet. "Trying to communicate with kids who think I'm speaking gibberish is forcing me to think outside the box. Gotta get inventive with my silly dances and comic facial expressions." He mimicked a pig's oink with alarming accuracy, forcing the tip of his nose into a snout with his index finger and waddling around like an overweight swine. The kids fell about with laughter, but not half as much as Kayla did.

Kayla wished she was good with kids. She tried blowing raspberries, sticking her tongue out, and playing the timeless "I've got your nose" trick her dad had always played on her, but could never illicit the same laughter that naturals like Sam could. Most children wrinkled their noses, looked at her like an especially smelly sock, and turned around to see where the real funny people were.

That night would essentially be the start of their weekend. They'd arrived in the Sangkhlaburi district on a Sunday and were thrown straight into the deep end on Monday morning, working long hours every day since. It was worlds apart from the party trip they'd been on thus far, and while Kayla had appreciated the change of pace, she was looking forward to letting her hair down a little. That she'd be asleep before nine P.M. was, however, entirely likely.

Russia ambled over to her. She had an altogether lackluster attitude toward children, and begrudged them for robbing her of precious sleep. She needed at least ten hours a night to function as a proper human being. Suppressing a yawn, she said, "What do you say to the idea that tonight, instead of partying in a club, because I'm too damn tired for that, we should chill out with some cheap wine, cheap cigarettes, and a little bag of somethin' special?" She winked at Kayla, patting the pocket of her faded denim shorts. It took Kayla a second to realize what she meant.

"Russia! You can't bring weed to a kids' community center!" Kayla hissed, though eh

he couldn't resist shaking her head and chuckling. She had to admire her friend's blatant disregard for socially acceptable behavior.

"Sure I can. It's not like I'm going to grind it up and put it in their rice soup. Although that would be entertaining . . . Please, Kay? Let's get stoned, laugh at nothing, and have the best night's sleep of our damn lives."

Kayla laughed. "Okay. Sounds good."

What harm could it possibly do?

"I'M GOING TO jump! I swear I'm going to do it!"

Cannabis, it seemed, did little to subdue Dave's hyperactivity. He was perched on the edge of Saphan Mon, the longest wooden bridge in Thailand. Though long, it didn't look as sturdy as it perhaps should. Dave had watched some native kids jump off the rickety structure into the lake below, and decided that he too should explore his rebellious side. Once he'd clambered up there, he had a change of heart, and had spent the last ten minutes as a performing monkey for his group of friends, who were rolling around on the lake edge hooting with laughter. "You sound like a bunch of owls! You twats. I'm going to jump! Honestly!"

Kayla thought her appendix might burst, as her sides were splitting with uncontrollable hysteria. Sam was clutching onto her knee, shaking silently with tears streaming down his cheeks. Russia lay on her back with her hands behind her head, sporting a dopey Cheshire Cat grin across her face. She was more of a seasoned professional when it came to smoking joints, and was much more relaxed than her desperately uncool companions. She gazed at them like a lioness might look proudly at her cubs. Her intoxicated, incoherent little cubs.

Bling, however, was completely sober and somehow impervious to the merriment of the situation. "Dave, get down from there, you idiot!" she called, met only by the echoes of her friends' howls bouncing off the wooden bridge.

Russia, in contrast, tried a different tactic. "Dave, if you jump off I'll shag you." Bling thumped her on the arm. "What? We've already done it, it's not like that's enough to make him ju—"

They heard a plunging splash, followed by the fizzing of foam and the splutters of a man who'd forgotten to take a breath before he leapt blindly into a lake. Russia grinned even wider, narrowing her eyes and nodding her head slowly. "Well, I think that says a lot for my sexual aptitude. Anyone want another drag?" She gestured toward Sam with the glowing remains of the spliff.

"Oh God, I'm the worst med student ever," Sam laughed, accepting the offer. "You know"—he inhaled deeply, barely disguising the violent cough he clearly needed to release—"I think I like weed after all. Maybe I'm more of a bad-ass than you all thought.

Next thing you know I'll be injecting heroin into my arms, gagging for my next hit."

They all laughed.

THE GUESTHOUSE WHERE they were staying in Sangkhlaburi was a tiny tin shack with a corrugated roof and a worn veranda out front. The plot it stood on was part faded grass, part overgrown plants with a wild floral border, and because the building was a bungalow, the flora seemed to dwarf the structure.

When they returned from Saphan Mon, dazed and sleepy and altogether a happy bunch of people, the owner was sitting in a grubby plastic chair on the veranda, smoking a roll-up and blowing lazy smoke rings into the warm evening air. There was no sign of the rest of the Escaping Grey group, who had left for a dinner reservation at a local restaurant a couple of hours ago.

As they were walking up the dusty path, Kayla felt a big hand gently close around hers. It was more fumbly than romantic, but it still gave her goose bumps. She turned to face its owner.

Sam was smiling at her, half coy, half relaxed. "Fancy going for a walk?" he asked, just quietly enough so the others couldn't hear him. "It's still so warm. Maybe we can catch the sunset if we hurry."

"Sure," Kayla said, returning his grin.

Shouting their excuses to the other three, she and Sam took off back down the path, trying desperately hard not to trip on the dusty, stone-studded ground. The others looked totally bewildered.

After slowing their pace to a canter and trying to catch their breath, they walked side by side for a few minutes. Sam chitchatted in disjointed half sentences, losing his train of thought and jumping straight onto another. A lingering effect of the two puffs of weed he'd smoked. Kayla couldn't help but grin as he erupted into borderline hysteria at the sight of a butterfly.

Eventually they found themselves down by a river. They'd had to navigate some rickety wooden steps and overgrown shrubbery to get to the banks, where Sam promptly flopped to the ground and lay back, sighing. Kayla sat down next to him with only a fraction more grace.

The gushing water, hazy evening light, and scent of frangipani made Kayla want to curl up and nap, but the sight of Sam's toned stomach poking out from beneath his gray cotton T-shirt as he stretched was enough to make her heart pound through her pot-induced haze. She turned on her side to face him, propping herself up on an elbow.

"Doesn't home seem like thousands of miles away?" she said dreamily, drawing out her words in a relaxed drawl.

"Kayla . . . home *is* thousands of miles away," Sam said, and laughed so hard that Kayla worried he'd rupture his spleen. "Five thousand, eight hundred and forty-seven miles, to be precise."

She shoved his shoulder playfully. His giant frame barely moved. He clutched his side, almost breathless with laughter. "Smart-ass. You know what I mean."

He shoved her back just as playfully, except Sam was much stronger than she was, and the push sent her rolling down the bank, laughing too hard to steady herself. He rolled after her—an inelegant log roll Kayla's sixth grade gymnastics teacher would have abhorred.

Sam ended up lying on his chest next to Kayla, their arms pressed against each other. He made a pillow with his hands, palms flat against the ground, and rested his temple sleepily on top of them. His eyes were crinkled and twinkling as he gazed at her. "You know I just saved your life."

Kayla spluttered. "Saved my life? How?"

"Stopped you from rolling into the river. You'd have been swept away by the current and hurtling toward a waterfall if it weren't for me."

"You pushed me, you idiot—"

The words were stolen from her mouth as Sam leaned over and kissed her, so gently she could barely feel it. She shivered despite the humid river air. He pulled away, shyness creeping in, and gave a dimply smile.

Kayla pushed herself up and rolled him onto his back, lowering herself so she was lying on top of him, their chests pressed together and their legs intertwined. His hands rested on the small of her back, pulling her closer into him. His body was warm and hard. She sighed.

And in the moment before she kissed him back, there was something, something on the tip of her tongue—something she needed to say, except she couldn't quite figure out what it was.

Chapter 13

July 11, England

THE MORNING AFTER the first string of nightmares plagued her sleep, Kayla knew she had to get out for a run.

Peering out of her bedroom window, she saw that it was, at least, dry. The fog that often clung to the Northumbrian coastline sat stubbornly in her garden, a thick miasma enveloping her house like a sinister blanket. Hopefully the rays of the ever-optimistic northern sunshine would burn through the mist and the ground would visibly sizzle like they often did after a thunder shower on a hot day. She was starting to miss the heat.

Not allowing herself the luxury of forethought, Kayla pulled on her beloved grubby trainers, which were still peppered with teeth marks from when they'd brought Max home as a puppy, and slammed the door shut behind her. *Here goes.*

Kayla knew the first mile would be easy, as usual, then miles two and three would hurt. A lot. But if she could smash through the mile-three wall, it'd feel effortless, and she'd experience that euphoric, untouchable sensation of hitting her stride, finding a nice breathing rhythm, and letting the endorphins work their magic. And she desperately needed some magic.

As predicted, mile one passed by without much difficulty, and she weaved deftly through the trees that sprung up through the fog in front of her. It was nice to know that a three-month stint of sedentary living hadn't completely destroyed her stamina. After the first mile came the inevitable struggle. Her right knee twinged, causing her to put less pressure on that foot. The added impact on her leg left resulted in invisible shards of glass tearing into her shin. Breathing became labored and her chest hurt as she struggled to gulp down the furry fog that seemed to have completely replaced the fresh country air she was used to.

The urge to slow down to a complete halt was overwhelming. All she could think about was how much easier it'd be to stop and walk back. Until that wasn't all she could think about.

Last night's dreams flitted into her brain in rapid beams. A sadistic slide show.

Veiny hands around Gabe's throat. His eyes bulging.

Run through it.

Kayla tried to dial 999. She couldn't type in the right combination of keys. 997 #99 989. She crushed her phone in her hand, and pain shooting through her palm as the shattered glass screen sliced straight through the skin. Blood drenched the cream carpet.

Just keep running.

Gabe's face was purple. Frozen in a single expression of terror as his frantic gasps slowed and he realized that this was it. The end.

One foot in front of the other.

The light behind his eyes was snuffed out, like moist fingers crushing a candle flame.

The person whose hands were wrapped around Gabe's airwaves turned to face Kayla. Their face was blurred.

Maybe if I stop running, I'll be able to focus on the face.

Kayla stopped running, crouched down with her hands on her knees and squeezed her eyes shut.

But the image was gone. All that remained was a black canvas flecked with kaleidoscope splodges of light, caused by running too fast and not inhaling enough oxygen. She pressed her fingertips into her eyelids and the spots intensified, but the face wouldn't materialize.

"HOW ARE YOU feeling today?" Dr. Myers peered at Kayla, who hadn't even showered since her curtailed run, over the rim of her glasses.

Kayla paused. There were some things that shouldn't be shared with a near stranger. "I'm okay." She dug her nails into her palm again, searching for relief that would never last.

Her shrink leaned back in her chair. "Can you tell me a little bit about your childhood? How did you and Gabriel get along when you were growing up?"

The change of subject caught Kayla off-guard. It wasn't something she'd thought about in a while, and for some reason the mention of her childhood flipped her stomach. It was a sharp downward jerk, as if lassoed by an invisible rope. And it only happened once. But it happened. "It was fine, really. Average. We squabbled like most kids, but were perfectly happy to play Monopoly together five minutes later. Just a normal sibling relationship." As far as she knew, she was telling the truth. So why did she feel so uneasy?

Dr. Myers nodded. "What was the age difference between you?"

"He was younger than me by nearly three years."

"And do you remember as far back as when he was born? Do you remember how you felt when you had to suddenly share your parents' attention with him?"

"Actually, I do remember that far back. Before he was born, my mum drank a lot, though I didn't really understand that at the time. I just knew that the nanny had to look after me after hours, overnight, on weekends, because my mum wasn't able to. And my dad worked away a lot, expanding the business, I think. But when my mum was pregnant, she obviously didn't drink, so it was really nice getting to spend lots of time with her. Then they found out Gabe was really sick, and wasn't developing properly in the womb, and my mum had a few complications. So my dad was home much more, taking care of us. I just remember feeling really happy that we were a proper family, like my school friends seemed to have. I guess I was too young to realize how selfish it was to feel glad that my unborn brother was so ill."

Dr. Myers shook her head. "It's not at all selfish. When we're younger, we tend to see things in a much more A-plus-B-equals-C sort of way, because we don't really have a grasp of what's moral and what isn't. That's why young brains are so unfiltered, and a child will often tell an adult if they look ugly, or if they really need to 'go poo-poo.' Social protocols haven't registered, and we're much more primitive and to-the-point." She pursed her lips. "We don't censor ourselves quite as much as we do when we're grown up."

Kayla detected the less-than-subtle hint. Dr. Myers knew she was hiding something. "Yeah. I guess."

Dr. Myers leaned back in her chair and tucked a stray lock of hair behind her ear. Kayla noted, for the first time, how young she was. She couldn't have been a day over thirty. And the perfume she was wearing, rather than being the kind of thick and musky scent often chosen by more confident and mature women, was sweet, like vanilla and coconut. Instead of throwing Kayla off, and causing her to doubt the young doctor's capabilities, the realization made her feel more at ease. She liked that they were relatively close in age.

When Dr. Myers next spoke, her smooth voice seemed less polished, less sharp, though of course it hadn't changed at all. "How did Gabe's illness affect your childhood? If at all?"

Kayla puffed her cheeks up and slowly forced the air through her lips. "For the first few years, he was in and out of the hospital. At first, I didn't really understand what was going on. Just that whenever my parents had friends over, they'd speak in hushed whispers whenever they discussed him. I wasn't allowed to play with him, or even touch him. It was like he was a porcelain doll."

"That must have been difficult."

"Not really. I mean, I was little. I just did my own thing, and gave up trying to work out what was wrong. I just thought it was normal. It wasn't until his health went downhill a couple of years later that my parents sat me down, and said that maybe Gabe wouldn't be able to make it home from the hospital this time. I remember saying that was okay, because I could just go and visit him there instead. They just looked at me with these painfully sad faces, like I was too young to understand what was going on. Maybe I was. Anyway, from then on I barely saw them for months. They were constantly at his bedside, and I spent my evenings and weekends with Anna, our nanny."

"I see. And did you ever feel resentful that Gabe received so much attention while you were left behind, in a way?"

Kayla had never thought of it that way, but the pang in her heart told her that it must ring true on some level. Her eyes felt hot and prickly. "I suppose so. I used to try and draw these amazing pictures, or write perfectly rhyming poems to show my parents. They'd smile and say, 'That's great, sweetheart,' then never look at it again. I thought their apathy meant I was a rubbish writer, or a clumsy artist. Obviously Anna tried her best to make me feel special. She'd stick the drawings on the fridge and make me banana milk shakes and ruffle my hair. But there's nothing quite like the approval of your parents." Kayla laughed bitterly. *What kind of twisted psychopath holds a grudge toward her sick little brother?* "God, you must think I'm just some attention-seeking rich girl with Daddy issues."

Cassandra leaned forward. "I'd never think that, Kayla. I know there's something much deeper that's making it more difficult for you to grieve. And I'm determined to help you figure out what that is."

Kayla smiled. Not through happiness, but to show her gratitude. She was starting to see why her mother had warmed to Cassandra. "Thank you. I know I'm not doing it right, this whole bereavement thing. I can't stop thinking about it from a purely physical perspective. Like, we're all going to turn into dust, someday, it's a guaranteed energy shift. At Gabe's funeral, my nan read this poem about how when we die, we become a part of the earth, part of the elements. It was really beautiful, and it's stuck with me. It hurts much less to think of death in a literal sense, so I cling onto that. When I start to go any deeper, it's too excruciating."

"I understand that. But you need to go deeper, as hard as that is. And it's best to do it in a safe place like this, rather than by yourself in the middle of the night. I can help you, Kayla. It doesn't matter how long it takes."

Kayla knew she meant it. A cynic would interpret Cassandra's words as a moneymaking scheme, like a driving instructor who insisted a learner needed more lessons before they were ready to book their test. But something in Dr. Myers's eyes, a warm intensity, convinced Kayla otherwise. For whatever reason, Cassandra was invested in her struggles. "I know. I know I need to confront it. But whenever I think about the fact I'll never again hear Gabe sing, or Sam laugh, I feel like I'm being crushed. It's like a moment of extreme pain, then I detach myself from the thought and it goes away. I put up a barrier. I can't bear to stick around long enough to follow the thought pattern to the end."

Cassandra's voice softened, reaching an even gentler register than before. "That's the first time I've heard you say Sam's name."

Kayla swallowed hard. "Maybe it is."

A pause. "Do you feel ready to talk about what happened to him?"

Kayla doubted she'd ever be ready. But she found herself taking a deep breath and answering, "Yes. I think I am."

WHAT IS IT they say about watched pots? They never boil. But if you take an eye off them, for even a moment, they have a tendency to bubble over.

When Kayla got home from her therapy session, she took a long, steaming shower, flicked through one of the trashy but easy-to-digest magazines her mother was so obsessed with, and gave herself a manicure for the first time in years. It wasn't until she was blowing aggressively onto her fingertips, encouraging the varnish to dry, that she remembered to check her e-mails.

Being careful not to smudge the crimson paint, she typed her e-mail address and password into her laptop. *Inbox (38)* flashed onto her screen—another spambot had found her third e-mail address in as many years. But as she was deleting the penis enlargement offers and advice on "how to shed an inch of belly fat every day using this one weird old tip," one name in particular caught her eye.

Aran Peters.

Kayla's heart pounded as she waited for the message to load. It pounded even harder when she read the response.

He was going to help her.

Chapter 14

May 15, Thailand

THOUGH DAVE WAS a chatterbox, it wasn't until his health began to really suffer that he eventually told Russia about his condition. And even then it was through necessity, not guilt or obligation.

The group had completed their volunteering projects a few days earlier, and were allowed two days of downtime before taking to the hills, rivers, and forests of Sangkhlaburi on a two-day trekking and camping expedition. By the end of the first day it was clear Dave was struggling.

Having pitched up in an idyllic camping spot, nestled in the trees overlooking a vast lake, Dave, Russia, Bling, Kayla, and Sam were sitting around a paltry campfire that the boys had taken what felt like eight hours to gather and light. It felt too warm to be lighting a fire, but it seemed like the right thing to do on a camping trip. And besides, it helped keep the millions of bugs away.

The sun had not long set behind the hills, and the sky was a dusty shade of indigo streaked with pink and orange. Sam had pulled out his iPod and hit play on a nostalgic-sounding acoustic album, accompanied by a male singer's voice full of grit and melancholy. Russia, who'd found a full day of physical exertion exhausting, had laid her head on Dave's bony shoulder. It couldn't have been comfortable, but as the reflections from the campfire danced across her face, Kayla thought the moment looked like it belonged on a romantic chick flick, rather than one that was shared between the most dysfunctional couple she'd ever met.

She shuffled closer to Sam and laced her fingers between his. His cheeks dimpled as his lips curled into a smile. Her heart fluttered.

Dave took a deep breath. "Guys? I have something I have to tell you." Kayla looked up from their intertwined fingers and fixed a look of interest on her face—she wasn't supposed to know already. "I'm not very well."

Bling giggled. "Well, we knew that, you idiot."

For once, Dave didn't laugh. His expression remained steely. Bling looked immediately chastened and pressed her lips together, staring at her bare feet. "No. I mean, I'm really not very well. I have something called ALS, which affects my muscles. It's degenerative."

Russia sat up, frowning. "What does that mean?"

"It means my muscles will eventually deteriorate to the point where I'm completely paralyzed."

"What? Are you joking? If you are—"

"I'm not joking, Rush."

Russia stared at her boyfriend in stunned silence, unsure whether to shout at him for not telling her. Sam, who Dave had already told, reached across and slapped him on the back. "Sorry, mate. Wouldn't wish it on anyone."

"I'm sorry, Dave," Bling said. "That's awful. And I'm sorry I implied you were stupid." A sadness-laced twinkle in her eye. "I really thought you already knew," she added. Dave pushed her over and chuckled.

He turned to Russia and cupped her chin in his hand. "Russia?"

Russia's shoulders started to shake and her bottom lip trembled. "How did you . . . ? Why? Wh-When?"

"There is no why. It's a genetic defect. No rhyme or reason. It's supposed to run in families, but I don't have any relatives that have or had it. Do you mean how did I find out?" She nodded and closed her eyes. "Well, last year my muscles were twitching and cramping a lot, and they got stiff pretty easily after I went to the gym. I was finding it hard to run too, even though I'd been a sprinter in my early teens. I can't explain, really, but running and walking just didn't feel . . . natural. Which is a strange sensation when you've done those things your whole life. I put it down to being unfit, 'cause what else would you really think? I hired a personal trainer, which is pretty funny in hindsight." Dave laughed his signature laugh, but it didn't meet his eyes. He blinked hard. "Thankfully, my overprotective mum made me go to the doctors. And that's when they discovered I had ALS. At least, I think thankfully is the word. I still can't work out if I'd rather not know how ill I am. Ignorance is bliss, and all that."

A fat tear rolled down Russia's cheek, and Dave wiped it away with his thumb. Kayla desperately wanted Sam to turn off the downbeat music, but knew it'd be too obvious to do so. Russia asked, "When will it . . . happen? Fully?"

Dave turned and faced the campfire, staring intensely into the flickering flames. "That's why I'm bringing it up now. I'm losing movement in my right foot. And the toes on my left have no feeling." He ran his hands through his thick black hair, which somehow seemed less shiny than it had five minutes ago. "The process has started. And once that happens, it doesn't take long at all."

AT THE END of the second day of hiking, the group was exhausted, but they'd promised Dave a night out on which he could drown his sorrows. That morning, a minibus had taken him back to their guesthouse upon Russia's insistence that he couldn't possibly complete the hike with only one functional foot. He'd protested, but only meekly so.

When they'd met him in a Hawaiian-themed bar down a side street in town, his eyes were already glazed over and his face was slack—he'd been drinking all afternoon. The barmaids wandering around the tiki-bedecked bar in grass skirts and lays kept shooting him concerned glances. He was, after all, their only customer, and had been for quite some time, yet his wicker table was covered in small tumblers with tiny shot glasses inside. The deserted bar stunk of stale beer.

"I'll buy the first round. Five beers, five tequilas?" Bling said, heading to the bar without waiting for a response.

Russia pecked Dave lightly on the cheek and sat down next to him without saying a word. None of them knew quite what to say, or what kind of spirits he would be in. If it had been Kayla, she'd be sinking into a deep depression around about now. But she knew that Dave's happiness wasn't as volatile as most. If anyone could tackle this with a smile, it'd be him.

It took less than sixty seconds for him to prove her theory right. A dopey grin spread across his face and he announced, "You know what? You wanna know something? I love you guys. Like. I can't believe I've not even known you for eight weeks, and already you're like family. You know what we are? We're the famous fucking five."

Sam laughed. "Mate, the famous five was a series of children's books by Enid Blyton. You can't go around calling us that. It's tragic."

"Stupid foreigners," Bling joked, arriving back at the table with a tray full of glasses, wobbling precariously and splashing the already sticky floor with amber-colored liquid. "Come on, let's drink these and go somewhere more lively, where we can dance?" She froze, and glanced awkwardly at Dave. Thankfully, he was too intoxicated to pick up on the reference to physical activity. Bling shot a relieved look at Kayla, miming at wiping her forehead with the back of one hand and throwing a shot of tequila down her throat with the other.

"I'm just nipping outside for a cigarette. You coming, Russia?" Kayla asked, before realizing that Russia was too concerned with jamming her tongue down Dave's throat to listen.

Sam piped up, "I'll come." Kayla looked puzzled. "Not to smoke, obviously. Just to keep you company."

Once outside, Kayla stood with her back and one foot against the wall and sparked up her first cigarette of the day. Sam slid down the wall and sat with his back to it, resting his elbows on his knees. "Makes you think, doesn't it."

Kayla inhaled deeply and blew a stream of white smoke up toward the rapidly darkening sky. "What, Dave?"

Sam nodded. "Yeah. It's just so . . . shit. You know? How can a guy that great possibly deserve to be slowly paralyzed by his own faulty genes?"

"It makes me feel sick. Genuinely sick to my stomach."

Sam sighed. "Me too. I'd do anything to change things for him. You hear all these stories about people his age essentially digging their own graves, with drugs and whatever, when he'd probably kill to have a chance at a full life. It just seems so selfish. Stuff like taking ketamine, driving at a hundred miles an hour . . ."

"Committing suicide?"

Sam closed his eyes. "That's not what I meant, Kayla. I'm sorry, I didn't mean to—"

Kayla tapped the ash dangling from the end of her cigarette onto the pavement. "No, it's fine. If I'm being honest, sometimes I catch myself feeling pissed off at Gabe. That's an awful thing to admit, I know, and I understand that he was driven to it. Or at least, I try to understand. I loved him to pieces, and still do. But why couldn't he just have asked for help? Gone to the police, or deleted his Facebook, instead of throwing it all away? It seems like such a waste." She slid down the wall so she was sitting next to Sam, making sure to edge close enough to him so their shoulders and knees were lightly touching.

"It sucks that we have to learn life lessons like this the hard way," Sam said. "I guess you never really have perspective until you go through severe grief, or meet someone like Dave. You can't teach it in schools, can you? My school uniform had a little castle sewn onto the top pocket of the blazers with Carpe Diem embroidered underneath. I've never really understood that saying until now. Seizing the day back in high school meant having a double cheeseburger for lunch, or nipping behind the sports hall to meet up with a girl instead of going to maths." Sam glanced quickly at Kayla. "Not that I ever did that . . ."

Kayla smiled, crushing the stub of her cigarette beneath her battered flip-flop. She leaned in a little closer to Sam, trying not to feel too self-conscious that she almost definitely smelled of smoke. Brushing her hair out of her face, she asked softly, "And what do you think it means now?"

"I'm . . . not sure. But I'm starting to understand the power of good moments." Sam reached across and cupped Kayla's tiny hand in his oversized one.

She turned to him, relinquishing all attempts at appearing coy or cute. Gently pulling him toward her, she kissed the only man in the world capable of making her stomach flip and her chest ache the way it did whenever he smiled, or talked, or laughed.

His lips were warm and soft as he brushed them against hers. The blaring sounds of the karaoke seemed to die down into the background, and the scent of warm pavement and barbecue smoke faded away. Kayla closed her eyes, relaxing into Sam as he stroked the nape of her neck with his thumb. Gentle pecks became firmer, more insistent. She shuddered despite the warm night.

Kayla thought back to that first night in the park. How she'd regretted not kissing him back almost as soon as she'd pulled away. How she kept lying awake at night, imagining how things could have been if she'd reciprocated. How good it would feel to kiss him. How good it would feel to never stop.

Yeah. This feels good.

As she erupted into a huge grin, the rhythm of the kiss was broken. Sam pulled away—but just a few millimeters, so his nose was still touching hers—and mirrored her smile. "What? Why are you smiling?" he mumbled.

"I think you know," Kayla whispered.

Then the sound came back. Bling stumbled through the exit, which had strands of beads in place of a traditional door. She didn't seem to notice—or care—that she'd interrupted a moment. She exclaimed, "They're firing up the karaoke machine! Dave is warming up. He sounds like a duck caught in a blender." Holding out her hands to help Sam up off the floor, she asked, "Who wants to sing Shania Twain with me?"

THREE HOURS LATER Kayla was fumbling around in her bum bag for the key to her bedroom. She'd left the Tiki Bar feeling more drunk than she had the entire time they'd been in Thailand. The bar had swooped and plunged into oblivion around her, swallowed by the edges of her languishing peripheral vision. It had become busier and busier as their sparkling renditions of pop classics floated into the street and seduced passersby into joining them. She had taken her seventh fall into a fellow clubber as her cue to go back to the guesthouse, and in typical inebriated fashion, she hadn't considered it necessary to warn anyone of her departure.

Trying the handle and realizing the door was already un-locked, she pushed into the bedroom, and was immediately hit by the smell of men's aftershave. Which was strange, considering it was an all-girls dorm. Kayla flicked on the light switch, blinking fiercely in an attempt to adapt to the fluorescent beams glaring aggressively overhead.

"Hi, Kayla," a gravelly, slurred voice greeted her.

She turned to face her bed, and saw Oliver perched on the wrinkled sheets. He stood up and walked toward her with a carnal smirk etched onto his tanned face. "Wait, wh-what are you doing here?" she asked. "How did you get into my room?"

"Are you pleased to see me?" Oliver tilted his head and bit his bottom lip. She was too drunk to work out whether he was in a similar condition.

"Indifferent. I'm pretty smashed."

"Just how I like my women," he grinned.

"Er, right. Well, I'm going to go to bed now. So I'll see you to-morrow?" Kayla couldn't be bothered to chat. She felt drowsy and longed to rest her head on the lumpy pillow.

"How about I join you?"

"Well, yeah, you'll have to. You're our tour guide?"

"I meant in bed." He edged closer to her, until she could smell the Thai beer on his sour breath. He'd definitely been drinking.

"Oh, erm, no thanks."

"Why not? I've seen the way you look at me." He grabbed her by the waist, and she tried not to visibly squirm. "You're so curva-ceous. Just looking at you makes me hard. Feel." He took her hand and yanked it toward his crotch.

"Again, I think I'll pass." She pulled her hand back to her side.

Oliver emitted a doggerel groan and pressed his lips forcefully against hers. *Am I drunker than I thought? Am I really giving off signals that I want him?* Kayla tried to pull away, but found the wall to be a mere inch behind her. Her back met the plasterboard. "Get off, man. This isn't funny."

"Stop complaining, love." His tongue was covering an alarm-ing amount of surface area on her neck, leaving a trail of slobber behind it. His stubbled chin was like sandpaper on her pink, sun-burnt skin. She put her palms on his shoulders and feebly tried to push him off. His hand found the zip on her denim shorts.

"I'm not fucking kidding, Oliver, get off me," she snapped, trying not to let her growing fear seep into her voice.

She felt her shorts drop to her ankles, and he pushed pain-fully against her. She tried not to let panic rise in her throat. Was this really happening? Why hadn't she told anyone where she was going? That third shot of tequila was making it difficult to think straight. Would anyone hear her if she yelled for help? *Wait, now there's something else rising in my throat.*

Kayla coughed violently, bile catching at the back of her throat, and vomit sprayed down the back of Oliver's shirt, sliding down the back of his neck and filling his ear with chunky, acidic puke. He recoiled quickly, his mouth gaping in disbelief. "You vile bitch! Did you just fucking puke on me?"

Kayla wiped her mouth and winked at him. She couldn't resist. He darted from the room in the direction of the communal toilet, and she hastily locked the bedroom door behind him, pressing her forehead against it and closing her eyes.

Don't cry. Don't even think. Just go to sleep.

THE SUN POURED through the curtainless window the next morning, and Kayla peeled one eye opened. Her mouth felt both dry and sticky, coated with a thick layer of sour fuzz, and an invisible fist was clenched around her stomach. She was in her bed, fully clothed, and saw that only half of her roommates had returned— Bling was nowhere to be seen. Russia was lying facedown in her pillow, her blond hair arranged like a bird's nest that had fallen from the highest branch of a tall tree. The room was quieter than it had ever been. It was like there was no longer a world outside.

The lingering stench of Oliver's aftershave on her sheets was enough to rouse Kayla from her bed. Slinging some sandals onto her filthy feet, she opened the door as quietly as she could. She had to find Sam. She had to tell him about Oliver.

She padded down the corridor and knocked on the boys' door. After a few seconds she heard heavy, uneven footsteps and Ralph's face emerged through the crack. He rubbed his sleep-edged eyes and groggily said, "All right, Kayla. How can I help you on this fine morning?"

"Is Sam around?"

Ralph grinned. "Well, you see, the thing is, Sam has company. The sly dog kept us up all night. Lucky bugger."

"Company?" A girly giggle wafted toward the door. A familiar girly giggle.

Kayla nudged the door wider and saw a tangle of thick black hair spread across Sam's bare chest. His muscular arm was wrapped around a petite, naked figure.

The girl's face was buried in his shoulder. But Kayla knew who it was.

It was Bling.

Chapter 15

July 12, England

ARAN PETERS HADN'T changed at all.

Sitting opposite Kayla, the sunlight illuminated the frizzy top layer of his wiry hair like a halo of fuzz. It was cut close to his scalp in a bid to tame the unruliness, but the effect was barbed wire curls cut off mid-bounce in a range of directions and lengths. Instead of stereotypical, thick-rimmed geek glasses, he sported dainty spectacles that perched delicately on his small pointed nose. His skin was the pallid shade of wallpaper paste with roughly the same cratered texture, and his small eyes were a watery blue.

If Kayla didn't know any better, she'd guess he had some sort of terminal illness. His frame disappeared beneath his two-sizes-too-big jeans, bunched together at the waist with a canvas belt, and a faded superhero T-shirt that had seen one too many washes.

"I hope you understand that what you're asking me to do is

dodgy." They were sitting in a window booth in a deserted pub—
Monday lunchtime wasn't exactly peak drinking time. He slurped
his lemonade through a straw, not bothering to lower his voice
despite the bartender's ears pricking up. "I mean, don't get me
wrong, I enjoy dodgy. I live for dodgy. But I sort of need to know
why I'm doing it. My days of wreaking havoc with the country's
technological defenses just for the hell of it are over. I'm much
more refined now. More mature." He winked, taking another gigantic slurp and reaching into his scruffy khaki backpack for his
laptop. It was covered in stickers and logos of dubstep bands Kayla
had never heard of.

She stifled a scoff. "So you want to know why I'm asking you to
do this?" Aran nodded, furiously typing in the third password his
system had demanded of him. She wondered what on earth he had
hiding on his computer to warrant such rigorous privacy mea-
sures. "Surely you heard about what happened?" News in their
tiny hometown usually spread pretty quickly.

"Yeah, I did." He didn't apologize for her loss or tell her how
sad it was. It was a pleasant change—his social ineptitude was refreshing. "But I still don't really get why you want me to do it. I
thought that was it, case closed, blatant suicide." Slurp. "So why
are you going through all this trouble?"

"I need closure," Kayla said. She decided to omit the fact that
her therapist had told her so. The fewer people who considered
her a raging lunatic, the easier it'd be to convince them to help. "I
need someone to blame."

Aran nodded, chewing the insides of his cheeks. His already
narrow face collapsed into itself, skeletal cheekbones jutting
through his skin. "That's good enough for me. So the game plan
is for me to hack into Facebook's servers and find out who created

the profile that sent Gabriel the hate mail?" Kayla nodded. "Easy. Though obviously I won't be able to find out exactly who made it, just where they did it. I'll get you an IP address, which should help narrow it down."

"You reckon you'll be able to?"

"Yeah, but I dunno how long it'll take. It's complicated, but simply hacking into the profile itself won't be enough. It'd maybe give me the e-mail address used to create it, but that wouldn't be much use either, as that'll probably be a ghost account too. Hang on, let me check." The clatter of touch-typing and a few bleeps later, Kayla was amazed that Aran had already found his answer. "Yep, as I suspected the e-mail address is just a series of letters and numbers." Aran polished off his drink, the ice cubes chinking against the empty glass, and he looked around to get the waiter's attention.

"Hang on, you've already signed into the account that sent those messages?"

"Yup."

"Can I . . . can I see?"

Aran sighed. "You sure?" Following Kayla's swift nod, he clicked off several private browser windows and turned the screen around to face her. She tried to prevent a gasp escaping from her lips, but it was too late.

Daniel Burns. The only messages sent from Daniel Burns's account were to Gabriel Finch.

It was nauseating to see them again in black and white, stamped with seen times over the course of a few weeks. The first: *Dirty faggot scum.* They progressed rapidly to rape threats, violence threats, death threats. The last one, on March 13, hadn't been read by its recipient. It simply consisted of two words: *Good riddance.*

It felt like she had been kicked in the stomach with a hard-toed boot. She turned away. "So that account was created with the sole purpose of tormenting my brother?"

"Looks like it. They don't have a profile picture, or any status updates. It's unlikely this account was made with the intention of posting every meal the guy consumed with the caption 'nom nom nom.' Or, indeed, targeting any other victims. It was made purely to attack Gabriel."

Kayla sat back in the leather booth, letting her hands drop into her lap. "And we have no way of knowing who made it?"

"No, I didn't say that. It's traceable, definitely. It just might take a while."

VEINY HANDS AROUND *Sam's throat. His eyes bulging.*

Kayla tried to dial 999. She couldn't type in the right combination of keys. 997 #99 989. She crushed her phone in her hand, and pain shot through her palm as the shattered glass screen sliced straight through the skin. Blood drenched the tiled floor.

Sam's face was purple. Frozen in a single expression of terror as his frantic gasps slowed and he realized that this was it. The end.

The light behind his eyes was snuffed out, like moist fingers crushing a candle flame.

The person whose hands were wrapped around Sam's airwaves turned to face Kayla. Their face was blurred.

She woke up drenched in clammy sweat. Her sheets were sodden, even though she'd left the window open to allow for a draft. Thai-style humidity had replaced the traditional British summer weather that rarely nudged the thermometer above seventy degrees. Her legs were tangled around the duvet—she felt like a bear caught in a trap too complex to unravel. Instead of wrestling with the linen and spiking her adrenaline, Kayla willed herself to go back to sleep, and tried to empty her mind of thoughts. She had to see that face.

But it was no use. She wriggled free of the duvet, rolled over and stared at the ceiling, wiping her sticky forehead with the back of her hand. The sweat felt cold.

The recurring nightmare that haunted her dreams every night was the only time she saw anything clearly, right up until the very last second when she inevitably, inescapably, woke up. During the day, she couldn't shake the mental fuzz—the fluffy pink candy floss clinging to her thoughts and memories, making them gloopy and impossible to process. But at night the visions were so vivid that she felt more alert than she did when she was actually awake.

She just wished she could stay asleep long enough to unearth what her subconscious was trying to tell her.

The lack of information surrounding Sam's death infuriated Kayla. Why had the investigation fizzled out so fast? No more questions from the British police. She hadn't heard a peep from Shepherd in weeks. And nothing had come of the police search in Thailand. They seemed to have all but given up when their initial hunts of the obvious locations presented no new clues.

If the news coverage had been sparse at the beginning, the measly mention his story currently received at the end of the regional news was nothing short of degrading. It seemed absolutely alien to her that a twenty-year-old boy could vanish off the face of the earth, under violent circumstances, and nobody would bat an eyelid. If it weren't for Sam's mum and her undisguised heartbreak, she might even suspect there had never been a Samuel Kingfisher at all. Her inability to grieve for him certainly suggested so.

And then there was the fact that she couldn't so much as think about Sam without then thinking of her brother. Her psychological disorientation was causing the grief for the two men she'd lost to merge into one ball of pain. She could no longer emotionally distinguish between the two tragedies. Both came with an identical matching nightmare, and both engulfed her with an uneasiness that wasn't usually synonymous with normal grief.

Both gave her the niggling feeling that something wasn't right.

THE TENSION AT Berry Hill was so thick it was almost tangible. Martha Finch had tripled her daily alcohol consumption, and Mark had quadrupled his quota of work-based stress. He would call Martha to say he would be home a couple of hours late from the office—something had come up. She would pour another drink to pass the time and ease the anger. Mark would dread coming home to a drunk wife, who screamed and yelled and insisted he was having an affair. The next night he'd come home even later, to an even drunker and even angrier Martha.

Even Kayla's nan seemed to be avoiding her. Yesterday morning Kayla had found herself making porridge while Nan was waiting for a pot of tea to brew. Neither woman had said a word to each other, and Kayla couldn't put her finger on why. She hadn't seen Nan for a few days. For an old lady, she had a fairly hectic social calendar, chock full of various coffee dates, garden center visits, and trips to the bingo hall. Usually, Kayla loved that about her nan, and hoped she would have just as much joie de vivre when she hit eighty-five. But lately she'd found herself getting frustrated when she knocked on Nan's door for a chat, or to ask if she wanted to go for a walk, and was met with silence. In a selfish way, she wanted everyone else to stop living their lives. She'd maybe feel less quarantined that way.

The boredom of being cooped up in the house all day—feeling like Rapunzel except with notably shorter hair and absolutely no Prince Charming to rescue her—had driven Kayla to consider the possibility of flying back out to Southeast Asia. She'd been the only one to fly home following Sam's disappearance. Dave, understandably, didn't want to waste his remaining days of mobility back in England when he could be continuing his adventure, and Russia had insisted on keeping him company. Kayla assumed Bling was still out there. At least, she hadn't heard otherwise. If all had gone according to plan, they'd be in Cambodia around now. Or maybe they'd stayed a little longer in Vietnam, taking time to properly explore, now that they weren't sticking to a preset schedule. Kayla felt a pang of longing.

Whenever she thought about the last month of the trip, a wave of white hot, self-directed anger surged through her veins. Sam had been so distant, but if she'd known it'd be the last four weeks she'd ever spend with him, she might have cut him some slack. Just thinking about how they treated each other filled her with self-hatred. She'd give anything to have those days back. She bit down on her bottom lip until it bled, feeling a strange sort of satisfaction as she dabbed at the cut and watched as the fine creases on the back of her hand filled with ruby red streaks.

After that hungover morning in Sangkhlaburi, she couldn't help but feel betrayed—by the people around her and by life itself. The feeling that nothing had turned out like it was supposed to clung to her everywhere they went. She'd think of Gabe, for one dreadful second forgetting he was gone, and then painful realization would hit her like a truck. Every time she smelled Oliver's syrupy aftershave, her stomach turned. Whenever she heard Bling's laugh or Sam's deep voice, she saw it all again. The tangle of black hair. The naked chest. The unmistakable smell of sex in the air.

The arm that should have been wrapped around her instead. The arm that now never would be.

Chapter 16

July 14, England

"YOU KNOW WHEN you're abroad, and it's absolutely scorching?"

Dr. Myers nodded. Kayla was starting not to notice the ever-present red light that recorded her every word. Perhaps it was the fact she had nobody else to talk to, but opening up to Cassandra was becoming much easier.

"Not just hot. The kind of sweltering heat that invades every pore and orifice in your body, and leaves you feeling suffocated, like there's no way on earth you can possibly stand it any longer. Like you can't move, or speak, or think about anything other than how hot it is. Then, just when you reach breaking point, there's a breeze. And even if it only lasts a few seconds, the relief is incredible. Suddenly, the heat is bearable again, if only for a few more minutes." Kayla looked away from Cassandra. She still felt embarrassed, discussing her feelings so candidly. "I guess that if losing Gabe was the heat, Sam was the breeze. He just made the overwhelming absence of my brother a little more tolerable, you know? But now . . ." Kayla met Dr. Myers's eyes. "Now, they're both gone. And the heat is relentless."

Dr. Myers was quiet for a moment, as if trying to process what Kayla was saying. After a while, she said, "Do you feel like there's been any relief, or 'breeze,' since you've been back home?"

Kayla's heart sank when she realized there hadn't. Dr. Myers nodded. She knew what the silence meant. "But in a strange kind of way, the heat has been less intense," Kayla mused aloud. "It's more of a dull warmth than all-consuming grief." She twirled a strand of hair around in her finger. "I know it must be so frustrating for you that I just can't seem to connect with what's going on. I really am trying."

"Of course not, Kayla. This isn't about me."

"Yeah, I know." *But for some reason, I care what you think.* Kayla leaned back in her chair and started to pluck stray pieces of fluff off her jumper. She couldn't stop fidgeting. There was something she wanted to say, but she didn't know how to bring it up. She took a deep breath. "Can I tell you something? And you have to promise not to think I'm crazy?"

Dr. Myers chuckled kindly, like you would to an elderly relative. "Go ahead."

"Well, I just feel like there's more to it than everyone thinks. Sam . . . Sam wasn't a hardcore druggie. He really wasn't. And I'm not blinded by grief, or love, or whatever else. I genuinely think the police have got it wrong. And it's . . . unsettling. To think we're all missing something big. Like, why did none of us hear the commotion if he was dragged out kicking and screaming by brutes? We were all the way out at the lake, but nobody saw or heard a thing. Anywhere. I just think that's weird. And for there to have been *that* much blood, he must have been in the room for a while before he left. Which doesn't really line up with the theory.

"I dunno. It probably sounds like I watch too much TV. But the gut feeling I first had when I was sitting in the Thai police station, and they were telling me it was drug-based . . . I can't shake it." Kayla debated telling Cassandra about the dreams, but decided against it. She must have seemed insane enough already. Her therapist's pixie features were perfectly composed as usual, giving away nothing about what she was thinking. "What do you think?"

"Honestly?" Dr. Myers shrugged. "I'm a little relieved. It's the first real sign you've shown to suggest that you're beginning the grieving process over Sam. Stage one is, famously, denial. Denial about what's real, and what . . . isn't."

Kayla felt disappointed. She closed her eyes, trying to mask her dismay.

She doesn't see it.

KAYLA KNEW THERE was one person who'd listen to her theories, no matter how outlandish. Not just to humor her, but because Sam meant more to her than he did to anyone else.

Kayla had the house to herself. She was sitting at the breakfast bar—the kitchen was her favorite room at Berry Hill—cradling a cup of coffee in her ring-covered hands. The frothy cappuccino smelled delicious but was too hot to drink immediately. She was staring at the television set mounted on the wall. It was on mute, but she hadn't even noticed. She was too nervous.

She clambered off the bar stool and wandered across to close the French doors. She'd opened them to allow a bit of fresh air to breeze into the room, but she needed privacy for the phone call she was about to make. Not that the gardener trimming the hedges could hear her over the roar of the machine and the crackling of chopped twigs, but if there was one thing crime dramas had taught her, it's that you can never be too careful when it comes to making assumptions about who you can trust.

Kayla squinted up at the surveillance cameras nestled in every ceiling corner, and wondered whether they were equipped with sound recording facilities. It was possibly something she should know, as the daughter of a surveillance mogul. She never could understand why her dad had them installed in their own home—it seemed like an unnecessary security measure, given the wrought-iron gates and buzzer system that prevented outside access to the property. In any case, their presence made her feel uneasy. Why had she never noticed how claustrophobic they were?

Maybe the garden was a better idea after all. She slid the doors open, grabbing her phone and her coffee off the counter, and made her way to her favorite spot in the world.

At the bottom of their main lawn—they had several—there was a rope swing. It was neither a fancy, ornate wooden beauty nor a tatty, childish tire on the end of a fraying length of cord. It was a simple plank of twisted driftwood, secured to the branches of a grand old willow tree with beige rope and intricate knots. When Kayla was little, she'd loved brushing aside the curtains of willow leaves and visiting her special place. The willow made her feel like Pocahontas, and she'd wish the gnarled old trunk would talk back to her as it had in her favorite childhood movie. When she reached the age of twelve, her dad assumed she'd be more into boys and makeup than playing football in the garden with Gabe before fighting over who got to sit on the rope swing first, and she'd seen the gardener taking it down. She burst into tears—she wasn't ready to lose such an emblem of her childhood. Her dad had made the gardener put it back up. It had been there ever since.

Resting her cappuccino on the thick grass, Kayla perched gingerly on the swing, unsure if the years of neglect would have weakened it. Despite a few creaks, it seemed sturdy enough. She placed her phone on the ground next to her coffee and gripped the ropes on either side of the wood, but couldn't bring herself to kick her feet against the earth and start swinging. She weighed significantly more than the last time she'd swung on it, and dreaded the thought of causing the supporting branch above her to crack, taking a wealth of memories tumbling down with it.

As she peered up to examine the tree's strength, her stomach dropped. Tucked in the corner where the branch met the trunk was the last thing she'd expected to see out there.

Another camera.

It was covered in moss and looked rusty, like it hadn't been tended to in years. She supposed the lack of a blue light flashing from the tiny bulb meant it no longer contained working batteries. It definitely no longer operated. Still, that wasn't the point. The hours she'd spent out here as a child suddenly felt violated. She'd felt so free, so unfettered. But she'd been watched the entire time.

From a practical point of view, it made sense. A young girl named Abbie had vanished from her garden in rural Northumberland when Kayla was in primary school, so for her parents to take safety precautions was understandable.

But Kayla couldn't help wracking her brains for moments she'd thought were only hers but instead had shared with the person on the other side of the camera. The time she'd sat on the swing, dangling legs not yet able to touch the ground, crying hiccupy tears because her mum had barely glanced at the necklace Kayla had made her out of chipped seashells. The time she'd pushed Gabe off the swing in the midst of a childish fight and caused him to fracture his underdeveloped wrist—an incident they'd both later insisted was an accident. The camera had seen it all. The laughs, the lies, and the tears weren't a secret after all.

Kayla felt nauseated. How much of her life had been completely transparent? She squirmed, trying to shake off the invisible ants that were crawling up and down her arms and spine. If only as means of distraction, she leaned down, took a big sip of milky coffee, and picked up her phone.

Best get this over with.

KATHY KINGFISHER AGREED to meet with Kayla again.

That was the first hurdle jumped. Now to convince Sam's mum that she hadn't completely lost her mind.

The first time Kayla had met Kathy had also been the first time she felt there might be more to Sam's disappearance that everyone thought. She knew she needed to spend more time with that peculiar sensation to try and translate what it meant. She also trusted Kathy to voice her honest opinions. There were a lot of things Kayla hadn't told anyone back home that weren't related, exactly, but were gnawing away at the back of her mind: what had happened with Oliver; the complex emotions between her and Sam; Sam's growing hostility during the last few weeks in Phuket.

"I was surprised to hear from you again, I must admit." Kathy took a bite of her marzipan French Fancy cake. They were in Betty's Tea Room in York—Kayla had taken the train down to meet her just five days after their last coffee date.

"I know. I'm sorry for phoning you out of the blue. I know you must just want to start getting on with your life, without reminders of Sam's last few months following you around."

Kathy shook her head vehemently, spraying cake crumbs everywhere. She swallowed her mouthful. "No, that's not what I meant. You're a lovely girl, Kayla, and it's nice to know that Sam had friends who cared so much about him. I just meant that I thought I might have frightened you off last time, sitting there and crying like that. I am sorry, it must have been very awkward for you."

"No, not at all," Kayla lied. "I know how you must be feeling. It's . . . it's horrendous, really."

Kathy nodded, her lips pursed. "So why did you call me? I know you wouldn't ask to meet a middle-aged woman a few hours away from home unless you were either really struggling or wanted to know something about her son." She smiled warmly. "Either is okay, love."

Kayla sighed, stirring sugar into her Earl Grey tea. "A bit of both, I guess. I'm starting to miss Sam a lot." Kathy gave her an odd look, cocking her head to the side. Kayla backtracked quickly. "I missed him before, of course. But now that the shock is wearing off, it's sinking in that there are certain things I'll never have again. Talking to him about stupid things, laughing at his sarcasm and the way he always deliberately misunderstood me. Silly things, really." She looked down. How could she tell Kathy the truth? Time to bite the bullet. "The thing is, Kathy, I loved Sam. And I think he loved me too."

Kathy sat up, straightening her back. The illusion that Kayla and Sam had been nothing more than good friends had just been shattered. "I see. Were you . . . ?"

"Boyfriend and girlfriend? No."

Silence. Kayla guessed there were a multitude of curiosities zapping through Kathy's head. Had they slept together? Why had they not taken their relationship to the next level? Did Kayla know more than she was letting on? She waited for Kathy to ask the most burning question of all, but she never did. Kayla took that as her cue to explain everything, romantic or otherwise, that had happened: the uncensored version. How there had been endless almosts, mistakes with others, a rapidly diminishing closeness toward the end. It was important that Kathy knew all the details, though she left out the unsavory details of Oliver's and Bling's roles.

That still didn't mean she was keen to discuss her relationship with Sam further, to open questions to the floor. She launched straight into the next item on her agenda. "I wanted to know whether you'd been in contact with the police over here about the case."

Kathy looked surprised, her eyebrows jumping into her limp, greasy fringe. "Of course I have. At the beginning, I spoke to them every day. Have they not contacted you?"

"No. Well, sort of. When I first got back, I spoke to Shepherd. Mason Shepherd," Kayla added. Kathy nodded in recognition. "But he seemed . . . I don't know. Distracted?"

"Disinterested?" Kathy asked.

"Disinterested." Kayla gestured exasperatedly. "I thought it was just me. Was he like that with you too?"

"Yes. I found it strange. DI Sadie Winters has been much more engaged."

Kayla's ears pricked up. "Winters? I don't think I've met her." She couldn't keep the confusion from her voice. There was a whole other police officer working on the case who hadn't even bothered to contact her? "She's probably just overlooked me. I guess they all have a fairly strong belief in their drugs theory, so why would they need to talk to his friend twice? The Thai police had already grilled me." Kayla shrugged. "I dunno. I just think that if I was them, I'd want to check the box then check it again, just to be safe." *Just to make sure I didn't kill your son.*

Kathy sat back in her chair, exhaling loudly. "Well, as far as I'm aware the case isn't being investigated much further over here. The Thai police are on the lookout for the drug dealers Sam had been . . . contacting. But there's no new evidence, nothing to disprove their theory. Sam is assumed to have been murdered, with a drug conflict as the main motivation behind it." Kathy's face crumpled.

Oh no, she's going to cry again. Crap. This was a mistake.

"I hate the idea of my boy in pain. For there to have been that much blood . . . what must they have done to him? Murder . . . it's such a brutal word. I don't know what I'll do when they find the body. I can't bear to know what injuries he'd suffered. Oh God . . ."

Kayla didn't know what to say. There was more she wanted to ask Kathy, but she'd underestimated how fragile this grieving mother still was. Kayla couldn't bring herself to think about the pain Sam must have gone through. She wouldn't allow her mind to wander that deeply into the realms of misery.

She cleared her throat. "Kathy, I'm sorry to be insensitive, I really am. But would it be at all possible for you to give me some contact details for Winters? I have some things I want to ask her."

"Sure, Kayla," she sniffed into a soggy handkerchief. "Whatever you need. But please don't cling onto false hope. I know there are a few things that don't quite make sense. But digging them up isn't going to bring him back, is it?"

"No," Kayla sighed. "Nothing can bring him back."

Though she wasn't about to let go of the idea entirely.

Chapter 17

May 18, Thailand

"What happened between Bling and I meant nothing."

Sam's eyes looked as sad as Kayla felt. Large, shiny, and doe-like, they seemed an even darker brown than usual. If she had been watching as an onlooker, she'd have wanted to reach across and give him a hug.

Kayla smiled a little too widely. "It's fine! Honestly. You guys are cute together."

Sam groaned. "No, we aren't. It was a stupid drunken mistake. Bling and I are just friends, nothing more."

Kayla paused, pressing her lips together. Swallowing what she really wanted to say. "Yeah, well, so are we."

"I've fucked up, haven't I?" Sam bowed his head.

Kayla couldn't summon the energy to reply. She didn't feel angry at Sam. Or even Bling, for that matter. Neither of them owed her anything. Instead, she felt like her heart had been torn out with their bare hands, leaving her empty and sad, wishing it had never happened. Wishing she could un-see their moment of raw intimacy. Wishing she could forget the terrifying moments in her bedroom the night before. Wishing she never had to look at Oliver again. Wishing she could run away from it all. But wasn't that what she was already doing? Running away to Thailand to escape her broken life?

It had taken two full days for Sam to realize that she knew everything. Then, at first, he'd overcompensated with generosity, offering to carry her bags, asking her thoughtful questions, rubbing after-sun lotion into her sunburnt back. He'd mistaken her quietness for a fierce hangover. Conversations between him and Bling were stilted and awkward, and they never made eye contact. Kayla tried her best to act like nothing had changed, but the damage had already been done, and by the second day she was even more hurt that neither of them had bothered to tell her what had happened themselves.

Between visiting the Mon village, spending time with the tribe, and exploring the temple, the group had been busy enough that perhaps neither of them had thought it timely to enlighten her. But after the first day, when they had all retired to their rooms, utterly felled by their hangovers, Bling simply climbed into her bed and read a book on her Kindle before falling asleep.

The next day, a water-filled excursion river rafting and visiting hot springs similarly saw no confessions. Kayla was keen not to ruin the dynamic of the group. After all, it wasn't the others' fault that she'd developed inappropriate feelings toward Sam. So she'd kept quiet. As far as the others were aware, there had been no attempted rape, no drunken tomfoolery, and absolutely no heartache whatsoever. Even Oliver, though never meeting Kayla's eye, was carrying on as if nothing had happened.

It wasn't until two days later that the illusion was shattered. They'd been discussing how frequently Ralph and Thomas had "gotten laid like a brick" while in Thailand when the attention had turned elsewhere. Guffawing like the buffoon he was, Ralph said, "Sam is such a dark horse. You think he's all sweet and innocent, then *bam*, he's got one girl in his bed and another banging on his door looking for him."

Sam closed his eyes and dropped his head into his hands before looking up at Kayla and raising his eyebrows, silently asking her, *Was it you? Did you know all along?* She'd nodded, once. He looked like he might cry.

Bling giggled and slapped Ralph's arm playfully. Kayla couldn't help but wonder whether she liked Sam or not, and whether it'd be worse if she did. If the night really had been just a drunken mistake, then it hurt her less. It didn't challenge her relationship with Sam. But on the other hand, if Bling genuinely cared for Sam, then Kayla knew she wouldn't be suffering for nothing—Bling would have acted out of genuine longing.

And as a girl similarly enamored with Sam, it was something she couldn't hold against Bling.

THE FULL MOON Party. There isn't an aspiring traveler in the world who isn't familiar with the famous dance music festival. Held on Haad Run Nok Beach, it attracts passionate partygoers in the tens of thousands to enjoy the music, the breathtaking surroundings, and, more often than not, the thriving hallucinogenic scene.

It would also mark the end of their eight-week stint with Escaping Grey and, much to Kayla's delight, their time spent being herded like sheep by Oliver, the dirty pervert. Her skin crawled every time he cockily gloated about his conquests the night before—she wondered how many of them had been wholly consensual—or whenever she saw him checking out his reflection in a glass window.

She knew she should tell someone what had happened. She owed it to his next prey, whoever she might be. But from a purely selfish perspective, the thought of pressing charges and dealing with the aftermath—endless probing and probably a very public trial—seemed like too much for her to cope with. In six days she'd never have to see him again. For now, that was enough.

She couldn't help but imagine what Sam's reaction would be if she told him. He was, as far as half-giant men go, extraordinarily gentle, if not always graceful. The kind of man who scooped up intruder spiders with an upturned glass and a sheet of paper to return them to the great outdoors rather than flushing them down the toilet without a second thought. But Kayla had seen how protective he was over his friends. Whenever Russia attracted unwanted attention on nights out, Sam would wrap his arm around her waist and glare at her admirers, who would take one look at his houselike build and run for the hills. Or when Ralph had one too many drinks and slurred racists remarks in the presence of Bling and Dave, Sam would say, in a friendly but firm parental tone, "All right, mate. That's enough."

Kayla wasn't the type to desire a knight in shining armor to protect her, but a small part of her wondered what it'd be like to have Sam defend her honor and pummel Oliver's perfectly pointed nose until it resembled a bag of wrenches. Either way, she'd never know.

That night, the group would board an overnight bus, then take a boat to the island of Ko Pha Ngan, where they'd spend two days relaxing on the illustrious gulf coast beaches before celebrating their frankly astonishing survival of the tour at the Full Moon Party. The next morning, a bus would take the whole group back to Bangkok airport. Except Kayla, Sam, Russia, and Dave, who weren't entirely sure they'd be on it.

They were visiting the Khao Laem Reservoir when they first discussed the possibility of staying in Asia. Oliver had long since given up on providing any sort of insight into the culture or history of Thailand, and they hadn't seen Chanarong since Bangkok, so they wandered aimlessly around the vast expanse of water. As with most stunning sights, they could appreciate its staggering beauty but weren't entirely sure how to react or behave in its presence. It was pretty, sure. But dedicating two hours to appreciating it seemed rather excessive, when really, two minutes would do.

It was Sam who first voiced what they had all been thinking. He'd been examining his left hand, which he'd fractured in a drunken fall. He'd fallen off the karaoke stage while singing a sparkling rendition of "Ain't No Mountain High Enough," and in traditional Sam style, landed crushingly on his hand. Testament to just how much tequila he'd consumed, he hadn't noticed the break until the next morning, when he had to make a trip to the emergency room and put his foreign health insurance to good use. He winced as he made a gripping motion with the bandaged fist, then looked up at the group. "Does anyone else feel like it'd be completely and utterly ridiculous to go home?"

Dave slid his hand into Russia's, lacing his skinny fingers through hers. "Completely. Home seems like another planet."

"Not to mention one that's light-years away from my home country," Russia said. "I'd never see you guys again!"

Sam threw a pebble into the water with his one working hand. "I just feel like we've got so much more to do here. I'm not ready to go back to reality."

"At least your reality," Dave replied, "doesn't involve waiting patiently until the day you're confined to a hospital bed, mate. You're off to med school to become a hot-shot doctor. Maybe if you're quick about it, you can cure ALS before it kills me."

Sam looked away. "Yeah. Maybe."

Russia frowned, deep in thought. "Why don't we just . . . stay?"

Kayla's mouth curled upward of its own accord. She hadn't been particularly looking forward to going home either. "Stay? How?"

"Well, I mean there are practicalities," Russia said. "We'd have to get jobs and save up a bit of money before we traveled to Cambodia, Vietnam, and Laos. Or at least I would! And there might be a bit of hassle getting the right visas. But if we all wanted to, I don't see why it wouldn't work? We could rent an apartment?" She'd begun talking faster, her eyes wide.

"I'm in," Kayla said. "No questions asked."

"Me too!" Dave and Sam said in unison.

"Bling?"

Bling hadn't said a word. She was chewing her top lip. "I'm not sure. I'd have to make some phone calls."

"What? Why? Check you out, Miss In-Demand," Russia teased.

"Well, I kind of have a job lined up for when I'm back." The group stared at her. They'd almost forgotten about the existence of careers and such trivialities. "And I can't really push it back."

"Dude, make the phone call," Sam said. "Now! We can't do it without you," he insisted with force. His eyes were intense with urgency. Bling looked smug at his overt desire for her to stay.

Kayla's stomach turned—maybe Bling did like Sam. Her delight certainly suggested so. Worse still, maybe the feeling was mutual.

"I don't know . . ."

"But Bli-i-i-ing. You have to stay," Russia whined.

"Why?"

"Well, you just do."

Bling laughed. "I could eat a bowl of alphabet soup and shit out a better argument than that." But she looked like she was considering it, burrowing her eyebrows together and putting a finger to her lips. Kayla suspected she was milking it, keen for Sam to keep trying to convince her.

She looked away, trying to ignore the flesh-searing surge of jealousy that pulsed through her veins.

Chapter 18

July 15, England

THE FIRST DROP of alcohol that touched Kayla's lips since returning from Thailand was bought for her by a police officer.

DI Winters—"Call me Sadie"—couldn't have been a day over thirty. She had pale skin, gray-blue eyes, and a long, prominent nose that sat above a wide, toothy smile. Her angular face was framed by straight blond hair, which was half pulled back with a bejeweled clasp. She wasn't in uniform—they were meeting after hours. The slouchy black jumper and tight navy jeans made her seem even younger.

"You're much younger than I thought you were going to be," Kayla admitted. "In a good way."

"Well thank you, I guess," Sadie beamed at her. She had too many teeth for her mouth, and the effect was a clumsy, crooked grin. "I hope you know that I shouldn't really be meeting you like this. It's not very . . . official of me. I've been doing this for a good few years now, and I've never felt inclined to meet a victim's friend in a cocktail bar before." She scanned the room as though waiting to be caught out.

"So why now? We aren't breaking any rules, are we? I don't want to get you in any trouble."

"No, no rule-breaking. I can meet with whoever I like, as long as I'm not discussing the details of any cases." Sadie shifted in her chair. "As for why now? I've been asking myself the same question. I suppose I just want to make sure all avenues have been explored. I'm thorough like that." She brushed a stray strand of golden hair away from her face and tucked it behind her ear. "You and Sam were close, huh?"

"You could say that." A vivid image of Sam's grinning face flashed into Kayla's mind. It was intense; a high-definition shot in which she could make out every stubbly hair, delicate dimple, and crinkle in the skin surrounding his eyes. It disappeared almost as quickly as he had. Kayla blinked away a hot tear. "I miss him. And my brother too. Did you . . . ?"

"Know about that? I did, I'm afraid. I'm so sorry, Kayla. I lost someone close to me when I was a little older than you. Family." Sadie rubbed her eyes and took a large swig of rosé, swallowing hard. It looked like she'd had a tough day.

Kayla didn't know what to say. To share details of deep, dark grief with someone you'd only known for ten minutes—and a police officer, no less—felt rather awkward. Thankfully, the detective was already talking again, masking her discomfort. "There's just something about Sam's case I'm drawn to. Maybe it's because, like I said, I lost someone too. Someone his age. And it's not that the case is out of the ordinary or unprecedented, which it isn't. Just that some of it . . ."

"Doesn't add up?"

"Maybe. Maybe not. I just want to get another perspective on things, I guess. Is that why you're here too? You're worried some of it doesn't make sense?" Sadie asked. "You sounded unsure on the phone."

"Kind of. I'm finding it hard to get closure. It's like I can't get over the discrepancies in the story and start grieving for Sam. I need to know exactly what happened and why—a mere theory won't cut it."

Sadie sighed. "I don't know what to say, Kayla. The case is all but closed. We reached a conclusion." She paused, her frown lines deepening before relaxing again. "My heart skipped a beat when you called. Nobody else close to Sam seemed lucid enough to talk to me properly while we were conducting interviews. His parents were completely distraught, understandably. I'm sure they still are. And your other friends from the trip aren't in the country. Was there anything in particular you wanted to talk to me about? Anything new to add? To consider?" She swallowed. "Anything Shepherd might have missed?" There was an edge behind her voice.

Kayla shook her head. "I don't know about that. To me, the most inexplicable part of it all is Sam being that into drugs. It's just so . . . out of character. Although I know that doesn't help you." Kayla thought for a moment. "Okay, so if the story is that he was beaten and kidnapped, or . . . murdered . . ." The word stung the back of her throat. "How was there so much blood in the room? If he'd been instantly removed from it by the drug guys, or whoever they were?"

Sadie nodded slowly. "And why were there no footprints in the blood other than Sam's?"

Kayla shuddered. Another question without an answer. Was it possible Sadie didn't buy the official conclusion either? That she was willing to dig a little deeper than Shepherd had?

Sadie hunched her shoulders over the bar, grabbing a handful of salted peanuts from the little wooden bowl in front of them. "I mean, I know a lot of the bigger drug circles out there have a whole group of 'bailiffs' who chase up debt. They know what they're doing and wouldn't be so careless as to leave any traces behind. It does fit, I guess. That they wouldn't leave any evidence."

"Is that what *you* think happened?" Kayla asked.

"It's the only theory that makes any kind of sense." Sadie paused, crunching another handful of peanuts. "Okay. These bailiffs. Usually they'll give someone who owes a *lot* of money—like, not just petty debt—two warnings. They'll add significant interest to the debt to make it even harder for victims to pay up. They're sadistic like that. The warnings are violent ones, like snapping a finger or putting a hammer to a knee." Kayla felt sick. The gin she'd had churned on her empty stomach. "After that, it's game over. They'll beat them to a pulp, without caring much whether the victim survives. And for us investigating Sam's case, it's difficult. Because without a body, we can't analyze his injuries to see if any of them were older. Consistent with this theory. If they were, it'd fit in with the timeline and suggest that they'd been chasing him for a while."

Kayla's stomach had fallen through the trapdoor that opened where her intestines used to be. Sam's hand, she thought. "He was injured," she whispered. She hadn't meant to drop her voice. She cleared her throat, trying to sound more assured. "He fractured his hand. Said it had been a drunken accident."

Sadie blew air through her teeth. "Did anyone see it happen?"

"I'm not sure. We never really discussed it like that. We just laughed at him for being clumsy, as usual."

"I suppose you weren't to know there was an alternative explanation. Can you think of anything else that happened that could explain it?" Sadie's eyes were widening. She crammed nuts into her mouth like an excited squirrel stocking up for hibernation.

Kayla thought about it. It was difficult to know what was relevant—you could attach significance to anything in retrospect—but there was one thing in particular that had been bothering her of late. "I don't know. Did Sam's mum, Kathy—well, you know her name—did she tell you he'd asked her to borrow money?"

Sadie choked on a stray nut. "No?"

"Yeah. Three grand."

"Wow." The detective's frown lines deepened once more. "Well, it certainly points to drug debt."

Kayla sighed. It did.

"But you said it would be out of character for Sam? To get himself in that kind of mess over drugs?"

Kayla nodded.

"Well, that's all that matters, isn't it. You can have the most conclusive evidence in the world, but if it doesn't make sense to the people who were closest to the victim . . . well, it'll never fit properly, will it?" Sadie unclipped her hair and let it fall around her shoulders, then tilted her head back and shook it all out of her face. She turned to face Kayla. "I want to do a bit more digging. Even if that just means thinking some more about it. Thinking about whether there's something we're missing. You know?"

Kayla nodded again. She knew.

After Sadie left, Kayla stayed in the pub a little while. Small panels of the pub's windows were made of stained glass depicting flamboyant birds of paradise. The sun was low in the sky, its rays turned red and blue and orange and gold as they shone through. It was relatively quiet, and the lone barman was squeakily polishing glasses and chatting to a cluster of regulars. In the small empty space near the kitchen doors, a young girl was assembling a gig set, tuning a guitar and fumbling with a microphone stand.

Kayla stirred her gin and tonic with the flimsy plastic swizzle stick it came with. The ice had long since melted. She didn't know how to feel about her meeting with DI Winters. On the one hand, the detective had made her see that the signs definitely did support the police theory. Shepherd's theory. There was no denying that. But there had been something . . . something resembling curiosity on Sadie's face. Like there was more to know. More to uncover.

Or am I just desperate? Desperate for something, anything, to cling onto?

The girl at the microphone stand struck the first chord. Very few people turned around to listen—most were still deep in conversation or patting snooker balls around the scuffed velvet pool table. Kayla rolled the bead of her friendship bracelet between her fingertips. It was cool and smooth. *Was it really only three months ago Sam gave me this?* A tug on her heart caught her off-guard. It felt like a different lifetime ago. A lump formed in her throat before she could stop it. *Oh, Sam. Where are you?*

"*I will keep you close . . .*"

The young girl had started singing. Her voice was ethereal, haunting.

"*As long as the wind blo-o-ows . . .*"

The two middle-aged men playing pool stopped and turned. The girl was blond and beautiful, with a tiny frame and a celestial voice. Her eyes were closed and her head tilted skyward as she strummed the guitar gently, like she was scared she'd break it if she plucked too hard.

"I will try to keep you safe . . . safe as our memories. Droplets on the window, they roll down, like you'll come back to me-e-e . . ."

The lump in Kayla's throat reappeared. *If only.* A fat tear rolled down her cheek before she could stop it. It splashed off the table, which was bathed in azure light from the stained-glass reflections.

Everyone was watching the girl now. The barman had abandoned the glass-cleaning rag on the bar and he stood, transfixed, just like the locals he'd been chatting to a few moments earlier. Her chords were so delicate that between lines you could hear the faint din of traffic passing through the village nearby.

"Oh, oh, a glimmer of hope . . . Oh, oh, a glimmer of hope . . ."

The girl had opened her eyes and was gazing out of the birds-of-paradise window, though it felt to Kayla like she was staring straight at her. Like she knew, and that she was singing to her, telling her to hold on. That there was a glimmer of hope. Just a flicker, like a dying candle flame. But a flicker nonetheless.

Logging onto Facebook was a strange feeling. Kayla had deactivated her account after Gabe's death—she wanted nothing more to do with the toxic environment that had provided an incubator for vindictive abuse.

Scrolling through her timeline, over four months later, absolutely nothing had changed. There was a whiny status about how all men are shallow, a racist joke, and a cryptic, please-ask-me-why-I'm-sad post. Kayla tried with all her might not to roll her eyes, but alas, it happened regardless. *All right. Let's just do the necessary and log straight back out.*

She typed three names into the search bar she never thought she'd have to: Minya Pavlova, Daivat Singh, and Ai Ling Brewer. They had no mutual friends, so scrolling through pages and pages of total strangers took time, but eventually she found the right Russia and the right Dave. There was no sign of Bling, but Kayla remembered she had her phone number stored in her mobile. She'd just text her instead.

She sent them all the same message:

Hey guys, hope you're all well. Wish I was still out there with you! England sucks, I've never been so utterly bored (or cold) in my life. Anyway, this sounds really weird, but did anyone actually see Sam break his hand? We were all drunk that night, I know, but I just wondered whether anyone actually saw it happen. It probably isn't important, but I want to know either way. Love and miss you all! Kayla xx

Finally, she took out her phone and punched in a number that by now had been etched onto her memory. Kathy Kingfisher's number.

Two rings, followed by a click. Voice mail.

Chapter 19

May 23, Thailand

"HAVE YOU SEEN this?" Russia asked, without even saying good morning.

The day before they were due to return to England, the Escaping Grey group were bundled into a tiny café, taking over two of the five tables. While most of the eateries they'd visited in Thailand had been a little frayed around the edges, this one was sleek, modern, and air-conditioned, with chrome fittings, white walls, and an industrial-sized coffee machine that looked more like a spaceship fixture than a beverage maker. There was a middle-aged British couple standing behind the counter—they looked like the owners—muttering in hushed, urgent voices. The atmosphere was tense.

"Hello to you too," Kayla said, flopping into the one empty seat. "What's happening?"

Sam gestured to the flat-screen TV mounted on the wall. It

was tuned into a British news channel, and flashing along the bottom of the screen were the words: BREAKING NEWS: TERRORISTS TARGET LONDON WATERLOO.

"What the . . . ?" Kayla stammered.

"Yesterday afternoon," Dave said. "No one was hurt. Police foiled the attack before the bombs went off," Even he was subdued.

"Bombs?"

"Yeah. Bombs planted all over the place. A staff member found one in the baggage area and alerted the police. Had to evacuate the whole building. Madness."

Bling, whose face was so pale it was almost translucent, muttered, "Christ. I have family in London."

Sam rubbed Bling's shoulder, and even despite the terror, Kayla felt a twinge of jealousy. *Get a grip, Finch.*

One of the owners upped the volume on the TV. The news reader was saying, " . . . emerged that a consulate from the Chinese embassy was on a southbound train traveling to Waterloo yesterday afternoon. It remains unclear whether his journey is linked to the planned attack on the station."

"Do you think they were targeting him?" Bling asked no one in particular.

"Looks that way," said Russia. "God, can you imagine if they'd gone off?" She shook her head. "The world is so full of evil people. It's terrifying."

"S'cuse me," Bling mumbled, gripping her phone so tightly as she left the table that her knuckles went white.

"Probably off to call her family. Poor girl," Sam said. Kayla clenched her fist.

Oliver, who'd been ordering more coffee, sat back down and sighed. He smelled of stale beer and even staler cigarettes, and several weeks of partying were etched onto his tanned face. He looked older than his twenty-six years. "All right, team. As you all know, we're due to fly back to the UK in four days' time. However, things are a little uneasy in London right now, what with last week's incident and now this. Tension is running high, and the UK authorities are insisting everyone remain calm and travel as usual, but—"

"Last week's incident?" Kayla interrupted. "What happened last week?" The rest of the group mirrored her ignorance.

"Oh, right. Well, while we were hiking, there was another terrorist incident. Heathrow. More bombs. They got to all of them in time . . . except one. Three people killed—a little boy and his young parents. Tragic."

"What the hell? Why didn't you tell us?" Sam said, trying to keep the anger out of his voice. Sounds of frustration rippled through the group. The couple behind the counter had stopped talking and seemed to be listening to the discussion intently. Neither were making any attempt to make the coffees Oliver had ordered.

Oliver shrugged. "Didn't want to ruin the party vibe. No one likes a buzzkill. Besides, more people were killed in Afghanistan last week than in Heathrow. Want me to update you on all of the global deaths every morning?"

"Wait, was it connected to the Waterloo bombs?" Ralph asked. "Heathrow? Was it the same people?" His long wavy hair had gone past the point of hipster cool and was now closer to the tramp end of the spectrum.

Thomas, who was sitting next to Evan and staring at his iPhone, said, "Sounds like it. BBC News says three northern MPs were flying into Heathrow that day. Too much of a coincidence for them not to be linked, surely? Powerful people being targeted?"

Oliver shrugged again. His nonchalance grated on Kayla. He had the ambivalence toward tragedy of someone who'd never had anything bad happen to him. "Anyway. The folks at Escaping Grey are keen for us fly back on tomorrow, as we originally planned. That cool with everyone? Nobody too scared to board a plane?"

"Actually," Dave said, exchanging glances with Russia and Kayla, "we're going to stay on for another month or two. Do a bit more traveling. That okay?"

Oliver frowned. "S'pose. Who's we?"

"Me, Russia, Sam, Bling, and Kayla."

Oliver stared at Kayla. She squirmed uncomfortably in her hard plastic chair, wishing her coffee would arrive so she'd have something else to look at. "That should be fine," he said coolly. "Will have to check with my superiors, though."

Kayla debated whether to nip outside and call her family. She knew her father sometimes did business in London and flew down to Heathrow when he did. But she was sure she'd have heard by now if something unthinkable had happened, and besides, she was starting to cool down for the first time in weeks. The air-con was a godsend.

The group chatted amongst themselves for a while, glancing at the television every few minutes to check for updates. Nothing. Nobody was in a particular rush to leave. It was over a hundred degrees outside, and the idea of traipsing around another national park in the blazing sun wasn't too appealing.

Bling eventually returned to the table, at least fifty-two percent of the color back in her face. "Everyone's okay," she said, slightly breathless. She grabbed a condensation-coated glass of icy water from the table and downed the whole thing in one gulp. Her flowery sundress was damp with sweat and clung to her skin, and her oversized sunglasses kept sliding down her shiny forehead. She did not look well.

"You all right, Bling?" Russia asked.

"Yeah, yeah, fine. Any more news?" She turned to the television. The news was showing footage of evacuated passengers standing outside the train station in hoards. Many were taking pictures and videos on their smart phones as events unfolded, and a young woman in a dishevelled suit was crying. There was no mention of any links to the Heathrow attacks.

"Ah, well," Dave said, ever the optimist. "All the more reason to stay put in Thailand."

FOR ONCE, KAYLA was grateful for her nan's inconveniently timed phone call. It interrupted the graphic daydream she was experiencing in which Sam was showering Bling's impossibly pert breasts with passionate kisses.

"Hi, Nan. How are you?"

"Hello, is that you, Kayla?"

"Yes, Nan, it's me. Can you hear me?"

"You're having a beer? Lovely, sweetheart." Her nan's amicable northern accent, full of whoops and twangs and vaguely Scottish notes, jolted Kayla with a pang of homesickness. "I just thought I'd check in with you. Nasty business, all these bombs. Still, I'm glad you'll be back home and safe with us soon. Are you keeping well?"

Kayla looked around. She was lying on one of the world's most beautiful beaches, Thong Nai Pan Noi, wiggling her toes in warm sand with the baking sun searing her skin in the most pleasant of ways. Together with its twin cove, Thong Nai Pan Yai, the beach on a gentle double bay, it formed a buttock-shaped imprint in the coastline. It was softly curved with white sands that tipped the rain-forest-swept mountains behind them.

The waves didn't so much crash in the background as fizz onto the shore like an ice cube being plopped into a glass of cola. Her best friends were laughing in the distance. Russia had scooped Dave up in her arms and was twirling around in the shallowest parts of the sea, threatening to dunk him under. Bling was delicately flicking water at Sam, who ripped his arms through the salty water and drenched her from head to toe in return.

No, Kayla thought. She definitely wasn't keeping well.

"I'm fine, thanks," she said to her nan. "How are you?"

"Just fine? It sounds like you're having a great time out there. I can hear people laughing in the background. Are they your pals? Oh, I do hope you're making friends out there. I'd hate for you to be lonely."

Having friends isn't a fail-safe against loneliness. "Yeah, I have an awesome group of friends."

"Good! That's good. Are you looking forward to coming home? It's this weekend you're due back, isn't it? We're all so excited to see you, poppet, it really hasn't been the same without—"

"Actually, that's what I've been meaning to talk to you about," Kayla interjected with a little white lie. She hadn't given her family much thought at all in making her decision. "We're planning on staying out here for a little while longer. We're having fun, and what with the terrorist attacks and all . . . Is that all right?"

"Oh. Right. Well, I'm glad you're having fun, I suppose." Kayla heard a fumbling with the phone, followed by a short, sharp sniff. "It's just that we all thought you were only away for eight weeks. It's been hard for us, you know, and —"

"Yeah, well, it's not exactly been easy for me either, Nan," Kayla snapped. She gulped, already regretting it. "I'm sorry. I just can't bear the thought of coming home knowing Gabe won't be there. I'm missing you all, obviously. Of course I am. It's just easier to forget, out here. Forget everything that happened."

The line went dead.

KAYLA ISOLATED HERSELF for the rest of the day. Her nan's animosity in hanging up had caught her off-guard. She tried to call back, thinking that perhaps Nan had accidentally pressed End Call, but there was no answer. Lying on the beach, she felt utterly detached. Detached from her friends, from her family, from her brother's memory. From herself.

Bling skipped over to her then. "Are you coming for a swim?" She flicked a starfish in her direction, giggling childishly. It narrowly missed Kayla's thigh.

Kayla paused. Then, in a voice so low it was almost a growl, she muttered, "Get the fuck away from me."

Both Kayla and Bling recoiled simultaneously. Bling blinked incredulously several times in succession. The sun was smothering, wrapping a blanket of heat around Kayla's mouth and nose. Bling took a few steps backward, her mouth curved into an O, and turned to run back toward the sea.

What just happened?

It was the pause that scared Kayla. The pause had given her the opportunity to stifle her rage—to swallow it, bury it, do anything but let it escape. But she hadn't.

She'd wanted to release it.

It had felt good.

THE FULL MOON Party was too much of everything.

Too many people, too much noise, too much alcohol. Too much heat, too much sand lodged in places it should never be lodged. Too much freedom.

Not enough air, not enough solid ground, not enough time to breathe. Kayla was spinning out of control, away from her friends, away from who she once was.

Bass, beer, a heart bursting through her chest. Was it her own? She didn't know.

Everyone blurred into one person, one pulse, but not in a good way. Panic scorched through her eyes, blinding her. Her hair was stuck to her forehead with gloopy sweat. She staggered from body to body, bouncing, playing human dodge 'ems in a fairground of fear.

Someone offered her something. Who was that? What was it? A small white pellet. Smooth in her palm, she stroked it with her thumb, momentarily entranced by its minuscule stature. This pill was tinier than a popcorn kernel. This pill could make her mind implode. It could kill her. Or it could fill her with ebullience, make colors theatrical and smells flamboyant and sounds carnivalesque. It was only a deep breath and a millisecond of bravery away.

It could make her feel joy, or it could kill her. Euphoria or euthanasia.

Win-win.

She swallowed the pill.

Chapter 20

May 24, England

Now it was her turn to apologize.

Last night came back to Kayla in flashes. The initial euphoria. If she'd been sober, perhaps she would have forced herself to assess whether she'd have preferred the alternative, but she was too happy to care much. She'd loved everyone. Race, gender, orientation became one; she was in tune with the heartbeat of humanity. She recalled grasping the hands of strangers and making them twirl her round and round like a tetherball around a pole. Her hands had frolicked through the air, rippling and swooping in a special kind of dance they'd choreographed of their own accord. She'd been carnal—horny for happiness.

Her friends made her chest swell like a river bursting its banks, overflowing with affection. Even Bling's china doll appearance and delicate voice had become endearing, not infuriating. Sam's crooked nose and swelling eye made her caress him in a motherly swoon, treating him like an injured toddler and cooing.

Wait, why did Sam have a swelling eye?

She didn't have time to rest on the thought for too long. There were too many other shameful snippets to work through. She'd save the worst recollection for last.

Next, out had come her phone. She left a voice mail for Nan. She couldn't remember what she'd said, exactly, but hoped the theme of forgiveness had been understood. She had also left a voice mail for Gabe. In Ecstasyland, she still had a brother.

A handsome stranger had appeared before her, conjured from the sand as if by sorcery. He had certainly been a magical sight—a topless concoction of tan and abs and fluorescent body paint, handing her a plastic cup containing a clear alchemist's potion of cheap vodka and very little else. She had taken a hearty pirate's swig. Love—or was it lust? All of her sentiments were blended in one big melting pot of passion—propelled her forth. She was kissing him, and he was kissing her back, and Sam was watching.

Something within Kayla fluttered excitedly. Presumably, the same feral part of her that had experienced such pleasure in biting back at Bling. She kissed the stranger harder, faster. In that moment, she knew beyond any shadow of a doubt that she was the finest kisser in the Northern Hemisphere. She laced her fingers through her enchanting companion's velvety hair, nibbling his lip, grazing his soft neck with birdlike pecks. Out of the corner of her eye she saw that Sam had turned away. It became clear that she needed to up the stakes. Random Gorgeous Man wasn't enough to pierce Sam's very core in the same way hers had been.

Without warning her suitor, she had swung on her heel, over-shooting slightly and lurching sideways before staggering to find her feet. Her hands flung out to both sides as if she was learning to surf and she remained in that position, scanning for her next prey.

Her eyes had locked onto his. Her random man was staring hungrily at her. Suddenly, she too was ravenous.

Kayla had taken one last glance at Sam, drinking in every inch of his agonized expression, and pounced.

"Kay-laaaaah," Russia half sang, half whimpered as Kayla attempted, unsuccessfully, to dash to the bathroom before her roommates demanded an explanation. "What happened last night, you saucy minx?"

Kayla sighed and gave up trying to escape. She flopped back onto her bed and emitted a long, deep groan. Her head was killing her. All she could think about was water. How sweet would an ice-filled pint glass of water taste, so cold the outside was speckled with condensation. *Maybe even a slice of lemon. . .*

Bling, who was lying with her face to the wall, muttered, "What a player." Her words were tinged with jest rather than malice. Kayla was pleased her frighteningly friendly persona last night had helped soothe the ill effects of her earlier malevolent words.

"Come on, then, spill the beans," Russia said. "What happened with Mr. Tall, Dark, and Handsome we saw you talking to last night? Well, by talking to I mean—"

"Yes, I know what you mean," Kayla threw a pillow at Russia, who sat cross-legged on the floor, rolling up her clothes and stuffing them into her backpack. They were due to leave in an hour. "God, I was an idiot last night."

"You were funny! I've never seen you like that before."

"I've never been like that before," Kayla admitted.

"Had you . . . you know, taken something?" Russia tried to sound casual.

"Ugh. Yes. I hate myself." Russia stared at her, unblinking. Kayla said defensively, "What? You're the Queen of the Stone Heads!"

Russia laughed awkwardly and shrugged. "Yeah, weed. That's different from . . . whatever you took."

Kayla was disappointed in herself. Her best friend's words stung.

Thankfully, Russia wasn't one to rub salt in the wound. "Hey. Cheer up, buddy. I'm not here to judge. Did you enjoy it?"

"Honestly? Yeah. At first, anyway. I was literally in love with everyone I bumped into. I've never felt happiness like it. I wouldn't do it again, though, it was really stupid. I have no idea who gave it to me, what was in it, nothing. It could have killed me."

"Didn't you think of that before you took it?"

Kayla shook her head. It was easier than explaining that the risk had been a coin toss she wouldn't have minded losing.

"Anyway, you rascal. Tell me what happened next!" Russia had abandoned her haphazard packing and was staring intently at her.

If she told her the truth, Kayla realized, she'd have to confess all of the events she'd failed to share. The creepy levels of admiration, the leering, the near-rape. She'd wanted to bury it, forget it ever happened. And until now she'd been successful. But she'd dug it back up all on her own, exposing the shallow grave she'd tucked her secret into just over a week ago. Now she was sitting beside the fresh, moss-free tombstone, surrounded by dirt and shame and clutching a shovel, with no choice but to deal with the consequences.

Kayla couldn't meet Russia's eyes. "I kissed Oliver."

Chapter 21

July 17, England

"HYPOTHETICALLY . . ." SADIE paused to take an enormous bite of something so crunchy it could only have been a raw carrot. The sound of her teeth gnawing through the hard orange flesh rattled through the phone like screws caught in a vacuum cleaner, followed by an emphatic gulp. "Do you think Sam had any plausible reason to . . . do this to himself?"

Kayla had rung DI Winters, who'd dashed out of her office to take the call, and informed the detective that neither Russia nor Dave had seen Sam fall and drunkenly break his hand. She'd also recalled the mysterious black eye that materialized at the Full Moon Party, with little explanation of its origins. She had instinctively reached for her phone to call Sam and ask what had really happened before realizing she couldn't. When you've lost someone close to you, those fleeting moments of forgetfulness, followed by sharp pangs of painful remembering, are more gut-wrenching than the acres of dull grief stretching out before you.

Kayla considered Sadie's suggestion. Sam might have been troubled, but he seemed far too stable a character to resort to such a drastic means of escape. Then again, she knew better than anyone that depression can be hidden—nobody had seen Gabe's death coming. Besides, Sam had been acting strangely during those last few weeks abroad. She shuddered at the possibility that her actions might have contributed to his end. *No. I refuse to entertain that idea. I'm already dealing with enough guilt.*

The garrulous detective mistook the brief break in conversation for uncertainty and set about articulating her train of thought. "I mean, I know the logistics don't exactly fit. How would he slit his wrists, or something like that, bleed all over the apartment, then disappear off the face of the earth?"

The mental image of Sam crawling around in agony, trying to find a ditch to disappear into forever, made Kayla want to vomit. Sadie was lovely, but not exactly tactful. She was more concerned with the science of the mystery than the human angle.

Another carroty chomp. Kayla envisaged her standing on a busy pavement outside a high-rise office block, waggling the vegetable around to illustrate her points to oblivious passersby. "All the facts suggest he was removed from the apartment by an external figure. But who? The lack of any concrete suspects does make you wonder, doesn't it?"

It did. It was exactly that—the lack of anything concrete—that was torturous to Kayla. She was sick of looking through a cloud of mist at vague theories and lethargic conclusions. "Honestly?" she said. "I can't see Sam killing himself, or even trying to. For one, he was a med student. Don't they, I don't know, value life? And secondly, his tolerance for pain was pretty low." Kayla remembered his near-hysteria over a wasp sting at the beginning of the trip. "I doubt he could . . . inflict any on himself."

"Ah. I see. And I suppose most people with such a disposition would opt for a less . . . violent method if they were to . . ." Sadie paused. Her train of thought had reached a station, and another passenger got on board. "Did Sam have any enemies?"

The question took Kayla aback. "You mean outside of his drug-dealing friends?"

Crunch, crunch. "Yeah, I guess the theory's already been explored. I don't know."

Kayla wracked her brains. Could there have been anyone? "I don't know either. I mean, outside of his friends from university, his family, and the Escaping Grey group, I can't think who else he's been associated with in the last year."

Sadie lowered her voice. "So maybe it's time to go back further?"

KAYLA WAS BEGINNING to grow tired of Kathy Kingfisher's answering machine. "Hi, you've reached Kathy. Sorry I can't take your call right now, but leave a message and I'll get back to you as soon as I can."

So much for getting back to her. The list of questions Kayla wanted to ask Sam's mum was growing by the day—more about the money she couldn't lend him, the tone of Sam's voice the last time they'd spoken, whether he'd signed off their final phone call with a final-sounding message of love. Not only was it frustrating for her queries to remain unanswered, but it was also difficult losing contact with the one person on the planet who loved Sam more than she did. Nobody else understood how heart-meltingly warm his dimpled smile was. Or how cold everything became in its absence.

Kayla wondered what Dr. Myers would say if she knew how much time and effort she was putting into solving the riddle of Sam's disappearance, which was supposedly already solved. Or that she was now officially referring to it as "disappearance" rather than death. Or that she was now analyzing all of her own actions through the eyes of a therapist.

Maybe it was the detachedness that appealed so much. Working with Sadie meant seeing the events from a scientific vantage point, laying out the cold, hard facts for the sole purpose of solving a crime. It was unhealthy, yes. Futile, perhaps. But, more important than anything, having a focus cured the crippling boredom that engulfed her every day.

Kayla's dad had started to hint at the idea of her completing her internship at Greyfinch and going on to formally train in marketing. Since realizing that she wasn't suicidal—hell, she barely even seemed depressed—he seemed to largely be glossing over the events of the last few months. Maybe it was too painful for him to think about, let alone talk about. Or maybe, in what would be a typical Mark Finch move, the thought of having any form of emotional conversation made his toes curl up tightly inside his shiny black brogues.

Her mum, on the other hand, adopted a much more hands-on approach. When Kayla edged back into the kitchen after her phone call with Sadie—and unsuccessfully ringing Kathy three times—she'd found Martha clattering around the kitchen cupboards, her trembling hands fumbling with an unopened sachet of ground Ethiopian coffee beans.

"Mum?"

Her mother jerked backward in surprise, as though she'd been caught doing something terrible. Her eyes were pink-rimmed and bloodshot. "Honey! Where have you been? Oh, help your mum, will you? I can't get this damn packet open."

Kayla took the coffee from between her mother's shaking fingertips and tore it open with ease. "Just getting some air."

"Oh, I don't blame you. It's so lovely outside." The kettle perched atop the Aga whistled for their attention. Martha picked it up and poured bubbling water delicately into their expensive French coffee press and closed the lid. Her gaze remained fixed on the swirling brown liquid for a few moments before she turned to face Kayla. "How are you feeling, love?"

"I'm fine. You know, considering." Kayla absentmindedly rolled the bead of her friendship bracelet between her thumb and forefinger.

Martha stepped forward and pulled a wooden chair out from its position beneath the huge oak dining table. "I mean how are you really feeling? You can't fool me, you know. I've been around for a few years—I know what loneliness looks like. Come on, let's sit down and have a chat. I feel like we haven't talked properly in ages." Kayla half expected her mum to pat the seat encouragingly. She didn't.

Kayla sighed and slumped down into the chair opposite. "I guess I am feeling a little lonely, if I'm honest."

Martha placed the cafetiere and some mugs heavy-handedly onto the oak table and sat down, picking up Kayla's hands in her own. "That's understandable, Kayls. You've barely seen or spoke to anyone other than your father and I since you got back. Why don't you give Juliet a call? The pair of you used to get on so well."

"Mum, I haven't spoken to Juliet since she spread those rumors about our family back in high school. I told you about that, remember?"

"Oh right, yes, sorry. I do remember that. It's hard to keep track of all these teenage dramas." Martha pulled her hands free and slowly started pushing the filter through the coffee. "How about Alexa? What's she doing these days?"

"She went to uni in Cardiff. She's staying there over the summer, doing some bar work, I think. She's glad to see the back of Northumberland."

"I see. And what about—"

"There's no one, Mum. I'm not isolating myself out of choice."

"Oh honey, I'm sure that's not true! You had so many friends in school." Martha poured coffee into both mugs and plopped two sugar cubes into Kayla's. After a moment's hesitation, she added a third. "Anyway, I had a thought. Bear with me a second."

Martha lifted herself out of the chair, with what looked like heavy reliance on the table as support, and crossed the kitchen. She delved into the third drawer down on the kitchen counter—the drawer that nobody ever dared open, as it contained a chaotic plethora of batteries, gas bills, pen lids, and sticky tape. Amidst many, many other random items that had no other home, even in a mansion as big as theirs.

Kayla couldn't see what her mother was carrying until she returned to the table with a proud expression forming on her face. University prospectuses. Martha sat back down and spread the thick brochures across the table. They smelled of fresh paper and printer's ink, all the covers adorned with smiling faces and scattered textbooks—politically correct groups of mixed ethnicities and genders sprawled happily on a lawn outside their grand, red-bricked schools. The message was clear enough: learning is *fun*!

"Mum, I—"

"I know what you're going to say," said Martha firmly. "I know you're maybe not ready yet, and that's okay. But I think this is something you should really think about, sweetheart. It would give you a goal, take your mind off things, help you meet people . . ." She trailed off, realizing that her daughter's face had hardened. "What do you think?" She took a sip of her coffee.

It looked to Kayla like her mum was using the mug as a shield. She felt bad. She could tell her mum was genuinely trying to help, and so she tried to take the edge out of her voice. "I can't, Mum. I mean . . . I don't even know what I would study. There's nothing I want to study."

"Well, what about English? You've always loved reading?"

"I hate Shakespeare. We'd have to study Shakespeare."

"Oh, he is a difficult bugger, isn't he? Well, what about exercise science? You've been getting back into your running recently, haven't you?"

Kayla stared intently into the palms of her hands. "Yeah. But it's just a hobby. I don't want to make a career out of it, or anything."

Martha persisted. "Well, I certainly think you should consider it. There's bound to be something out there you'd enjoy studying. Newcastle and Durham are great universities, and you could commute from home! You got such good grades all the way through school, and it'd be a shame to waste all your hard work. You're such a bright girl, and—"

"Actually, Mum, I'm not feeling too great. Think it's the heat in here. I'm going to go and lie down, but I'll think about it. About uni. I promise." She squeezed her mum's hands and left the table.

The heartbreaking look of motherly concern on Martha's tearstained face stayed with Kayla for the rest of the day.

She knew, deep down, her parents were only trying to help—even her dad, pushing her to join Greyfinch again. She wished she could stop being so stubborn and accept that life had to go on. Being stuck in limbo was no fun. She wasn't sad enough to do nothing all day, nor was she emotionally ready to move on and do something with her life. It was a deep rut, and one she couldn't foresee herself clambering out of anytime soon.

She couldn't see past the present. Past her emptiness. The idea of flying back out to Southeast Asia to resume her travels had, at one time, seemed feasible, but now that her suspicions surrounding the incident—as she'd taken to calling it—had piqued Sadie's interest, she couldn't bear the thought of leaving the country without playing a part in the miniature investigation.

DI Winters had promised to keep rooting around the jumble sale of Sam's past, hoping to pick up a rare gem that might possibly tie into the tragic events of exactly one month ago today. For now, she would cling onto that.

KAYLA THOUGHT THAT Sadie's loquaciousness might be rubbing off on her, or maybe she'd spent too many hours out of the last week cooped up in her bedroom. During her fourth therapy session, she could barely contain the rainstorm of words from gushing out her mouth. She explained all about her new detective friend and her dedication to seeking justice for Sam.

Dr. Myers's reaction was one of concern. "Just be careful, Kayla. I don't want you to—"

"Cling onto false hope, I know."

"I didn't mean it like that. I just don't want you to put off confronting your emotions for the sake of a misplaced inkling that there's more to the story."

"But there is more to the story. There has to be. Nothing adds up, and it's infuriating."

"Kayla . . ." Cassandra leaned forward and stared at her intently. "If there was more than meets the eye, the police would have found it. You know that."

"No, I don't. Weren't you listening? Sadie—the detective— admitted there might be more to it." Kayla's voice was quickening. In the absence of friends, it was thrilling having a third party to discuss these conspiracy theories with.

Dr. Myers didn't bite at the bait. She asked calmly, "Don't you think, on some level, you're using this surreptitious investigation simply as a scapegoat for your grief?"

Kayla didn't answer. Cassandra's irritating ability to pinpoint the root of her problems was becoming annoying. Kayla's eyes cast a glance at the usual features of the room: the ticking clock, the aggressive red light, and very little else. She wondered whether her psychiatrist ever actually listened to the recordings on her dictaphone.

Dr. Myers tried another strategy. "Have you considered taking up a hobby? I mean that in the least patronizing way possible. I just think it might do you some good. Finding something to occupy both your body and your mind, I mean. And that doesn't have to be a huge life step, like choosing a degree program or finding a new job. It can be anything. Swimming, knitting, yoga . . . of course, I know that it'll take time to process what's happened. These things always take time, and that's why you have me here." A warm smile. "For as long as you need me to be. But in the meantime, this could help you begin to start your life back up."

"I guess. Does it have to be a new hobby? I used to run a lot."

"Used to?"

"Yeah, used to. It was once my favorite thing. But I've only tried once since I got back."

"And?"

"The thing I used to love about it has become the thing I hate about it."

"What's that?"

"Too much time to think."

Chapter 22

May 24, Thailand

"KAYLA." SAM SMILED gently, genuinely. "It's okay. Really. And I'm not saying that in the passive-aggressive way you did when I messed up." He chuckled and tucked a lock of damp hair behind her ear. She'd just showered for half an hour, scrubbing harshly at her flaming skin to wash every last trace of Oliver down the plug hole. Then, with her tail between her legs, she'd knocked on Sam's door. Best to get this over with. Suddenly she understood why he was always so apologetic and overly kind when he'd done something wrong—she was desperate for resolution. A metaphorical ice bucket in which to plunge her aching conscience.

Sam had answered, taken one look at her bloodshot eyes, and cuddled her into his chest. He smelled of sun cream and warm skin. His heart pounded against her ear, strong and steady, and Kayla was, in that moment, eternally grateful that he was a much better person than she was. That he could forgive imperfection. If only she could forgive herself. "It's not okay, Sam. Nothing about last night was okay."

"I mean, yeah. It wasn't great to watch. I'm not sure which was worse, the ridiculously good-looking guy with the abs or the slimy creep that is Oliver." He felt Kayla squirm in his arms. He nudged her chin upward with his index finger, her eyelashes fluttering to disguise her watery pupils. "As long as you're okay, though?"

Kayla pressed her forehead into Sam's chest. "I'm an idiot."

"No, you're not, you're only human—"

"No, Sam. I am. I am." *You have to tell him. Deep breath, then go.* "Wh-When we were in Sangkhlaburi—the night you broke your hand—Oliver . . . he tried to rape me." The hand that had been tenderly stroking the back of her head stopped abruptly. Sam didn't say anything, but Kayla felt his body go rigid, his muscles tensing against her cheek. "I didn't tell anyone because . . . well, I didn't want to ruin the trip. Or deal with the consequences of an allegation like that. But that's why what I did last night was so awful."

Sam gripped her shoulders and forced her to look him in the eye. "Please tell me you're joking. Please, Kayla."

She pursed her lips and shook her head, staring down intently at her feet.

Sam let go of her and clenched his unbandaged fist, biting into the whitening knuckles. Through the gaps between flesh and teeth, he said, "I'm going to fucking kill him. That bastard. That vile, vile bas—"

"Sam. Last night was . . . by choice. I took something I shouldn't, something I swore I never would, and I actively sought him out. I kissed him first." She felt it was in good taste to omit her reasons.

"That makes no difference. Jesus Christ, the thought of his greasy hands all over you, his disgusting lips kissing yours, that's vomit-inducing enough. But to think it was forced..." He thumped his already fractured hand against the flimsy hostel wall, wincing on impact but too pumped with fury to acknowledge the pain. He was visibly shaking, his eyes narrowed. His black eye was swelling, framed by a perfectly straight cut that traced his brow bone.

"Sam, what happened to your—"

"Sorry, Kayla, can't chat. I have vermin to kill." He pushed past her, through the doorway behind her, and stormed down the corridor, flip-flops slapping against the linoleum floor. Kayla didn't bother shouting after him. She'd never seen that look on his face before, and had a feeling it wasn't one she wanted to mess with.

If she didn't detest Oliver with every fiber of her being, she might consider warning him.

WAVING GOODBYE TO the vast majority of the people they'd spent the last two months with was a strange feeling. While some of them would not be missed—Ralph's obscene poshness and Xiang Qiang's complete lack of personality hadn't made them the most likable travel companions—there were certain quirks and dramas that had provided endless entertainment, such as Francesca's unique sense of humor (she was "grieving" on behalf of them all, wailing as she embraced Russia, Kayla, and Bling).

There was a sense of uneasiness too, on account of the terrorist attacks over the last few weeks. Officials were still insisting it was perfectly safe to travel and that they had the situation under control, but Kayla, for one, was glad not to be traveling home today. And, for some reason, even more glad that Sam wasn't. The thought of anything bad happening to him made her shudder. She absentmindedly drew a row of crosses in the dusty sand with the edge of her flip-flop, the dried out weeds tickling the inside of her foot. Before Gabe died, she'd always thought tragedy would never happen to her. Now that it had, she felt personally targeted—like a threat was around every corner. Waiting for the people she loved.

She chanced a peek at Oliver. He was sitting in the front row of the bus, checking names off the list and ensuring everyone's luggage was on board. Through the glaring, sun-dappled glass windows, she couldn't make out whether his face was beaten or if his expression showed he was hurt. She nudged Sam, who was standing next to her, trying to disguise the fact that he was breathless. "Sam? What happened? What did you do?"

He offered a strained semismile. "Don't worry about it."

"I have every reason to worry about it," Kayla hissed. "Anything you did, you did because of me."

"I said don't worry about it, Kayla." His voice was alarmingly neutral. He walked away toward Ralph to say goodbye—an awkward pat on the back and "See y'later, mate" in a predictable display of testosterone.

Case closed, then.

Several farewells, baggage checks, and tearful waves later, the remaining group was finally alone. After watching the bus drive off down the dusty Thai road, a contemplative silence ensued. The realization that being on their own for the first time was scarier than they'd expected struck them all at once. Like birds flung prematurely from their nests, they blinked rapidly and looked around as if dazed by the sudden blinding freedom.

"Right, then," Bling said authoritatively to her four remaining comrades. Sam was staring at the ground. "Guess we better find somewhere to sleep tonight."

RATHER THAN STAYING in a place Kayla had tarnished with her paintbrush of emotional destruction, the fivesome decided to move on to Phuket. The heat had engulfed their desire to sightsee and explore—relaxation and recovery were at the top of their agenda. Russia had insisted on a trip to Phang Nga Bay, and after one quick look at the relevant *Lonely Planet* pages, the group agreed that the sheer limestone karsts jutting vertically out of the emerald-green water were worth making a detour for. Promising to visit the bay after they'd settled in, Bling worked her magic in a run-down estate agency in Phuket Town and found them a relatively cheap, not-overly-dingy villa on the outskirts to rent for a month.

The town itself was bursting with character. Sino-Portuguese splendors and funky shops lined the heart of Phuket's sleepy provincial capital. But despite its intrigue, Kayla was secretly pleased not to be staying in the center. She didn't know whether she was just experiencing a paranoid come-down, but the leers of local men sent invisible ants crawling up and down her goose-pimpled skin. There was a vise grip on her guts, alleviated little by the pungent smell of warm fish flesh and moldy apples seeping into the air from the nearby market. She thought she might vomit.

Why won't that man stop staring at me? Kayla shakily smoothed down her wrinkled sundress and turned away from the fruit and vegetable stallholder who'd cocked his head and refused to break eye contact. *And why is it so bloody hot?* Her sweaty inner thighs were beginning to chafe. The rawness made every step burn. She squirmed uncomfortably, wishing their taxi would hurry up.

An hour later they'd eventually made it to Villa Phleng Chat. It was a small bungalow with little in the way of modern amenities, painted in a palette of pretty pastel shades. Its exterior was a sky blue color, with a cobalt corrugated roof, window shutters, and front door. The small patch of backyard was overflowing with tropical plants that looked like they might bite your hand off if you dared pluck the flowers from the stems. A few hundred meters away was a vast, glistening lake surrounded by rolling hills and smatterings of leafy mango trees.

The Lotus Agency, the villa specialists they'd rented the property from, had said the reason the bungalow was so cheap was because it was in an authentic residential area away from the tourist hot spots. This had sold it to the group—the village was deserted in the middle of the day as the natives worked, and this, in turn, meant a capacious lake became their own private swimming pool.

Russia, Dave, Bling, and Sam rushed excitedly around their new home like bluebottle flies buzzing frantically in a greenhouse. But Kayla stood back. She felt faint, as if she hadn't eaten in weeks, and was growing tired of the tickling paranoia that sat on her shoulder, breathing coolly down her neck and whispering eerie messages in her ear. *I'm watching you. Then, I will find you.* Even worse, *There's nothing you can do to stop—*

Russia grabbed Kayla by the waist. She flinched as if she'd been stung. She hadn't even seen Russia approaching. Beads of sweat trickled down the sides of her forehead and dropped off her jawbone. Her friend looked at her quizzically, raising her eyebrows. Though their friendship had never been touchy-feely, Russia clearly hadn't expected her spontaneous hug to have such an ill effect on Kayla.

"We're just going to dump our bags in our rooms then head out to explore," she said. "I can't wait to skinny dip in that lake! Are you coming?"

"I think I'm going to take a cold shower and lie down," Kayla replied. Her own voice sounded miles away. "I don't feel great."

"Yeah, you don't look it either." Russia smiled and squeezed her clammy hand. Kayla shivered. "Do you want me to get you anything? We're going to stop by a supermarket to pick up some fridge supplies. You look like you could do with some soda?"

"That'd be great, thank you." Kayla could barely finish her sentence. It felt like too much energy—energy she no longer had. She had a strong urge, an inescapable urge, to drop to her knees and sit on the floor in the exact spot she was standing. She mustered one last burst of animation and propelled her wobbly legs into the bathroom, locking the door behind her.

Steadying herself with both hands on each side of the small porcelain sink, Kayla retched, gagging on the musty air. She switched the shower on. Partially to allow it to run cold, and partially to disguise the sounds of her dry-heaving into the washbasin.

Once her stomach had rid itself of every last drop of nonexistent vomit, Kayla peeled her dress off and climbed into the shower in her underwear. The water was warm—not the icy-cold stream her body, mind, and conscience had so intensely desired. It was a lukewarm trickle that did absolutely nothing to assuage her aching joints. She slid down and sat in the shower basin, the irregular jet of tepid water pounding her back in staccato bursts.

For the first time since Gabe's death, Kayla allowed herself to cry.

GRIEF DIDN'T STAND a chance against the pounding dance music and the group of ladyboys parading in front of Soi Bangla's moonlit bars in feathered, sequined outfits.

"We *have* to watch the Moulin Rouge Cabaret Show later!" Bling yelled over the roaring bass line that was yet to drop. She was sucking her fluorescent straw furiously. Kayla stared at her feet.

Picking up on the stilted conversation and awkward glances between Sam and Kayla, Russia gripped Dave's hand and said, "Sounds good to me! Dave, let's go and play giant Connect 4. Bling, you can take on the winner."

Bling looked reluctant to leave Sam and Kayla alone. "I'm okay, I don't really fancy—"

"Bling. Now." Russia hissed, shooting her a death stare. Bling meekly followed her and Dave into the crowd, leaving Sam shuffling his feet and staring around three feet to the left of Kayla's shoulder.

Kayla couldn't bear awkward silence. The compulsion to fill it was often the cause of her verbal diarrhea. "I don't usually like this kind of music, but it's quite good to dance to, isn't it?"

Sam nodded. "Yeah. It's good."

More silence. Kayla thought back to the very first night in Thailand, and how much had happened since then. They'd been so carefree, laughing and misunderstanding each other. It had been the first time she felt anything close to happy in a long time. And the night by the river . . . the contrast between that night and the present moment caused tears to prickle behind her eyes once again.

Sam's blank expression was agonizing. Kayla felt her phone vibrate in her pocket, but didn't have either the energy or the wish to answer it. She clicked it off and forced herself to look at the man who used to make her feel giddy with infatuation. "Listen, Sam, I—"

She froze. Sam's neutrality has morphed into something far worse: a blend of shock, horror, disgust. She followed his line of vision. When her eyes planted on the source of Sam's abhorrence, the wind was knocked out of her sails in one fell swoop.

Oliver was standing at the bar. Watching.

Chapter 23

July 17, England

THE LAST PERSON Kayla had expected to see sitting on her beloved tree swing as she jogged breathlessly past was her nan. Even when they were little, nobody had ever come to this part of the garden. It was her and Gabe's private den. Kayla stopped running and walked over, tapping her nan on the shoulder before realizing just how strange the scene was.

A paperback novel was open, facedown, on the grass—Kayla cringed at the thought of the damp grass staining its pages green— next to her nan's slippered feet. Nan was wearing a tatty old dressing gown and very little else, and her eyes were bleary and pink. It was the first time Kayla had seen her without glasses in years.

Iris didn't jump in surprise. She turned around slowly, sniffing. "Oh hello, Kayla love. I'm sorry I'm dressed like this, I'd just got out of the shower and felt a little dizzy. I think I ran the water too hot." Her eyes were out of focus and her body was slack and droopy.

"Are you okay, Nan? You don't look too good . . ."

"Nonsense, I'm fine." A watery smile. "How are you doing, anyway, poppet?"

Kayla sat down cross-legged on the grass. She was less than half a kilometer from the house and her legs were already starting to cramp. "I'm all right. Missing Thailand and my friends a bit. And Gabe, of course." She plucked two daisies from their beds and busied her hands making a daisy chain.

"We all do, Kayla. We all do."

Kayla knew instinctively that telling Nan about Aran's mission would do more harm than good, but the words were already spilling out of her mouth by the time she'd changed her mind. "I'm finding out who did this to him," she blurted out.

Iris appeared confused, narrowing her eyes and tilting her head. "But he did this to himself?"

"I mean who sent him the messages. Who drove him to it." Kayla waited for her nan to ask how, but all of the color had drained from her face. "Oh, Kayla," Iris's bottom lip quivered. She pressed her lips together to steady it. "Why would you do such a thing? We're all just starting to move on with our lives and—"

"How? By running away and drinking and never talking about it?"

"Please." Nan's voice was almost a whisper. "Please don't make us go through this again. I don't know if I can deal with it . . . I'm sick of crying myself to sleep every night as it is, and if we had to go through a trial too . . ."

Kayla hadn't considered the criminal implications—she had selfishly focused on providing a face to direct her own internal anger toward. *Typical me.* "I'm sorry, Nan, I hadn't thought of it like th—"

Iris let out an animal-sounding wail. She was trembling violently. "Promise you won't chase it Kayla. Please. I can't—"

"Nan, I promise. It's okay." Kayla clambered to her feet and hugged her grandmother, rubbing her back to try and warm her up. "I'll leave it alone. I'm sorry, I didn't think." Nan's tears soaked through her cotton workout tank top. Kayla felt terrible. Her nan never cried.

Iris conjured up a tissue from somewhere deep inside her sleeve and dabbed gingerly at her face. "I'm sorry for getting so upset. It's been a horrible day. You go for your run, sweetheart, don't let your silly old nan keep you. It's nice to see you out of the house, you look so sporty in all your gear." She smiled bravely.

As Kayla jogged away, she was surprised by how hard the wave of love for her nan hit her.

AROUND TWO MILES into the run, Kayla's mind started to wander. Gabe.

Could any of them have saved him? Could this have been stopped?

How could we miss the signs that he was so depressed? So alone?

But we didn't, she thought, her trainers pounding the woodland trail. We didn't miss the signs. They were all there. We just didn't know what to do with them,. How to help him.

Five months earlier—or was it six?—she'd tried to talk to Gabe. Tried to interject.

His voice had never sounded so cold. "Go."

"Gabe?" she'd whispered, kneeling down and gently touching his shoulder. It was bonier than it used to be.

"Please. Go." A frosty mutter. Each word formed icicles as they curled past his lips.

They had been in their father's study. Gabe was sitting on the floor, elbows on his sky-facing knees and his back leaning against a rich mahogany bookcase. The room smelled of tangy wood varnish, musty books, and freshly vacuumed rugs. It was eerily silent. Kayla's footsteps echoed around the bookcase enclaves and high ceilings.

She'd sat down next to him and crossed her legs, trying to position herself so she looked less like a worried older sister and more like a warm friend. She plucked a rogue piece of fuzz from her jeans and rolled it absentmindedly between her thumb and forefinger. "Talk to me. Is it Zack?"

Gabe had scoffed. "If only." He sat stock-still. Like he was frozen.

"What is it?" she persevered, attempting to keep the edge of frustration out of her voice. Why was he being so hostile toward her? she had wondered. Toward their whole family? They'd always been supportive of him. But lately . . .

"Trust me, Kay. You don't want to know. It'll gnaw on your insides like a parasite." Wisps of exhaustion spiraled around him like steam off tarmac on a hot, rainy day.

"Gabe, you're worrying me. Please—"

"I said go." A glacial glare.

She'd gone.

Kayla thought about that day a lot. About how different everything could have been if she'd stayed.

SHE HAD ANOTHER nightmare that evening.

Veiny hands around Sam's throat. His eyes bulging.

She tried to dial 999. She got through to an operator, who kept demanding credit card payment in order to complete her request. She kept insisting there was no time—he'd be dead before then. The operator hung up. She crushed her phone in her hand, and pain shot through her palm as the shattered screen sliced straight through the skin. Blood drenched the tiled floor.

Sam's face was purple. Frozen in a single expression of terror as his frantic gasps slowed and he realized that this was it. The end.

The light behind his eyes was snuffed out, like moist fingers crushing a candle flame.

The person whose hands were wrapped around Sam's airwaves turned to face her.

Their features started to come into focus. A dainty nose, long glossy hair, gaping red lips painted on like a creepy clown's mouth.

It was a woman. A laughing woman.

Chapter 24

June 8, Thailand

OLIVER BECAME LIKE a shadow in Phuket. Wherever the group went, he was always there.

On that first night they spotted him in Soi Bangla, Kayla had stormed up to him and demanded to know what he was doing there, how he'd found them, why he wasn't back in Bangkok awaiting the arrival of the next Escaping Grey group. He explained that his bosses had received some complaints of indecency, petty theft, and a lackluster approach to his job as a rep. He'd been sacked.

Typical Sam, Kayla thought, hiding a smile. He was too smart to punch Oliver square in the nose, or to reveal the sexual assault and land them with a trial.

Oliver had also explained that he was friends with Bling on Facebook, and she'd posted a picture of their villa online with the caption "Our Phuket home for the next few weeks!" He said he'd caught several buses back to the area to join those he considered his friends, and Kayla had assured him that he was by absolutely no means their friend, nor would he ever be. Oliver didn't even flinch, he just took another swig of beer and smirked. Kayla found herself feeling irrationally angry at Bling for betraying their location. Then she felt angry at herself—if she'd reported the incident when it happened, she would never have had to worry about Oliver's whereabouts. He'd be behind bars, hopefully rotting in a Thai prison cell.

They had no idea where Oliver was staying or what he was doing. Especially not why he was there, though Kayla could hazard a guess. Every time she caught him staring at her from a bar or market stall, or every time she turned around to see him following them down the street, she felt queasy. She was constantly on edge, wondering when he'd pounce. When he'd finish what he started. What *she* started.

Without a regimented itinerary, the group was finding it hard to go out and do things. The extreme heat had hit the region later than usual that year, and the lure of an air-conditioned flat beat the desire to explore, hands down. Russia and Sam, with their confidence, charisma, and above-average looks, had both gotten jobs on the clubbing strip as a shot girl and flyer boy respectively, cleaning the bars before opening hours for some extra pennies. The other three spent their time alternating between watching the geriatric television set in the bungalow and lounging by the lake, deepening their tans and daydreaming about where they were going to go after Thailand. Kayla had been offered a job too but didn't know if she could handle spending eight-hour shifts out in the open for any male predators to prey on her. Not that the bungalow felt any safer—she found herself double- and triple-checking the locks every night, ensuring that every last window was bolted shut.

One night, she was restless. Lying in bed in the small hours of the morning, the nasal snore next to her prevented the fuzzy edges of sleep from forming around her overactive mind. The same mind that had, in turn, started to play cruel tricks on her. The creaking of the old building, the tin roof rattling in even the slightest breeze, and the oddly shaped shadows of eccentric tropical plants—everything seemed amplified through the lens of fear, became imposing, intimidating, inhuman. The branches were warped, the leaves distorted, the flowers eerie, and her imagination had them dancing a tango of terror across the bedroom wall. It was like a morbid version of the Disney film *Fantasia* they'd been made to watch in middle school.

She and Bling were sharing a room, as were Russia and Dave. Sam was alone, in the tiny box room at the end of the corridor. Kayla imagined an intruder forcing his way into their villa, into her room. Bling's petite stature would render her helpless against a muscular man—Kayla didn't know why, but she pictured her potential attacker as beefier than Oliver, with bulging biceps.

Whether it was lust, terror, or an electrically charged combination of the two that propelled Kayla through the hallway toward Sam's bedroom, the anticipation caused the hairs on the back of her arms to stand on end. She knocked timidly on his door. No reply. She tried again, a little louder. A muffled sound vaguely resembling a response echoed through the thin door, and she pushed it open.

Even in the near blackness she could tell Sam was surprised to see her. He propped himself up on his elbows and blinked rapidly, trying to force his eyes to adapt to the dark. The white cotton bedsheets were tangled around his legs, and his tanned torso glistened with a thin layer of sweat—the fan overhead had stopped spinning. Kayla flicked it back on using the dial next to the door frame. "Hey." Her voice croaked. She was in desperate need of water, but the need to be next to Sam, to feel his skin on hers, was far greater.

"Kayla?"

"Yeah. Can I come in?"

"Oh, um . . . sure. What's up?" *Where do I start?*

"Can't sleep." *I'm petrified.*

"Me neither." He unraveled the sheets and shifted his body to the side of the bed. He didn't have to spell it out. Kayla crept forward and closed the door behind her. The room smelled of sweat and after-sun lotion, and she could still taste the strawberry cider on her tongue from earlier.

Banishing her hesitance, she padded across the smooth tiled floor, but the bravado only lasted until she reached the bed, where she perched awkwardly on the edge. Sam chuckled. "Do I smell that bad?"

Kayla blushed more furiously than she had since she was fourteen. She was grateful for the dark. She slid her legs down the length of the bed and inched closer to Sam's warm body. After she had lain rigidly on her back and stared at the ceiling for a moment, his hand found her hip. He rolled her body slightly away from him and curled his own around her, tucking his arm underneath hers and looping it around her waist. His face nuzzled her neck, and she could smell the sweet coconut shampoo on his hair.

"You fit perfectly," he mumbled, planting a delicate kiss on the back of her neck. The spot of skin his lips brushed tingled. She wished he'd do it again, all over her body.

She tucked her knees up toward her chest as if curling around a ball, pushing her back even closer to Sam. She could feel him pressing against her, hard and firm, and wished she wasn't wearing pajama shorts. An overwhelming longing pulsed through her veins; a delicious aching that, until now, she hadn't fully realized Sam reciprocated.

The air-conditioning had kicked in and the room was cooling rapidly. Sam wrapped his arms tighter around her. He slid her tank top strap halfway down her upper arm and swept her hair out of the way, kissing her warm, bare shoulder with tender pecks that lingered longer each time. She laced her fingers gently through his, careful not to squeeze his fractured hand. She started pulling him down toward the waistband of her shorts, edging his fingertips underneath the elastic.

"Kayla . . . are you sure you—"

An aggressive ringing cut through the quiet. Kayla jumped with fright and crushed Sam's hand, who yelped in pain like an injured puppy. On the bedside table next to Kayla's head, his phone was vibrating and ringing shrilly, much louder than it seemed to during the day. Squinting at the screen, Kayla could only make out two words: *Unknown number.* The phone's clock told her it was 3:33A.M. *Who on earth calls at this time?* It might have been someone calling from back home who didn't understand the time difference, much like her nan. But something in the panicked expression on Sam's face told Kayla it was more sinister than that.

She climbed out of bed and made for the door, not wanting to intrude on what she assumed would be a very private conversation.

Sam picked up the call without greeting the person on the other end. His voice went cold. "Now isn't a good time. No . . . No!" He shot Kayla an apologetic glance and gulped. "I don't know what you're talking about . . ."

She left the room.

Chapter 25

"So nobody saw Sam break his hand?"

"Nope." Kayla once again met Sadie in a bar, off hours, for a conspiracy and gin session. While she was backing away from Aran Peters—for her nan's sake, if nothing else—that didn't mean she was about to surrender all suspicion without any answers.

Bling had eventually texted Kayla back to inform her that she hadn't seen the injury happen, and Kayla jumped at the chance to meet with the detective. She missed having people around her, and Sadie was young enough and nice enough to almost pass as a real friend.

"Which means that the theory about a drug dealer's bailiff chasing Sam for money, and providing physical incentives to pay up, makes sense." DI Winters was making light work of the wasabi peas on the bar, crunching loudly through the fiery balls. Kayla swore that her mouth was even bigger than last time, her teeth even more crooked. That didn't make her imperfect smile any less attractive, though. "Did Sam receive any threatening phone calls? Or appear to be on edge?"

"It's hard to say, really. Obviously I never heard what the person on the other end of the phone was saying, but there were a few times that pleasantries weren't exactly exchanged, and Sam seemed unsettled. As for being on edge the rest of the time, he definitely was. But it's hard to know why." Kayla polished off half her gin and tonic in one fell swoop. "It's a little complicated, if I'm honest. This guy Oliver, who we all hated, had followed us to Phuket and wouldn't leave us alone. So Sam was a little aggravated by that. And since he'd apparently asked to borrow money from his mum, who then declined, he'd have been stressed about that, I guess. I've tried to call Kathy to ask her more about it, but she hasn't got back to me.

"I don't know," she went on. "My memory is so fuzzy, like it didn't actually happen to me. Feels like a lifetime ago, like I can't distinguish between what I think happened and what actually happened. Looking back, I wish I'd paid more attention."

"Everyone wishes that," the detective replied. "If only you'd read the signs, if only you'd done something differently. It's natural for people to obsess over how they'd live the past differently if they could." She took a gigantic swig of gin to wash down the five kilograms of wasabi peas she'd just inhaled. "This guy Oliver. You've never mentioned him before. Tell me about him."

"Ugh. Do I have to?" Kayla dreaded the thought. Sadie said nothing, just looked at her expectantly. The stakes were too high not to share the story. She inhaled deeply, steadying herself. "When we were in Sangk—Sangkhlaburi—sorry, I still have no idea how to pronounce it, I'm such a tourist." She laughed, but her false giggle did little to soften Sadie's intense stare. Kayla went on then and told the detective about what happened between her and Oliver. No matter how many times she said it aloud—albeit it only a few—it never got any easier.

Sadie choked on her mustardy snack and hastily took a sip of her drink. "He tried to rape you?" Kayla wished she'd keep her voice down. People were starting to stare, and it wasn't something she'd wanted to announce to the whole bar. The stereo system was between songs, and Sadie's voice rang through the silence, lingering on the word rape. "Did you report it?" Kayla shook her head. She felt like a naughty schoolkid. The music started up again. "Why the bloody hell not?"

"I don't know . . . No, I do. It would have been difficult to prove, for one thing. And after everything that had happened with Gabe, all I wanted was to move on and not cause any more stress or heartache for my family. Can you imagine how my parents would feel losing a son to suicide, then a few months later it comes out that their daughter had been assaulted? It would've broken my mum. My dad would pummel Oliver to a pulp, then probably go to jail for murder. Even if he didn't, we'd all be stuck in Thailand until the trial was over, and God knows how long that'd take. At the time, I thought we were only lumbered with Oliver for another week and then he'd be back in Bangkok with the next Escaping Grey group." *Preying on his next victim.*

Kayla realized she was rambling, and was aware that she sounded incredibly selfish. She hadn't meant to imply that as long as Oliver was no longer her problem, he could do what he liked to who he liked. But that's the way it sounded. Sadie looked shocked.

"I didn't mean it like that," Kayla said, her cheeks flushed with embarrassment.

"No, I know you didn't," said Sadie, a little too quickly. She gestured for the barman to bring her another gin. "I really think you should report it, Kayla. I know it's been a while but . . . I shudder to think of him doing the same to countless other girls and getting away with it. Did you say he followed you to Phuket?"

"Yeah. He lurked near us all the time. In bars, down the street, at the market. He was a bit . . . obsessed by me."

"And how did that make you feel?" Sadie asked, before erupting in laugher. "Jesus Christ, I sound like a therapist." Kayla thought it'd be too awkward to tell her that she really did have a therapist. And actually quite liked her.

"It's hard to explain. Trapped, I guess? Suffocated?" She couldn't bring herself to drop in the small detail of her entirely consensual kiss with Oliver a week after the initial rape attempt. She cared far too much about what DI Winters thought about her. "Observed. I felt constantly observed."

Sadie nodded. "Have you heard from him since Sam went missing?"

Kayla opted for honesty. "Yeah. He texted me about a week after it happened."

"What saying?"

"Basically, that he was really sorry to hear about Sam and that he was a nice guy, blah blah blah. And that if I needed anything, I knew where he was."

Sadie's eyebrow jolted upward in an arch, as if caught in a fish hook. "That's a little strange, isn't it? Why on earth would he assume that you'd want to go to him for comfort after what he did to you?"

"I suppose it is odd."

"Well, forgetting the fact that I think you're utterly bonkers for not reporting the assault—which I do, but it's your decision—let's look at it in another light. Do you think Oliver was so obsessed that he might have let jealousy over your and Sam's relationship . . . influence his actions?"

The idea had crossed Kayla's mind once before, if only briefly. It didn't seem compelling enough a hypothesis to run with. Obsession in itself was a powerful force, sure, and it had been enough for Oliver to follow her to Phuket. But enough to commit murder? She didn't think so. Plenty of people experienced obsession in various forms: a band, a teenage crush, a sports team. It was largely harmless.

The only aspect that caused any doubt, in this case, was the carnal nature of most of Oliver's actions. At times he seemed almost doglike, unaffected by morality, a slave to his urges. "I genuinely don't know if he was jealous. Sometimes I think absolutely not. But that's maybe because I myself can't imagine a crush driving me to homicide. It's hard, isn't it—as a normal person—trying to wrap your head around the thought processes that would drive someone to be so . . . evil? Murder. It's just such an absurd solution. One that no ordinary person would resort to."

"I know," Sadie said. "It's something I used to struggle with a lot. Couldn't understand the reasoning behind it. I've always been a logical person, so to work with people every day that were so far from logical, so far from normal . . . it was difficult. So I went back to uni, a few years ago, and started studying for a master's degree in criminal psychology. It was fascinating, really amazing." Sadie's pupils were dilated, her skin flushed, her hands gesturing animatedly. Her passion was written all across her face. "It meant

I would be able to apply so much of what I learned to my work, help me get into the brains of rapists and murderers. It was an uncomfortable place to be, but that's when I started to really engage with the messed up people I deal with on a daily basis. It sounds so weird, I know, but I genuinely love my job."

"So what happened?"

Sadie looked confused. "What happened with what?"

"You said a lot of that in past tense. It was fascinating. It *was* an uncomfortable place to be. You *started* studying for your masters. What happened? Didn't you finish it?"

"No," Sadie admitted. "And I wish I had. Sometimes I dream about going back, but . . . it's complicated."

"Why? Did you drop out, I mean? I'm sorry if that's too personal . . ."

Sadie sighed, looking around to see where the barman was in the gin-and-tonic-making process. Not very far along, it seemed. His attention was entirely focused on the bosomy brunette at the other end of the bar. "A few reasons, I guess. Some were circumstantial. Because my work had improved so much, I was offered a promotion. I took it, of course. Who wouldn't? But the increased workload meant I missed a lot of my classes. I was studying part-time—six to eight, two nights a week—and found myself staying in the office until long after seven. Juggling both got a lot harder. I finished my first year, then got so caught up in work that I just never went back for my second. So I deferred it a few times. I'm supposed to go back this September, but . . . I don't know. I could pick up exactly where I left off, but it feels like there's something stopping me. I can't work out what, though. I just get to the start of the semester, and when I'm prompted to re-enroll, I just . . . don't."

"Do you think the disturbing things you've learned made you subconsciously not want to go back?" Kayla speculated.

"No, I don't think that's it. I wouldn't throw myself into a job dealing with psychopaths on a daily basis if I'd become squeamish toward crime. The only thing I can think of is that my young cousin—he was only twenty—died as I was doing my exams, and it hit me pretty hard." Sadie chuckled, a little sadly. "Again, you'd have to ask a therapist."

"Your cousin died? I'm so sorry."

Sadie shook her head dismissively, the words *you didn't know* left unspoken. Selfishly, Kayla didn't want to let it go, though. She remembered the initial reason Sadie had felt so connected to Sam's case was because she said that she too knew what it was like to lose a young loved one.

"How did he, or she . . . ?"

"Drug overdose. Stupid. He was a pretty shitty person, actually, but he was family, you know? The funeral was the worst."

Memories of Gabe's funeral hit Kayla with a pang of sadness. She knew how gut-wrenching they were. She thought, for a split second, about how death was hard on everyone, no matter what walk of life they were from or what the circumstances were. "I know it's messed up to wish this . . . but part of me feels like it would be so much easier to have closure on what happened to Sam if there had been a funeral. Maybe that's why I'm so hell-bent on discovering what really happened the day he vanished."

"And maybe that's why I'm so hell-bent on helping you." Sadie smiled, a glint of determination in her eyes.

There was a lull in conversation—something that didn't often happen when drinking with Sadie Winters. Kayla took a deep breath, trying pluck up the courage to ask her something that had been troubling her for a while. "Why do you think there hasn't been much on the news about Sam? Usually when this kind of thing happens, especially to a guy from such a tight-knit community, it's on the news for months on ends. But not with Sam."

Sadie swallowed, not quite meeting Kayla's eye. "Shepherd seems keen to bury Sam's case as soon as possible." As soon as the words left Sadie's lips, they rang true with Kayla. The half-assed questioning. His complete disinterest.

Kayla was taken aback by her honesty. "Really?" She stirred her drink with a swizzle stick, pushing the ice and lemon around in the small glass tumbler and trying to seem nonchalant. "He seemed distant and apathetic, but I didn't get the impression he actively wanted to bury it, yet it seems that's what he's doing. Why is that? Sorry if that's inappropriate to ask you, it just seems weird."

"No, it's fine. I probably shouldn't be saying this, but I think there were a few cock-ups in the process of handing the case over from the Thais to us. Nothing drastic, just sloppy reports and huge time delays. Shepherd is relatively new to the DCI role—he only started a few months ago, and everyone thought he was the wrong man for the promotion—so he probably doesn't want to attract attention to it. It'd reflect badly on him."

"And the rest of us are just supposed to forget about it too?"

"Yes. But *I* haven't, Kayla. I hope you know that."

SADIE ASKED KAYLA for her version of the events that occurred five weeks ago, on the seventeenth of June. The proper version, not the curtailed, disjointed notes she'd given Shepherd.

"You want an objective account of what happened?"

Sadie clicked the top of her pen, poising it above her lined notebook, ready to record her every word. Kayla liked that she used pen and paper, not a dictaphone. It felt like she was properly engaging with her.

"Yes, please. If it's not too difficult for you, a timeline would be great. As accurate as possible too. Down to the minute." Sadie pushed her reading glasses farther up her nose.

"Why are you only asking me this now?" Kayla blurted out. "Why not ask me the first time we met?"

Sadie looked taken aback by her assertiveness. "I guess I was treading lightly because I didn't want to undermine Shepherd. In theory, he's already asked you everything we needed to know. In theory . . . all avenues have been explored." She tilted her head to the side. Kayla knew what she was thinking. *But they haven't.*

Kayla recounted the events of the morning and early afternoon with relative ease. Practically, not emotionally. But when it came to the nitty-gritty details of the disappearance, she was surprised to find that her memory had failed her. Everything was foggy. Sadie tried to help her out. "So you estimate that you knocked on Sam's door around quarter to seven, is that right?" Kayla nodded. "And what were you met with?"

"Silence. It sounds cheesy, but my heart skipped a beat at that moment. Like I already knew that something weird had happened. The way the door was slightly ajar, when he usually shut it to keep the coolness of the air-con inside. Does that sound daft? I mean, I couldn't possibly have known."

Sadie shrugged. She didn't write that part down. "Intuition's a funny thing. Depends what you believe in, I guess. And how long had it been since you last saw him?"

"I'm not sure. Around half an hour, but it could have been more."

"What happened next?"

"After I knocked? I pushed the door open, and saw . . . well, you know what I saw. Blood."

"Then you collapsed, right? Into the pool of blood, which is why your clothes were soaked through with it?"

Kayla cocked her head. She couldn't possibly have detected a note of suspicion in Sadie's voice, could she? "Yes, that's right."

"And how long would you say you blacked out for?"

"I haven't a clue. No more than a minute or two, I don't think."

"And then?"

The words caught in Kayla's throat. Her skin prickled. This felt more like an interrogation than a casual chat. She took a drink. "I—I don't remember."

"You don't remember?"

"No . . . I think I went outside. To find the others." She instantly regretted her choice of the word "think."

"They were by the lake?"

Kayla nodded. Sadie had obviously done her research. "Yeah. Russia started screaming at the sight of me covered in blood. I think she thought I'd been hurt myself."

"How did the others react?"

"Dave came rushing over and asked if I was all right. Bling went white as a sheet—she's terrified of blood."

"So that's when you told Dave what you'd found?"

"Yeah. Although I remember struggling to get the words out."

"Who called the police?"

"I don't know," Kayla admitted. "I'd be lying if I said I did. What I do remember is feeling like it took them an eternity to show up. Russia wouldn't stop screaming, and Dave was pacing up and down, muttering about whoever had done this getting farther and farther away. Bling vomited, a lot."

Sadie stopped writing abruptly. "Don't you find it strange that you can't remember who dialed the police? I know who did, for the record. It's just weird that you don't."

Kayla lowered her voice. "I know. It *is* weird. I feel like I forget a lot of things now. Everything is so blurry all the time. Maybe it's grief. Maybe I'm losing my mind. Or maybe it's that thing . . . what's it called, PTSD? Post-traumatic stress disorder?" Sadie said nothing. "Who did call the police? Out of interest?"

"Daivat."

Kayla nodded. "Makes sense."

"I'll be honest, Kayla. Something's bothering me."

"What's that?"

Sadie removed her glasses and rubbed the red indents left on her nose where they'd been digging in. "The timing. You say you saw him half an hour before you realized he disappeared. At that point, he was uninjured. Then, a mere thirty minutes later, an absurd amount of blood was found in his bedroom. A volume of blood that couldn't originate from a struggle or punch-up. So even if he went to his room and was attacked instantaneously, the rate at which he must have bled would suggest one of his main arteries had been hacked. Now, why would a drug dealer do that, then take him away? Surely he'd just knock him out and shove him in a sack or something?" *Delicately worded, as ever.* "And you've pretty much said Sam wouldn't have done something like that to himself. I'll admit that doesn't make sense either, because why would he try and kill himself, then vanish?"

"I have no idea."

"Exactly. Me neither. Which leads me to suspect one of two possible scenarios. The first is that the perpetrator was simply sadistic. Loved the sight of blood. Considering the kind of people we're talking about . . . it's not beyond the realms of possibility. The second is that whoever did that to Sam could have done it as a warning, of sorts."

"A warning? How do you mean?"

"As in, they wanted you all to see his blood."

Kayla felt sick. "But why?"

Sadie puffed air through her cheeks and turned to face her. "I have no idea. It's the 'why' part that's got me stumped."

Kayla walked back to her car after meeting with Sadie. It was late—much later than she'd realized. The inky blue sky told her it was well after eleven.

She knew she probably shouldn't drive home. She'd had two fairly strong gin and tonics, and her vision was a little fuzzy around the edges. But she didn't particularly savor the thought of waking up early on a Sunday morning to come and collect her car.

Something new was playing on her mind. The thought had struck her when she was talking to Sadie about how on edge Sam had been in the last few weeks they'd been together. And now that the thought was lodged in her brain, she couldn't unthink it.

Sam and Gabe. The way they'd both acted in their final few weeks was eerily similar. Like they were scared and angry and helpless. Like they couldn't see a way out. Like . . . like something inside them had irrevocably changed.

Rounding the corner into the deserted car park, a cool breeze sent shivers down her forearms. She wrapped her thin cardigan tightly around her. Wasn't it supposed to be summer? She reached her car and started rooting around in the bottom of her handbag for her keys.

Then she heard it. It was a muffled sound, like a stifled scream, followed by a pounding of footsteps. Something surged through

Kayla's veins—the closest to adrenaline she'd felt in a long time—as she swiveled around, trying to pin down the source of the sound. But it had already died down.

She shivered again, but this time it wasn't because of the cold. That had definitely sounded like a struggle. *Should I go and investigate?* Her feet felt like they were cemented to the ground.

Somewhere not too far away, a vehicle door slammed shut and tires screeched and skidded on tarmac. Just as Kayla turned away from her car, she saw a white van with no headlights fly past the entrance to the car park.

Her fingertips found her keys. She dove into the driver's seat, quickly locking the doors behind her, and fumbled to stick the key in the ignition.

Her sense that danger was never far behind was starting to feel exhausting.

Chapter 26

SINCE KAYLA SNUCK into his bedroom that night, Sam had become more and more guarded. She'd tried, unsuccessfully, to fall asleep after she left his room. For five minutes or so the muffled sound of a heated conversation seeped through the thin walls—but that wasn't anywhere near as eerie as the silence that soon ensued.

Kayla lay awake, staring at the ceiling until she couldn't bear it any longer. She'd tiptoed back along to Sam's bedroom and knocked on his door. When there was no response, she tried again, this time whispering, "Sam? Are you okay?"

His sharp reply cut through the quiet like a sword. "I'm fine. Just leave it, Kayla."

And so she left it.

While she'd anticipated a certain level of embarrassment during the aftermath of her visiting him earlier, she hadn't bargained for the hostility Sam fired her way. The next morning, as they were pouring their breakfast cereal, she'd asked him politely—suppressing the blushing as best she could—whether he could possibly pass her the milk, please. He'd shot her a death stare and plonked the carton aggressively in front of her. The lid had been removed, and the jerking motion caused some of the milk to splash on her, for which Sam did not apologize. An hour later they were at the bus stop waiting for a coach to arrive to take them into town. Kayla had struggled to decipher the timetable and jokingly said to Sam, "This might as well be written in bloody hieroglyphics for all the sense it makes to me."

He'd snapped, "Stop acting stupid, Kayla. Doesn't suit you."

The permanent fixture of Oliver Gilmore hardly helped matters. He was still everywhere they looked. The only solace came when they returned to the villa—it seemed as though he hadn't yet plucked up the courage to climb on the same bus as them.

Suspense within the group of friends was soaring in line with the temperature. For one thing, the snide comments directed at Kayla started to feel less lighthearted. They'd evolved from jesting quips like, "Maybe if you weren't so bloody gorgeous, Oliver wouldn't be so obsessed. Can't you just shave your head, or something?" to snappier remarks, such as, "Bet you didn't expect this when you kissed him," and, "We're half tempted to leave you in Phuket and bugger off on our own." Only one other person in their group of five knew what had really happened between her and Oliver—what he'd done to her—and Kayla didn't know if those who didn't know would be more or less likely to resent her if they were to discover the truth. She couldn't blame them. If roles were reversed, she wasn't sure how she'd be acting either.

The minuscule size of the bungalow, which they'd initially found so charming, was beginning to feel claustrophobic. Russia

decided to take healing action and suggested they leave Phuket
for a few days. They were all crowded together in the tiny living
room—four on the sofa, Dave sprawled across the floor massaging
his feet—and watching a bizarre Asian game show on TV, when
Russia stood up suddenly and authoritatively. "Let's just do it.
Okay? Oliver will never know where we are. It'll give us all some
precious bonding time away from that psycho, and hopefully,
when we come back, he'll think we've left and will leave us alone.
I'm also pretty bloody bored of this house. I mean, we'd never
planned on staying in the same place for so long, and outside of
work, we never do anything. So I vote we bail. Yes?"

They all replied affirmatively.

Kayla had wondered, for a second, whether she was invited.

DESPITE BEING MERELY a few miles away from Phuket, Koh Phi
Phi could have been on another planet. Gone were the smoky
scooters and the dusty roads, the greasy street vendors and the
omnipresent stench of rotting; nature's handiwork was infinitely
more awe-inspiring. The archipelago of six islands rose from the
vivid sapphire sea like a fortress, sheer cliffs towering overhead
before they made way for beach-fronted jungle.

It had been Dave who suggested swimming with sharks. His
rapidly deteriorating health meant none of the group had it in
their hearts to deny him a few more life experiences before he
became bed-bound for the rest of his life. Russia had kicked up
quite the fuss, insisting that it'd be dangerous for someone with
limited function in his feet to swim with infamous predators, but
Dave simply laughed and kissed her whenever she tried to argue.
Eventually she'd given up and agreed that it would be fun.

Meeting outside Ja Soh's curry house at 5:45 the next morning, however, their enthusiasm level had taken something of a knock. Emphatic yawns and bleary eyes had replaced the chirpy voices of yesterday. Early mornings had recently been a thing of the past. With Sam and Russia working at night, and the others with a distinct lack of motivation to rise early, sleep-ins that sprawled lazily into mid-afternoon were becoming increasingly regular. It was one of the reasons why Russia had insisted they shake up their idle routine. It seemed like a waste to be living in such a spectacular place and spend half of their time in bed. Breaking the habit, though, was much easier in theory.

Through a voice thick with lethargy, Bling grumbled, "Where is the bloody guide? Why ask us to be here this early if he's not even going to turn up himself?" Despite the early hour, the air was already clammy with humid heat.

As if on cue, a deeply tanned man, who looked to be in his mid-twenties, bounded around the corner. In an Australian drawl, he said, "G'day, kids! M'name's Zach. Zach Fletcher—but you can call me Fletch. Everybody does. So who's ready for an adventure? I know I am!" Fletch grinned, a wide and easy smile that flashed a row of perfectly straight, pearly white teeth. His face was attractive, if a little angular, with a chin that jutted ferociously in front of him. He was impossibly alert considering the time of day.

Kayla rolled her eyes at Russia, who appeared to be slipping into an upright coma. It was, in a way, rather refreshing to meet a tour guide who fit the stereotype of a charismatic, hyperactive character, with energy levels akin to a cocaine-addled springer spaniel. Oliver had been a despicable disappointment in a multitude of ways, of which apathy toward his job was just one.

A tired sea of murmurs bubbled groggily around him. "Now

c'mon, guys, I'm going to need more enthusiasm than that! I said, who's ready for an adventure?"

"Oh, for God's sake," whispered Russia. "Just our luck to get a guide who'd be more at home in a pantomime." Raising her voice ever so slightly, she mock-shouted, "He's behind you!" Kayla suppressed a snigger.

After Fletch had briefed them on how to snorkel alongside a black tip shark and not scare it away, they headed toward the beach, where they found a native boatman organizing his longtail boat. The sun had reached the tops of Tonsai Cliffs, flooding the bay in a golden blaze. When Fletch wasn't talking, which was a rare occurrence, it was extraordinarily peaceful. The only sounds Kayla could hear were the soft crunching of sand underfoot and the lapping of tiny waves against the side of the small wooden boat. The wooden boat that, as it transpired, would be taking them to their destination.

Twenty minutes later they'd reached Shark Point. Everyone was quiet. Even Fletch had dropped his voice, as though apprehensive of imminent danger. Kayla wasn't sure whether it was all part of the show or the "timid" breed of sharks they were soon to encounter actually posed a real threat. She tried to believe the former.

They pulled their snorkels down over their faces. Hers was too tight and pinched the bridge of her nose painfully. She'd never worn one before and wasn't sure how well she'd adapt to breathing through the mouthpiece. It felt unnatural and flimsy, and tasted of tangy salt and the previous tourist's saliva. She felt suffocated. A wave of panic coursed through her limbs and tightened her airwaves. She was scared.

She glanced across at Sam. He looked utterly terrified. Kayla wondered whether it was the vicious sea creatures he was most afraid of, or something else. Something worse.

Moving into position, upstream of the stronger currents, Fletch led the small band over the shallows, to be swept east by the surge of water. Floating an arm's length apart from each other, the group followed his cue and peered down into the water beneath them.

At first it seemed too murky to see anything clearly, but Kayla's eyes soon adapted. She instantly wished they hadn't—the broken coral and jagged rocks just a few feet below looked like they could slice her open if she got too close. The urge to tap Fletch on the shoulder and ask to be taken back to shore was intense, but her pride wouldn't allow her to go through with it. Plus, Sam was watching. She cared what he thought of her.

Then she saw it. A black tip shark pup darted past, fleeing from the group as soon as it sensed their presence. Kayla looked around, but nobody else had reacted. She was the only one to see it. Adrenaline flooded her senses and she grinned involuntarily, allowing water to slip around the snorkel and into her mouth. She bobbed her head above the surface, spluttering and coughing violently.

Sam, swimming next to her, surfaced next. "You okay?" he grunted, licking his lips vigorously. Kayla knew how he felt—the sea salt coating her mouth was crusty and thick. She was already desperate for a drink.

"Yeah. I advise you not to smile and inhale at the same time." She laughed, but found herself praying he wouldn't snap at her for being idiotic.

His face remained stony. "I don't feel good." In fairness, His face was completely drained of color. It was the whitest Kayla had seen him look in weeks.

"Wanna get Fletch to take you back?"

"I dunno," he said. He looked like he might faint. "You think I should?"

"You don't look great, Sam. Maybe it'd be best?"

"Yeah. I feel dizzy."

Fletch's head cut through the surface of the water, and he shook like a wet Labrador. Water whooshed around his ears, spraying Sam and Kayla, his floppy, sun-bleached hair matted to his forehead. He spat out a mouthful of water and yelled, far too loudly, "Guys! What are you doing? There are two glorious females down there! Just circling us like they haven't a care in the world. You gotta see it, guys. Almost two meters long each. Beauties, they are."

"I, um—" Sam coughed. "I gotta go back. Feel faint."

"What's up buddy? Happens often, mind you. People get scared and freak out. They're fine, I promise you. Lovely creatures. I still got all my limbs, ain't I?"

"No, it's not that. I feel ill. Like I might throw up."

Fletch swept his hair out of his face and scanned around to make sure the others hadn't traveled too far alone. Reluctantly, he said, "Well all right, then. If you don't think you're gonna feel better soon, we'll go back. Such a shame, though. Amazing day for it . . . just amazing."

Sam looked ashamed. "I'm really sorry. I'll go myself, though, you guys carry on."

"No can do, mate. Can't be sending you off yourself through shark-infested waters. We'll all go back with you, drop you on the beach, then if the others are keen, we can all come back. That okay, buddy?"

That was the moment Kayla realized just how bad Sam must be feeling. Ordinarily, he'd never even consider causing such an inconvenience. It wasn't his style. But today he turned away and said, meekly, "Yeah. Thanks."

Yeah. There's more going on than a bug.

Chapter 27

July 24, England

AT A DESPICABLY early time—barely even eight A.M., for goodness sake—there was a tap on her bedroom door.

Kayla groaned, pressing the only button on her phone to check the time; 7:49 A.M. Her background picture of the group at Tiger Temple induced a sharp pang in her chest.

Another tap. "Kayla?" It was her mother.

"Yeah? Com'in," she mumbled, thick with sleep.

Martha walked in timidly, as if Kayla was an animal that might lash out and bite her. She was wearing skintight white jeans, cork wedges with black straps, and a black jumper. And pulling a wheeled suitcase behind her.

"Mum? Wh-Where are you going? What's—"

"Shhh, Kayla, don't worry. Nothing's wrong." She abandoned

the suitcase and perched at the end of the bed. Kayla propped herself up on her elbows, trying to force her eyes to adjust to the light. "I'm just getting the train down to Surrey for a few days. To stay with your auntie."

"Okay . . ." Kayla rubbed her eyes. Her mum was leaving? At a time like this?

"If you need me here, I'll stay," Martha said quickly. "Of course I will. If you need me, I'll be here. But . . . well, I booked this trip while you were in Thailand. Your aunt Elsie is so stressed with work, and I'm worried about her. I was going to take her away to a spa for a day or two, just to make her relax a bit, but . . ." Doubt flashed across her face. She frowned, accentuating the deep lines on her weary face. "Oh, Kayla, what am I saying? I shouldn't be leaving you here. Not now. I'll cancel—"

"Mum, relax," Kayla interrupted. "It's fine. It's only for a few days, right?"

A small smile. "Right. But are you sure—"

Kayla laughed. Nothing was funny, she just didn't want her mum to feel guilty. She probably needed the break as much as Aunt Elsie. "Go. Have fun. Catch up with your sister. I'll be completely fine."

Martha ran her hands through her dark hair, which she'd recently had cut into a bob. It suited her. "I'm so lucky to have a daughter like you," she whispered. "You're so strong." She shook her head. "Much stronger than I am."

Kayla's eyes felt hot. "Thanks, Mum. But I don't feel it, most of the time."

Martha edged up the bed until she was next to her, leaned over and tenderly kissed her forehead. She hadn't done that since Kayla was a little girl. "I'm proud of you, Kayla. I really am."

Kayla gulped. "Mum? Is it . . . is it safe to travel? I know there hasn't been an attack for over a month now, but . . ."

Something else flashed on Martha's face. Was it fear? Anguish? Or . . . indifference?

"Sweetheart," her mother said, clearing her throat. "The government are urging people to travel as normal. We can't let these . . . these *terrorists* win. We can't show fear." She stroked Kayla's cheek. "Besides, isn't lightning only meant to strike the same place once? You've suffered through two strikes. I think we're immune from a third."

"Outside of your sessions with me, have you anyone to talk to about what you're going through? Any friends around you?" Dr. Myers looked especially pretty today. Her skin was dewy and glowing, like she'd been spending a lot of time outside, and her eyes had the vibrant quality of someone who always gets enough sleep.

Kayla hesitated. She never knew quite how much it was acceptable to share with Cassandra, especially where her secret relationship with DI Winters was concerned. "I'd love to say yes. It's weird for me to admit how lonely I am. I was so sociable during school and had such a big group of friends . . . but we've all grown apart, I guess. Ever since Gabe died, it's like they haven't known how to act around me. So I haven't really seen any of them since I got back from Thailand."

"What about family?"

"Sort of. My mum's away now, visiting her sister, and my dad works a lot. I mean, I've always been close to my nan. But it's been weird lately. The atmosphere in the house doesn't help. She's away on a walking holiday this week, up near Oban. I already miss her being around. How sad is that? Even when we aren't talking much, it's just nice to have her there."

"It's not sad at all. It's lovely." If Dr. Myers was shocked that her family were deserting her, she didn't show it.

A moment of silence. Perhaps Cassandra sensed that she wanted to say something else.

"There are a couple of people I've been meeting up with recently," Kayla began.

Cassandra cocked her head. "Well, that's good. Who?"

"One is a guy I went to school with, the other is . . . just a friend. That police officer, actually. The one I told you about a few weeks ago. Sadie." Kayla smiled weakly. "But now I've lost contact with both of them. My nan asked me to stop seeing Aran, and Sadie has been ignoring my calls since Saturday. Even Sam's mum, Kathy, won't return my messages." She pulled her phone out of her pocket. Still nothing.

"Why do you think that is?" Dr. Myers looked genuinely intrigued. She'd been fidgeting absentmindedly with a dangly charm bracelet on her left wrist, rolling the white gold dove between her fingertips, but was now focusing intently on her.

"I have no idea," Kayla admitted. "It does seem weird that everyone I've gotten halfway close to over the past two months has suddenly disappeared from my life. Not necessarily literally," she added quickly. "Honestly, though, I feel like a leper."

"Why did your grandmother want you to cut ties with . . . Aaron, did you call him?"

"Aran. If I'm honest . . . I was stepping out of line. Wanting to dig stuff up that related to my brother's death. She found out and got really upset, said she couldn't bear to go through all of that again. I completely understand where she's coming from. I guess I wasn't thinking straight." Kayla couldn't meet Cassandra's eye.

"So you weren't meeting him as a friend? Just to talk about

what happened to Gabriel?" Kayla said nothing. "Oh, Kayla. I know it's hard for you, I really do. It's fine to talk about him—great, in fact. Healthy. Just as long as you're not searching for answers that don't exist. I'm here to help you get through this, to guide you through—"

"I know," Kayla snapped. "Sorry, I just . . . I think I'm going insane. I can't shake the feeling that I'm missing something. Yes, before you say anything, I know how mental that sounds. They were thousands of miles apart, three months apart. I know that. Maybe I was clutching at straws with Aran, but it helped." She chewed her lip. "And my memory seems to be getting worse and worse, I can barely remember what happened yesterday, let alone in Phuket. How am I supposed to make sense of it all if my mind is so damn foggy all of the time? It's just frustrating. I feel like my body is letting me down. If I don't feel physically well, how am I ever supposed to heal emotionally?"

Kayla dropped her head into her hands and groaned. "I'm sorry. This must be so frustrating for you. Have you ever had a patient so messed up her own body prevented her from grieving?"

"You'd be surprised. The best I can do is talk it through with you, and hope that at some point, your subconscious lets down its guard. So we can work through whatever it's trying to protect you from."

"You think my brain is trying to protect me from something?"

Dr. Myers shrugged. "It's certainly possible."

"Like what?"

"That's what we're going to have to work on discovering. At what point do you usually feel everything start to cloud over, mentally?"

Kayla thought. "Mostly when I'm thinking about Gabe or Sam.

Not just them, generally. More like when I try and wrap my head around the nitty-gritty details of what happened to them. And why. It's the why that gets me." Kayla sighed. She saw Cassandra jot something down on a notepad for the first time since she'd started seeing her. "I can't make sense of the why."

Dr. Myers was quiet for a moment. There was something else bothering Kayla, but she knew it was even more ridiculous than not believing the police. She knew that if she voiced her thoughts, Dr. Myers would lose all respect for her. Hell, she might even have her locked up in a mental hospital.

What the hell. What have I got to lose? "What if what happened to Sam and Gabe was . . . connected, somehow?"

"Connected? Why would you think that?"

Kayla squirmed in her chair. "Well, firstly, the way Gabe and Sam both acted in the weeks leading up to their . . . deaths." The word tasted cold, metallic. "So twisted and resentful. And scared. I know, I know, their reasons have been explained. But it just seems odd, doesn't it? For them to go in such similar ways. Fear, then blood. Most people go their whole lives never losing someone in such a . . . bloody way." *There was so much blood . . .* "And yet it's happened to me. Twice. In the space of three months. And they were both the men I loved most in the world . . . Doesn't that seem at *all* strange to you?"

"But Kayla," Dr. Myers said, clearly exasperated. She dropped her pen onto the pad and shook her head. "What could possibly link Sam's and Gabe's deaths?" She flinched at her own faux pas. Nobody knew for certain whether or not Sam was dead. But her patient hadn't even noticed.

"Honestly?" Kayla swallowed. "The only thing I can think of is me."

KAYLA DIDN'T DRIVE straight home.

Instead, she drove north. Specifically, to the northernmost town in England: Berwick-upon-Tweed. She'd had family here, once upon a time, but like everyone else in her life, they'd moved on to better things. Moved away from her.

There was a spot. A spot she felt compelled to visit—one that she could drive to in her sleep. In the month just after she'd passed her driving test, at the ripe old age of seventeen, she'd been to the spot six times. Her first love had just dumped her for another girl, and, at the time, it was the most inconceivably horrific tragedy that could possibly happen to her.

Irony's a bitch, she thought bitterly.

Perched on top of a steep grassy bank, she had stumbled upon Meg's Mount by accident while walking her cousin's Dalmatian, Baxter, around the town's historic walls one morning. It had been an early morning in late April, and the sun had only just risen over the horizon. The pale spring sky and bracing breeze gave her goose bumps. The spot overlooked the town's burnt copper rooftops, forest green leaves, and vast expanses of glistening water. Much to Baxter's horror, she'd sat down, enchanted, on the lone wooden bench, and gazed out onto the River Tweed as it flowed into the gray North Sea. Doves cooed, currents gushed, the scent of damp grass hung in the air. And she forgot everything else.

It was a blank feeling she'd come to crave, especially in times like today, when her loneliness was paralyzing. She'd always found crowds to be triggering rather than healing; embracing solitude and turning to nature was, for her, a cathartic antidote. Not that she had an alternative these days.

But today was different. She sat on the bench for nearly an hour, but no inner peace arrived. Maybe it was too busy, or maybe too late in the morning. Maybe it had been too long since she'd last been here, or maybe her pain was too severe. Because somehow, the spot had lost its magic. *Or maybe all that's happened is simply too much to come back from.* Kayla fought the thought away.

Delving into her jeans pocket, she checked her phone. No new e-mails, no text messages, no missed calls. She hadn't really expected anything else. She'd told Aran to stop working on his little project, without so much as an explanation. There had still been no reply from Kathy. And DI Winters? She'd been ignoring her since Saturday. *Probably because I came on too strong. Got too personal, asking about her studies and her cousin's death. What an idiot.* Kayla didn't know the hows or the whys. All she knew was that she was well and truly on her own. Yet again.

Just as she was going to slide the phone away it vibrated in her hand. It was a text message. She frowned at the sight of the name. It wasn't one she'd ever expected to see again, yet for a moment, deep down, she felt glad that she hadn't been forgotten altogether.

Kayla. I didn't know whether I should tell you what I know. About Sam, that is. I've been going over and over the possibilities in my mind, and perhaps it doesn't even mean anything but . . . it might. And I figured that "might" was enough to act on. Can we meet? I'm back in England. I'll come up north to see you. Please. Oliver x

Kayla's mind raced. The idea of seeing Oliver again turned in her stomach like a slab of congealed raw meat. Was this just a mind game? Was he trying to trick her? It seemed a likely explanation.

But what if he really did know something? Would it matter

if he did, or was it already too late? Did she even want to know? Would she ever know the answers to these questions if she didn't meet him? Without Sadie's help, it'd be nearly impossible.

Kayla knew what she had to do. She replied, hitting send with a shaking hand.

Chapter 28

June 12, England

THE THIRD TERRORIST attack was on Sam's birthday. London Kings Cross.

Huddled around the tiny television set, Kayla, Russia, and Bling watched as the news reader, who looked completely shaken up herself, shared footage of the explosion. Nineteen casualties. Countless more injured. Major roads blocked as many fled the city. The governor of the Bank of England was among the missing.

Bling was crying silently. She couldn't get through to her family. Her father worked in the City. Banking. Russia had made her a cup of herbal tea and was trying to console her, stroking her hair and murmuring something about being sure there was an alternative explanation for their radio silence. The apartment was hot and humid, reeking of old garbage and bleach, but Kayla had chills.

It had become a rarity for the group to spend an entire evening together. Between Dave's ill health, Sam and Russia's conflicting work-shift schedules, and Bling's disdain toward the town's sleazy nightlife, the fun nights out and thrilling adventures were few and far between. Tragedy has a way of pulling people back together.

As happens with many friendship circles, the gang was beginning to realize that none of its members were perfect. Gone was the polite laughter at unfunny jokes and automatic accommodation of each other's needs. They'd now gone beyond mere friendship into the murky realms of almost-cousinhood that came from spending every second of every day together. It was nice, in a way, that they'd become almost like family. But it didn't come without its downfalls. There were arguments. Lots of arguments.

Sam came into the room. He'd been oddly withdrawn over the last few days, especially considering it was his birthday. His expression was pinched, his T-shirt creased, and his hair sticking up all over the place. The exhaustion wafted off him in waves.

"Can we get a rain check on tonight's night out? I'm not feeling it," he mumbled, his eyes flickering toward the TV. They barely seemed to register the attack.

"But it's your birthday!" Russia said. "Why on earth would you want to stay in on your birthday? Gotta go out and drown your sorrows. Especially considering . . ." She gestured at the news on the screen. BREAKING: 19 DEAD IN KINGS X ATTACK.

"I just don't feel like it, all right?" Sam hissed. Russia recoiled as if she'd been slapped.

"Jeez. No need to act like a grumpy old man. Even though that's what you are." She tried to nudge him playfully but was met with a withering glare and no response. "Kayla? Tell him! We have to go out for his birthday, we just have to."

"Come on Sa—"

"I said no, all right?" Sam said, cutting Kayla's protest off. He turned back to Russia. "What makes you think I'd listen to Kayla? Don't treat me like a stubborn child."

"Whoa, I'm not. I just thought that—"

"Whatever. I'm off to bed."

"Sam! It's only nine o'clock. Please just come for one—"

Sam slammed his bedroom door before Russia had even finished her sentence. The news reader continued her updates. Another body. Twenty now.

Bling looked up from her phone and blinked rapidly, sniffing. Her eyes were pink-rimmed and her nose shiny. "What's with Sam?"

Kayla shrugged, trying to convey apathy, and probably, she imagined, failing miserably. "Who knows. He's been acting weird for weeks." *Like he doesn't even know me. Like he doesn't even care.* She cast her eyes back to the TV and immediately felt guilty for her petty troubles. ST. PANCRAS EVACUATED AND EUROSTAR LINKS CLOSED FOLLOWING KINGS X BLAST.

"Yeah, he has," Russia agreed. "Have you got no idea why? You two used to be so close. Though not as close as he and Bling were . . ." Bling giggled through her tears and pushed Russia off her perch on the arm of the sofa.

Kayla blushed. "Nah. He doesn't talk to me these days. I don't really know why. It . . . sucks." *It kills me.*

Russia lowered her voice, wary of the villa's paper-thin walls. "Did anything ever happen with you two?" Kayla shook her head. Bling had turned her attention back to her phone, repeatedly pressing the redial button. "But you do like him though, right? At least you used to?"

Kayla pressed her lips together and glanced toward his door. It remained firmly shut. "Doesn't really matter now, does it?"

The bathroom door opened and a billowing cloud of steam poured out, closely followed by Dave, who wore a towel turban and a dopey grin. "Look! I finally worked out how to do the twiddly towel thing you girls do on your head. I feel like a genie or something."

Russia giggled. "I think that's vaguely racist?"

"It's all right, I'm Indian. I'm allowed to be racist. Where's Sam? Gotta give him his birthday present."

"In a huff. What did you get him?"

"That's for me to know, Rush," Dave said, winking.

"Oh God. You're going to snog him, aren't you?"

"Perhaps. Are we off out tonight, then?"

Kayla and Russia exchanged a look. "Sam isn't the greatest fan of the idea."

"So what? Majority vote. If he's going to be a miserable sod, let's go without him. I might even wear my turban."

THANKFULLY, HE DIDN'T.

The strip was even busier than usual. The smell of fruity tobacco from a nearby shisha café hung in the air, and a fresh throng of party animals—completely oblivious to the terrorist attacks—had arrived since they'd last been out. Kayla didn't know if she was simply out of practice, but the music seemed louder, the crowds more fierce, than ever before.

Bling, who'd finally got through to her completely uninjured family, was furiously sinking Jägerbombs like her life depended on it. Kayla offered to get the next round. As she was on the way back from the bar, clutching four beers and forcing her way through the crowds, someone grabbed her arm. Hard. She twirled around to yell in the face of whatever overly pushy male had taken a fancy to her but the words never quite left her mouth. She froze, her mouth hanging open.

Oliver. Since the first night they'd spotted him in Phuket, he'd kept his distance.

"Kayla," he said urgently. "I need to talk to you. It's important."

"Go away, Oliver. And get the hell off me." She tried to shake her arm free.

"Kayla, I know I've fucked up in the past. Believe me I know. I hate myself for it. But I really, really need to tell you something. Please."

"What the hell—"

"Please." His voice had an overtone of begging. "I'm serious. This is serious." He tightened his grip on her arm. It started to hurt.

"Oliver, for fu—"

"Get the hell off her, you twat," Sam said, barging into Oliver. Sam's hand grasped his throat, and Oliver's eyes looked like they might pop out of their sockets. "What on earth do you think you're doing?"

Oliver flailed helplessly at Sam's huge hands, resembling a weasel caught in a trap. Sam let go and yelled over the pounding music, "Get lost. Now. And don't you *ever* touch her again." Oliver obliged and trotted away, his head bowed against the bustling crowds.

Sam started to turn and leave. Kayla touched his arm. "Sam! I didn't even realize you'd come out. I'm glad you're here. Happy birth—"

"Yeah, well, I was just leaving." His voice was flat. He didn't meet her eyes. Kayla desperately wanted him to gaze back at her longingly, lovingly, like he used to. "If he gives you any more trouble, just let me know."

Then he was gone.

She felt empty.

Chapter 29

July 29, England

"HAVE YOU SEEN the news?" Kayla asked, panting. She'd run up the stairs two at a time to grab her phone as soon as she'd heard it ring.

"Yes, I have, love," her mother said. "Don't worry, I'm fine. I hadn't set off for the station yet." She sounded a lot calmer than Kayla did.

There had been another attack. Just not a physical one.

A group of sympathizers of the Islamic State militant group had hacked all of the major travel Web sites—airlines, railways, bus timetables, car hire services—and replaced the homepage with IS propaganda videos. The message was clear: you aren't as free as you think you are. We are everywhere.

It was even more chilling than the bombings. Even more sinister.

Still, the government insisted it was little more than a prank, an act of vandalism rather than terrorism, and that citizens should continue to travel as normal. Martha was supposed to catch a train home that afternoon.

"Please tell me you aren't still planning to come home today?" Kayla pleaded, failing to keep her fear from seeping into her voice. She was starting to doubt her mum's logic that lightning wouldn't strike thrice.

"I've spoken to your dad," Martha sighed. "He thinks I should stay put. Just to be safe."

"Okay, Mum. Love you. I'll see you when I see you."

"Love you too, sweetheart. Take care—and don't worry too much. Continue your day as normal, okay?"

Kayla swallowed the urge to scoff at the word normal. "Okay."

After she'd called her nan, she stared at the phone in her hand. There was no one else to call. Nobody else in her life she needed to check up on at a time like this. The kernel of loneliness in her heart was growing.

She threw her phone across the room and pulled on her trainers.

KAYLA HAD ALWAYS thought the chilling sensation associated with being watched from afar was a myth; a paranormal phenomenon invented by horror film producers. Surely the human psyche wasn't powerful enough to sense true danger.

At least, that was what she believed until she experienced it for herself.

She was out for a run in the woods, shards of sunlight piercing through the gaps in the canopy, when the icy fingertip traced down her spine. It was most noticeable, she thought, because she was hot and sweaty—the goose bumps were otherwise inexplicable. *How do you act in such a situation? Do I slow down or speed up?* She opted to stop altogether. The air had been sucked from her lungs.

The uneasiness lingered. White spots danced across her vision from the physical exertion, and she crouched down on her haunches to try and regain a normal breathing rhythm. Fine hairs were standing on end all over her body. A branch crunched somewhere behind her; her heart skipped a beat. *It's just wildlife, Kayla. You're losing it. Properly, this time.*

She scanned the sparse woodland. Nothing. She loved this patch of woods, just a mile from the bottom of her football-pitch-sized garden, because of its lack of cameras, lack of noise, lack of company—it was as close as she ever got to pure happiness. But those very attributes suddenly felt eerie, isolating. If anything happened to her out here, she was well and truly on her own.

Shut up, you idiot. Nothing's going to happen to y—

Something flickered somewhere to the far left of her peripheral vision. She stood up and spun around. Still nothing. Just leafy trees with sunlight pouring through the gaps between them, a light dusting of dead leaves on the dry mud carpet, and—

No, there was definitely something. A flash against something unnatural, something that didn't belong amidst the bushes. Something metal. The sun bounced off it, reflecting back into her eyes. It only lasted a split second, then it was gone.

She could have gone over to the offending bush to investigate. After all, it was probably nothing sinister.

But she didn't. Something in her gut told her this didn't feel right.

So instead, she turned and ran back toward the sanctuary of

her house—her safe, secure, monitored house—as fast as her feet could carry her.

OLIVER HAD LOST WEIGHT.

He'd always erred on the scrawny end of the physique spectrum, but as he stirred a packet of artificial sweetener into his black coffee, his clavicle rippled beneath the skin on his chest. He was emaciated. If he hadn't maintained his terra-cotta tan, he would look ill. His angular collarbones jutted uncomfortably below his skeletal shoulders.

"It gives me great pleasure to tell you that you look horrendous." Kayla struggled to conjure up a single ounce of sympathy for him. Still, it was nice to be out of the house. Away from her thoughts—and that constant feeling of impending threat that crawled over her skin like menacing little ants.

"Yeah. Can't eat, can't sleep. I'm a mess." His mouth barely seemed to move as he spoke. It was as though he couldn't muster up the energy to properly articulate.

"I have to say, it's nice being within five meters of you and not being gassed out by that sickening aftershave you dowse yourself in. Guilt getting to you?" Kayla knew she should dial down the sass, but every time she considered it, vivid memories of that night in Sangkhlaburi barged into her brain. Being pressed against a wall, his sticky breath on her neck, begging him to stop. Him not listening.

"Look, do you want to hear what I've got to say or not?"

"Depends. If it's some bullshit excuse to lure me here, then no, absolutely not."

"Oh, get over yourself, will you?" It was the kind of sentence that should have been laced with venom, but Oliver seemed too exhausted for that. He stood up, disorientated, and bumped into the table, causing his untouched coffee to slop over the sides of the mug. The man at the next table looked up from his newspaper and glared across at them. "I'm leaving. I shouldn't have bothered. Forget it." He turned toward the door.

"No, Oliver, wait. I'm sorry for being a bitch." He stopped and closed his eyes, not turning back to her. "It's not helpful. I do want to know whatever you have to tell me, especially if it's about Sam. Please." *And I don't want to be alone. Not today.*

Oliver sighed and flopped back down into his chair with a thump. Kayla wondered if it was because he'd actually accepted her apology, or simply because he didn't have the strength to make it to the door. "Fine. Where do I start?"

"How am I supposed to know? I have no idea what you're about to say."

"Fair enough. Might as well come out and say it, then. Sam was being followed."

"What?"

Oliver took a sip of his coffee, wincing at the heat. "This is so embarrassing. Okay, so it wasn't exactly a secret that I'd become a bit . . . obsessed by you. You're an amazing girl, who could blame me?" He tried for a smile. Kayla didn't reciprocate. "I came to Phuket because I lost my job—probably rightly so, I was rubbish— and I didn't know what else to do. Things were weird between us, I know, but I couldn't come back to England. I've fucked up here too, but I won't go into that. That first night in Phuket, it was obvious you couldn't forgive me. Which is fair—I wouldn't forgive me either. I should have left then. I know that."

"But you didn't." Kayla found it hard to remove the bitterness from her tone. If it hadn't been for Oliver's constant presence during their last few weeks in Thailand, things mightn't have been so strangled between her and Sam. He might have been talking to her, and she might have been able to see what was happening to him more clearly. Maybe.

"But I didn't. Because I'm a royal twat. I just . . . lurked. Maybe because I had nothing else to do, and maybe because—as creepy as this sounds—I got addicted to looking at you." He stared intensely into his palms. His cheeks were tinged with pink. "That's why I started anyway. But then I started noticing things."

"What kind of things?"

"That I wasn't the only one following you. Well, not just you. Sam. There were two of them. Whenever he was working, whenever you were all out together, there they were. So I kept watching. And they kept being there. They never went close to him, really. I don't know if that means Sam might have recognized them if they had? Then you guys went away for day or two, am I right?" Kayla nodded. Phi Phi. "Well, I didn't see them around Phuket. I looked, you know? Went to the usual haunts, but they weren't there."

"Do you think that means they followed us to Phi Phi?"

He shrugged. "Possibly."

Kayla shuddered. How could she not have noticed? "What did they look like?"

Oliver reached into his backpack for his phone. "I tried to take a picture, but it was hard. It was usually dark, and the zoom on my phone is terrible. So is the flash. It's just all blurry, see?" Kayla looked. He was right, they were blurry. The shadowy figures on Oliver's phone screen meant nothing to her.

"Have you showed these to the police?"

"No. I thought about it. But all the fancy gear in the world couldn't make sense of these pictures—even the angle is bad, it's mainly the backs of their heads. And I just . . . I couldn't face explaining why I was there. Why I was following you in the first place."

Kayla nodded. She understood that even though going to the police was generally considered the right thing to do, it was often more complicated than that. She hadn't reported Oliver, after all. "Thanks for telling me. I dunno what to do with this information, though." *What does it mean, what does it mean, what does it mean?* Her mind whirled, trying, failing, to slot the knowledge into place.

"It might not mean anything, but given what happened, and more importantly, what the police think happened . . ." Oliver visibly shivered, and changed topic suddenly. "God, it's fucking awful, isn't it. Sam was . . . well, we had our differences, but . . . he was a good guy. Thought the world of you, of course. I can't stop thinking about it. My mind goes a million miles an hour, all the time, trying to work out what happened. What he must have been through. Poor guy."

Kayla felt sick. *So much blood.* "I know. But I'm kind of jealous of your overactive mind—I'm the opposite. I can't get my brain to cooperate. I want it to move quickly, sharply, not sluggishly, 'cause I feel like there is something more to the whole thing. And it should be so obvious but—"

"It's not."

"Nope. It's not."

Perhaps she was imagining it, but at that moment, she could have sworn she saw the angry man at the next table relax his shoulders and smirk into his newspaper.

Chapter 30

June 14, Thailand

THERE WAS A tap on Kayla's door. Soft, cautious. Unsure.

"Come in." She sat cross-legged on her bed in the villa, reading a battered paperback she'd found in a secondhand English bookstore.

Except she wasn't really reading it at all. She'd been thinking about Sam and chain-smoking for over an hour. Nothing new there.

The door swung slowly open and Sam himself stood there. Kayla blinked. He didn't make a move into the room, instead choosing to peer at her through the thick haze of cigarette smoke drifting through the room. She knew she must have been quite the sight, tangled amidst crumpled, off-white bedsheets in a faded T-shirt and black boxer shorts. Her hair had been haphazardly thrust up in a messy bun, and her ashtray was overflowing. *Sexy, Kayla. Really sexy.*

"Sam!" She was surprised to see him. Not only because she'd thought he was at work with Russia, but because they hadn't been alone together for nearly a week. He seemed to be avoiding her at all costs. If ever they found themselves sitting on the sofa without the others, or walking side by side toward the bus stop, he'd make his excuses and go elsewhere. Memories of how close they used to be felt alien now. Like they didn't belong to her. "What's up?"

"I'm sorry." His voice was hoarse, his eyes bloodshot.

"For wha—" Before she could finish asking her question, Sam was on the bed, kissing her. His lips tasted salty and his facial muscles were tense. He pulled away, almost as quickly as he'd arrived next to her, and closed his eyes. "Sam. What's wrong?"

"I'm just . . . sorry. I'm so sorry, Kayla." He ran his hands through his hair. He looked like he might say something else, but he didn't.

"What for?" It felt polite to ask, but she already knew why he felt sorry. It didn't matter. Nothing mattered. All she wanted was to be kissing him again, feeling his firm body press against hers. But the tortured expression on his face was impossible to dismiss.

"You know what. Everything. Just . . . everything."

"It's okay."

"No, it's not. Nothing is okay." He kneaded his thumb into the palm of his fractured hand, which had started to heal. At first Kayla assumed it was therapeutic for him to massage it, but then she noticed the force with which he was pressing down. The pain in his eyes. She took both of his hands in hers and kissed them, one after the other.

He whispered, "Why are you being sweet? I don't deserve it. I've been . . . horrible."

"Honestly? It's just nice to be talking to you now. And touching you . . ." She tilted forward to kiss him again, but he pulled back. The hurt must have been written all over her face, because Sam looked instantly guilty.

"No, but seriously, Kayla. Why do you even still want to kiss me?"

"I don't know." She leaned back. It felt colder, just moving a few inches away from him. She picked up the half-smoked cigarette balanced on the edge of her ashtray and took a long, slow drag. "I guess when you get older, and shit stuff starts to happen, you learn to appreciate the amazing things in your life when they come around. And part of that is realizing that something doesn't have to be perfect to be amazing. I mean, our whole group of friends is insanely flawed. We're all idiots, let's face it—we're selfish and immature and ignorant, like most people our age. But we like each other regardless, and we have a bloody good time together. It's the same with you. You're a twat sometimes." Kayla chuckled, and planted another kiss on the back of Sam's hand. "But you're kind of amazing, anyway. And that's why I want to kiss you."

And because I love you.

"By that logic, do you also want to kiss Dave?" Sam joked.

"Oh, hell yes. And Russia. The things I'd do to Russia . . ."

"What about Bling?"

Kayla screwed her face up in fake dismissal.

Sam laughed, but only for a second, then sighed and squirmed his fingers out of her grasp. She tried to keep her disappointment from playing across her face. "Kayla. There's something I have to tell you."

"Sounds serious."

"It . . . it kind of is."

"Oh." Kayla wondered, for a split second, if he was going to tell her he loved her. But if that was the case, he probably wouldn't look like a policeman on a doorstep delivering bad news to a newly bereaved widow. She slid her legs out from under her and closed her book.

Silence made way for more silence. Sam's internal battle over the next few minutes was so loud that Kayla could almost hear it: *Tell her. Just tell her. Just start talking, the words will come. You're not going to tell her, are you? Bugger.*

Kayla soaked up the image of the disheveled boy in front of her. She hadn't been in such close proximity to him for weeks. His broad shoulders and big arms were deeply tanned, and his hair was in desperate need of a good cut. His strong, masculine jaw was stubbly; it seemed red raw, like he'd been scratching at the skin below his patchy afternoon shadow. He wore a plain white T-shirt and khaki shorts, with a wooden beaded necklace dangling around his neck. He kept absentmindedly nibbling the shark tooth charm.

After the long silence, he sprung up abruptly from the sagging bed, as if a wasp had stung his backside. Or as if a pressing thought had suddenly leapt into his mind. "You know what? It doesn't matter." He walked toward the door.

"What? Sam?"

"Just forget it. Forget I said anything." He didn't even turn to look back at her. Kayla felt a dull ache form in her chest. She knew she was about to lose him again.

"No, Sam, I want to know," she said as he moved to the door. "Please. You can't just waltz in here, kiss me, say you have something important to tell me, then disappear as fast as you—"

Slam. The door shut mid-sentence.

Kayla hated herself for loving Sam despite his infuriating tendency to walk away from her.

Chapter 31

July 31, England

"How much longer do you think I'll have to keep seeing you?"

"Well, that's really up to you," Dr. Myers said. "Nobody's forcing you to come here against your will. Do you feel like you've made any significant progress in the past few weeks?"

Kayla was silent. She did not.

Her mum was still down south. Her nan was still in Oban. Her dad still worked all the time.

Loneliness. Fear. The omnipresent questions: What really happened? What am I missing?

What happens next?

"I really want to help you, Kayla. Your case . . . it's got under my skin, I have to admit. Between our weekly sessions, I've been reading journals and theories about why you're unable to connect with what happened, why you can't get into a mental place where you can start the grieving process."

Kayla nodded, but she felt sick. She was sick of the words "grieving process." The whole concept seemed totally abstract to her. Like the idea of being model-beautiful or Einstein-intelligent, it was something desirable but by no means attainable. It was tempting to give up all hope and exist eternally in state of psychological limbo.

"I have an idea. It's slightly unconventional, and some practitioners would . . . frown upon it, I suppose. It might make you feel uncomfortable, and if that's the case we'll stop straightaway. But it might help you, so I think it's worth a shot."

"You're not going to electric-shock me, are you?" Kayla joked.

Cassandra smiled genuinely; a rare occurrence. Kayla felt disproportionately proud. "No, I'm not. Though I'm not ruling that out just yet." She winked. She looked even younger when she smiled and winked. "Okay, the most important thing for you to know is that we can stop this at any time. If you feel uncomfortable, or triggered, or panicked, just tell me. And we'll stop.

"I'm going to get you to list the cold hard facts. We'll start with Gabe. I want you to tell me, in kind of vocal bullet points, exactly what happened on the day he died. Include as many details as you can. That sounds odd, but bear with me. You've probably never said any of this aloud, not in this way, apart from maybe to the police all those months ago. To say it all again once the shock has worn off might act as a trigger in making it seem more real. A psychological electric shock, if you will." Another warm smile. Kayla wondered if someone had slipped narcotics in her coffee.

"Okay. Sounds good to me." She actually didn't dread the

thought. Talking in cold, hard facts seemed much more appealing than being trapped in a web of gooey emotions.

"Ready when you are."

"Right. Well. As cliché as this sounds, it was a day just like any other. I just . . . went about my business, as usual. With absolutely no idea what was going to happen that night. You always think you'd have an inkling, a sense of foreboding. That you'd wake up that morning and know instinctively that something bad was going to happen. But you don't.

"So I went to work at eight-thirty, like I always did. I liked to get there early and read the paper with a coffee before my day started at nine. I was interning at my dad's business in central Newcastle at the time. I suspect you know all about that from my mum?" Cassandra nodded. "Yeah, well my day was just the same as all the other days I spent working there. Making tea, photo-copying documents, making sure databases were in order, stuff-ing envelopes. I had my lunch—a tuna baguette, isn't it weird the things you remember?—and the rest of my afternoon was fairly uneventful. At half five, I stuck my head around my dad's door. He looked stressed, and said he was going to stay a bit longer, as he had a conference call with some clients. I usually shared a car journey home with him. I could have driven myself and just let him get a taxi later on, but I decided to stay in the city and go to the theatre."

Cassandra's ears pricked up. "By yourself?"

Kayla shrugged. "Yeah? I was in a good mood, and I hadn't been to the Theatre Royal since school. There was an RSC show on that night, and my dad had been offered tickets he didn't want. Thought I might as well put them to good use. It was brilliant, the show. *King Lear*. Phenomenal. So then I came out and rang my dad, asking if he was ready to come home with me, but he wasn't. So I just drove back myself.

"I was so happy, I remember. I drove home with my favorite album blaring, singing along as loud as I could. It was early spring, and even though it was dark, you could just tell everything was starting to bloom. I'd just seen an amazing, inspiring show in a beautiful theatre, and I was going home to a nice warm cup of tea and a cozy bed. I can't explain it. It was the kind of happiness you sometimes experience for no reason at all. It just creeps up on you when the right song is playing, and you smell really good, and you remember something someone said that day that made you feel all warm and fuzzy inside. Nothing major, but the little things just add up and make you feel untouchable. Like you have your whole life ahead of you and you're so excited because you assume it'll be full of those little slices of pure joy. Those moments that make everything worth it. But now . . . now I can't imagine ever feeling like that again." A tear rolled down Kayla's cheek. Cassandra looked pleased at the emotional progress, though she tried her very hardest to hide it.

Kayla wiped the rogue display of emotion away. "So I got back to the house. No one else was in, apart from . . . you know. My nan didn't live with us at that point, and my mum was out at some charity ball. An excuse to get pissed, basically. So I expected the house to be quiet. I didn't know whether Gabe was in or not, so I just pottered around, made some dinner, watched some TV in my room. It's so weird to think that while I was doing all that, Gabe was just down the hall. Or at least, his body was."

Cassandra shuddered. She couldn't help herself.

"So nobody discovered . . . him . . . until your parents got home?"

Kayla paused. "Not exactly. I . . . I found him. But that's where it all gets a bit hazy."

Cassandra raised an eyebrow, just a fraction. She sat up in her seat, straightening her back. "What does?"

Kayla gulped. This wasn't going to sound good.

"It's so blurry. You'd think something like that would be vivid in my memory. But all I remember is the blood. How cold and wet it felt on my skin. How dark it was, and a little bit sticky."

Cassandra tried not to react. "Oh."

"And how much of it there was. I've only ever seen that much blood one other time in my life."

Veiny hands around Gabe's throat. Or was it Sam?

His eyes bulging.

Kayla dialed 999. She got through to an operator but hung up right away. She knew there would be no time.

The Sam-Gabe hybrid's face was purple. Frozen in a single expression of terror as his frantic gasps slowed and he realized that this was it. The end.

The light behind his eyes was snuffed out, like moist fingers crushing a candle flame.

The person whose hands were wrapped around Sam's airwaves turned to face Kayla.

Their features started to come into focus. A dainty nose, long glossy hair, gaping red lips painted on like a creepy clown's mouth.

It was definitely a woman. A woman Kayla knew very well.

After all, she'd looked in enough mirrors in her life to know her own face when she saw it.

Even when it did have its hands wrapped tightly around a man's throat.

Kayla woke up screaming.

Chapter 32

June 16, Thailand

KAYLA WAS HOT. Hot from sunstroke, and hot from anger.

Sam hadn't spoken to her since he came into her room and kissed her like he loved her.

I'm clearly bloody delusional. He doesn't love me. He never has.

He didn't even afford her the decency of hostile comments and evil glares this time. At least those had told her he cared, albeit in a negative way. Hate and love are cut from the same emotional cloth.

No, this time he preferred to act like she no longer existed. That hurt much more than she thought it would. You don't miss what you've never had, and she was starting to wish she'd never met Sam.

The wish became more intense one day when the group were lying by the lake, which was rapidly becoming one of Kayla's favorite spots in Thailand. It was one of the only places she could cool down, in more ways than one. That day, the water was glimmering in the mid-afternoon sun; flecks of dazzling light woven together with slices of deep blue water. Everything seemed still. There were no clouds in the sky drifting on the wind, or birds squawking overhead. Just a ball of fire in the sky, a heat haze in the air, and vast mountains surrounding the lake. Nature was staggeringly constant—human trials and tribulations were fleeting inconveniences in comparison. There was no better place for perspective.

It would have been quiet too if Russia and Dave weren't rolling around nearby, giggling and play-wrestling over the book Russia had stolen from between Dave's fingertips. "I'm a cripple! You can't be stealing from your crippled boyfriend! Rush!" Russia was laughing hysterically. She had a wonderful ability to be lighthearted in the face of Dave's illness.

Bling was lying flat on her back, spread-eagled like a starfish and lathered in baby oil to darken her tan. She had headphones plugged in, and Kayla could hear the vague pounding of the drum and bass music her friend was so fond of. She'd been quiet since the terrorist attacks. Pensive. Even though her family were all safe in the end, terror never felt too far away.

When would the next attack be? Where?

Why?

Although many decibels away from peaceful, the scene by the lake would have been fairly blissful had it not been for Sam. He was huddled beneath a tree, clinging to the shade for dear life. His face was contorted in a gargoyle replica of his formerly handsome features.

His personality had suffered a similar metamorphosis. The anxiety beamed off him in waves. Kayla thought it might be contagious, but it didn't seem to affect the other three the way it did her. Whenever she saw his twisted face, heard his strained voice, or sensed his tense presence, her mood plummeted, her stomach knotted. A rather different effect than the one he used to have on her.

She couldn't bear it any longer. She was tired of mourning what they used to have. She stood up and strode toward the lake, plunging into the cool water with no hesitation. She was in up to her waist, then her chest. She stopped and tilted her head back, soaking her long hair and splashing water all over her face. The cool relief soothed her, and she wanted more. She took a deep breath and sank her whole body into the lake.

Quiet. Real, genuine quiet. The loudest quiet she'd experienced for months. Was this what death felt like? Her thoughts and fears seeped out of her ears and melted into the water. It was peaceful. Purifying. She thought of Virginia Woolf, one of her favorite writers, filling her pockets with stones and walking into the River Ouse. *If I was to take my own life too, I'd like to drown in a lake.*

Kayla ran out of breath too quickly, and pushed herself up through the surface again. She felt relieved that her body instinctively forced her above water to gulp for air—sometimes it acted of its own accord, as though it knew what her heart wanted before she did. But today it wanted to stay alive. And she was thankful for that.

She didn't return to the bank straight away, though. She floated around on her back, the water lapping at her ears, and closed her eyes against the glare of the sun. After ten minutes she still couldn't face going back. So she stayed for ten more.

Eventually, her feet found the lake bed and she held her hand up to her forehead to shield the sun from her eyes. Her face felt hot and stinging. Sunburn. Peering across the grassy bank where her friends lay, she noticed Sam had gone, and there was a bottle of something alcoholic where he'd been sitting. Excellent. She had never swam back to shore so fast.

"Gimme that," she said, grinning at the sight of the dusty bottle of rum that had been in the bungalow since before they arrived. She flipped her hair around to her side and squeezed the excess water out of it before taking a seat next to Dave.

"Sure thing, Kay-layla," Dave slurred. Kayla laughed—he had always been a lightweight drinker.

"Jesus, Dave, I was in the water for less than half an hour. How did you manage to get so pissed so quickly?"

"It's my talent, Kayla, I'm a cheap date. It's why Russia loves me." His eyes were wide, his smile sloppy.

"Us Russians have a bit more stamina," said Russia, who still looked sober as a judge. She grabbed the bottle back from Kayla and took an impressively long swig. Kayla's throat was burning after a mere sip. It tasted like paint stripper. Russia offered the bottle to Bling, who shook her head. "Sweet. More for us!"

"Where did Sam go?" Kayla asked, attempting a casual tone.

"Dunno. I have no idea what's going on with him," Russia said, shaking her head. "He's acting so strangely. I'd ask him what's up, but . . . I don't know. He's kind of scaring me. Is that weird?"

"I know where you're coming from," said Kayla. "It's like he's fighting himself. He wants to be part of the group, he wants things to be good, he wants to . . . kiss me." She didn't look up from the ground to see whether her friends had registered the reference to her and Sam's romantic relationship, or lack thereof. "But something's holding him back . . . He seems so conflicted. I wish I could help, but he won't talk to me."

"Nor me," said Dave solemnly. "And I'm his besht mate." He took another drink of rum.

Russia lay back and rested her head in her cupped hands. "I miss old Sam."

Kayla smiled sadly. "Me too."

The group sat and drank, mostly in silence, as the sun dropped lower and lower in the sky. It smelled of earth and hibiscus, and the rum warmed them from the inside as the outside temperature was cooling. Most of the lake had already dipped into the shadows of the mountains, but it could still be heard tinkling and slushing in the background.

Just as the sun was about to duck below the farthest mountain peak, Dave took Russia's hand and spoke in the most hushed voice Kayla had ever heard him use. He spoke slowly. "I can't feel either of my feet. Or the tips of my fingers."

Russia drank deeply, then pressed her lips together. "At all?"

"At all."

There were a few moments of silence. Kayla drank next. "What does that mean?"

Dave plucked a wad of grass in his hand and threw it in front of him. It landed on his feet. Kayla wondered if he'd be able to kick it off if he tried. "It means this is all happening quicker than I thought it would."

More silence. Russia was too overwhelmed with sadness to speak. Her pretty face was frowning—something that didn't happen too often—and her full cheeks were wet with tears. Kayla filled the silence. "I'm really sorry, Dave. I don't know what else to say. It's . . . horrible. Totally bloody horrible."

Dave swallowed. He'd become much more sober in the last few minutes, and took a drink of rum to rectify the situation.

"What's it like? To know you have your whole life ahead of you? My body . . . it's a ticking time bomb. Except instead of exploding like a heart attack, it's just going to slowly fail. But my mind won't. Inside, I'll be like you. I'll still want to dive into a lake in Thailand and swim with sharks and stroke tigers and drink rum with my best friends watching the sun go down, but I won't be able to. I'll be trapped in my own body, staring at the same patch of hospital ceiling every minute of every fucking day until my organs have the courtesy to fail on me.

"But you guys . . . you can do anything. *Anything*. How does that feel? I used to have that too—not that long ago, actually. But it's something you take for granted, isn't it? That you're going to grow old? I didn't have the presence of mind to really think about how that felt until it was gone. Then it was too late. So tell me. How does it feel?"

The three girls weren't sure whether it was a rhetorical question. Instead, they all rose at the same time and went to sit around Dave—Russia behind him with her arms wrapped around his waist, delicately kissing his neck and head, with Bling and Kayla on each side, resting their heads on his shoulders.

And that's how they sat for ten minutes, until Dave broke the silence. "You know that in Hindi, Daivat means strong and powerful? Pretty ironic, isn't it." He laughed bitterly. "My body couldn't be further away from strength."

Russia nodded sincerely. "I know how you feel. In Russian, Minya means 'God reincarnated.' It can be a lot of pressure."

Just like that the melancholic spell was broken. The group fell about laughing, and Dave choked out, "Damn it, Rush, why did you have to ruin the whole pimp thing I had going on?"

He kissed her with the passion of a man who knew he only

had a few good months left. Kayla felt a pang of jealousy, before quickly chastising herself. Terminal illness was not something to lust after.

But she would kill for Sam to kiss her like that again, even just one more time.

Chapter 33

August 2, England

OLIVER'S WORDS KEPT playing on Kayla's mind.

Not purely because it raised a lot of questions—How? Why? For how long?—but because it deeply disturbed Kayla that she and her friends could be followed for such a long period of time and never notice. All right, so they were drunk at least eighty-two percent of the time, but it seemed her first instinct was right after all—the human psyche, no matter how powerful, did not have a sixth sense. Nobody could feel eyes burning into the back of their head. It was, as she had always believed, a myth.

Perhaps that was the reason that ever since her run in the woods, cut short by that strangely chilling sensation, she'd felt as though she was being watched. Was her brain overcompensating for missing a trick? Because she'd been followed for weeks without noticing, was her mind sensing danger that wasn't really there?

She was sitting at the breakfast bar, watching the evening news and eating Nutella straight out of the jar with a spoon. It was sticky and clammy in her mouth, but the sugar hit was like morphine, a painkiller for her psychological turmoil. She could never understand those who lost weight after going through something like this, as though grief was the best diet in the world. It was almost as if they *didn't* use food as an emotional crutch. Bizarre.

She would have loved to talk to Sadie about Oliver's confession. The DI's mind was much sharper than her own, much more honed in the realms of crime investigation, so Sadie could probably slot the piece of information into the case and make more sense of it than she ever could. But Sadie hadn't been answering her e-mails, texts, or phone calls. Usually, Sadie was so eager to speak to her. Had she been stupid to think they were actually been becoming friends? She just wished Sadie would give her some kind of reason for her sudden disappearance. If she was busy at work, or if Shepherd had discovered her persistent interest in Sam's case and put his foot down, it would explain a lot, and she could leave Sadie alone, knowing why the DI was ignoring her.

And then, there was always the possibility that Sadie's silence was linked to the case itself. Had she stumbled upon something controversial that she didn't want to share with her? Or worse, was Sadie starting to suspect her When Kayla had been giving her a run-through of what happened, she'd detected a trace of something in Sadie's voice: at best, niggling uncertainty, at worst, outright suspicion. Snippets of the conversation flashed back into her mind.

"I pushed the door open, and saw . . . well, you know what I saw. Blood."

"Then you collapsed, right? Into the pool of blood, which is why your clothes were soaked through with it?"

Kayla strained through her mental fog, trying to conjure up a mental image of the detective's expression at that moment. Her eyes had been narrowed, her attempt at a casual tone of voice a little too sharp. What had Sadie said then? It had been a comment on the timeline, Kayla remembered.

"And how long would you say you blacked out for?"

"I haven't a clue. No more than a minute or two, I don't think."

Sadie's response to her uncertainty had come a fraction too quickly. The words spilled out of her mouth before Kayla had uttered her final syllable.

"And then?"

Of course, it was Sadie's job to consider every possibility. It was in her nature, even—she was a born detective, there was no denying that. Kayla tried to put herself in Sadie's shoes. If she were a detective would her suspect herself? *Probably.* Still, that didn't stop her from wishing she'd masked her own uncertainty a little better. *"I think . . . I don't remember . . . I haven't a clue."* Expressions that didn't exactly paint a picture of an innocent bystander. Expressions that were rapidly becoming the soundtrack to her inner monologue.

She sighed, put down the jar of Nutella and muted the TV. There was never any mention of Sam now that the case had been essentially closed, but the news reader was talking about the terrorist attacks that had taken place while they were in Thailand. They still hadn't found the people behind it—or determined whether they were linked to the cyberterrorism of a few weeks ago. The propaganda videos that left her frightened mum stranded in Surrey, too scared to board a train home.

The memory of the first time they'd heard about the attacks—sitting in that sleek, modern café in Thailand—recurred to Kayla. The link between this life and that one. The memory of Sam next to her. Was it real? Was that ever her reality? She felt winded, couldn't breathe. Grief over what she'd lost, who she'd lost, choked her. She was suffocating, drowning in the memories, memories that—

Her spine tickled between her shoulder blades. She was being watched. Or was she?

Kayla stood up, trying to steady her erratic breathing, and wrapped her dressing gown tightly around her waist. It wasn't cold, but it wasn't as warm as it should have been in mid-August. She padded toward the French doors. Evening cigarette time.

She lit up, inhaled deeply and blew the smoke slowly out from between her lips. It was cloudy outside and the air was damp. Humidity not unlike that she'd experienced in Thailand, though without the soaring temperatures. What she'd give to be lying by that lake again—

There. She wasn't imagining it this time. Something, or someone, moved at the bottom of the garden. She couldn't make out the details—she wasn't wearing her contact lenses, and if she hurried back inside to get her glasses it'd probably be too late.

She couldn't quite tell whether it was a man or a woman, or even a child. It could even be Nan, home early from her travels. But through the trees and shrubbery, she could definitely see a human-shaped silhouette where there shouldn't have been one.

Someone was sitting on her tree swing, rocking back and forth.

KAYLA LOCKED HER bedroom door behind her and dived back into bed, pulling the covers over her head like a terrified child. Her heart was thumping.

Calm down, Kayla. It must just be your nan. How would anyone else have got onto the grounds? Her house was famously the most secure property in the county. Or so she thought.

She dug around underneath her pillow to locate her mobile phone. She punched in her Nan's mobile number, her fingers never quite finding the right digits, so it took much longer than usual.

Ring, ring. Ring, ring. Rin—

"Hello-o-o?" Her nan's voice was crackly—she obviously had poor reception. Kayla's stomach sank. Her house always had a great signal. She obviously wasn't home.

'H-Hi, Nan. How are you?"

"Kayla! How lovely to hear from y—"

"Sorry, Nan, I just need to ask you one thing. Where are you right now?"

"I'm in Oban, sweetheart! The hotel we're staying in is really lovely, you know. You'll never believe this, Kayla, but there's a bath in the middle of my bedroom! A big, old-fashioned, roll-top tub. I watched *Coronation Street* while I was washing my hair last night . . ."

Kayla had stopped listening. She felt sick. *If Nan is in Oban, who the hell is at the bottom of the garden?*

"Sorry, Nan, gotta go. Have fun."

She hung up. She was too terrified to feel guilty about her abruptness.

She couldn't call the police. She was sick of police.

Why did there seem to be something sinister around every corner?

Her heart hammered through her chest.

What am I going to do?

She tried to calm herself down with the idea that if the stranger on the swing was going to attack her, he would have done it by now. Her dad was at work, her mum still down south, and Gabe was . . . well. Gone. She had no choice but to try and stay calm, try and distract herself. She'd tell her dad about it when he got home. Though she had no idea when that would be—he'd been known not to arrive home from work until after midnight.

For a moment she was still too scared to move. Like when you're young and can't quite bring yourself to stick one leg out of the covers in case someone, or something, grabs it, she thought. That fear froze her whole body. It took all the willpower in her possession to reach out from her duvet and grab her laptop off the floor. *Why did I leave the bloody Nutella downstairs? Oh, calm down, Kayla. It's probably just one of the kids from the farm down the road. Probably.*

There were no cameras in her bedroom. There never had been. *If anything bad happened here. . .*

She shuddered. Something bad already had happened in one of these bedrooms. And she, for one, was glad there was no video footage of her brother slashing his own wrists.

What if he didn't slash his own wrists?

Kayla forced the thought away.

She sat up, propping a wall of cushions up behind her, and opened her computer. In school, she'd wasted hours on this thing when she was meant to be studying for her A levels. She watched funny videos, read magazine columns, conducted Internet searches seeking answers to questions that had bothered her for years. (Why are yawns contagious? Why do placebos sometimes work? When you watch a TV program and they quote statistics from a national survey about cheese consumption, when did this survey take place and why was she not asked?) The procrastinating influence of the Internet was made for days like this, when you had a lot of time to kill. Or a sickening reality you'd rather not face.

But of course, the days when you welcome distraction with open arms are invariably the days when there is no distraction to be found. She couldn't find any funny videos worth watching, the columnists were bigoted idiots, and the only question she wanted to type into Google was: Who is the stranger sitting on my rope swing and why are they there?

Kayla sighed and opened her e-mail account, expecting to find nothing more than the usual spam e-mails and LinkedIn requests.

She shook her head in disbelief. Right at the top of her in-box was the name of someone she'd asked to stop contacting her. Subject title: URGENT.

With a shaking hand, she clicked open the message.

TO: Kayla Finch
FROM: Aran Peters
SUBJECT: URGENT.

Kayla,
    Don't be mad at me. I know you asked me to stop trying to track down who sent Gabe those messages but . . . well, it had been proving pretty difficult, and I can't resist a challenge (as you know). Anyway, I did it. I found out the IP address. That means I tracked down the geographical address the fake Facebook account was created at, and where the messages were sent from.

The address is Berry Hill House, Upper Coquetdale,
Northumberland.
And yes, I triple checked.
Aran

The words on the screen bore deep into Kayla's retinas like
lasers. Berry Hill.
Impossible. That's just impossible.

Chapter 34

June 17, Thailand

THE SUN WAS only just beginning to dip behind the mountains when Kayla spotted Sam down by the lake. He sat on the bank, peeling a label off a bottle of spring water and bouncing his right foot up and down as though inflating an air bed with a foot pump. She knew that was Sam's sign of nervousness.

Instead of going straight over, she watched him for a couple of minutes. His shoulders were hunched together and his muscular back rippled through his pale gray T-shirt. Kayla imagined what it'd be like if they were together. She'd float across to him, kiss the back of his neck and massage the knots out of his tense shoulders. He'd turn around and start kissing her, laying her down on the firm bank and ...

Quit getting ahead of yourself, Kayla.

She took a deep breath and willed her feet to propel her forward until she was standing next to him. He didn't even look up.

"Hey, Sam."

He stopped peeling the label, stopped jiggling his leg, but didn't respond. He looked frozen in time.

"Can I sit down next to you?" she asked, already in the process of doing so. He shrugged. Kayla frowned. "Are you okay?"

"I'm fine. Just . . . you know. Getting some air. Spending some time alone."

Kayla chose to ignore the thinly veiled implication that she should leave. "Okay." They sat in silence for a few moments. "It's really beautiful out here. Especially when the sunset is that gorgeous."

"Yeah. S'lovely." The latter two words seemed to cause him great difficulty.

Kayla swallowed. She knew it was a bad time, but there didn't seem to be such a thing as a good time anymore. Sam was perpetually miserable. All she knew was that if she didn't get her feelings off her chest soon, it was possible that she'd either implode or explode—she couldn't decide which. She'd go down in the history books as one of those freaks that spontaneously combusted. Come to think of it, maybe the whole phenomenon wasn't really such a great mystery. Heartache is a powerful thing, as is desire. Combined, there was every chance that it could be fatal.

"Sam?" Kayla whispered. "You must know how I feel about you. I mean . . . you have to, right?"

The words might as well have been torture devices, given the pain they looked to be causing Sam. "Kayla—"

"No, just let me talk. I have to tell you how much you mean to me. We have to talk about this. We owe it to ourselves."

His whisper was even quieter than hers. "Please don't."

"Why not? I can't just be imagining this. We have something, Sam. Something that's not just a straightforward, platonic friendship. I can't work out what it is, exactly . . . it seems hasty to call it love. Though that's probably what it is. At least on my part." She couldn't look at him. She wished she had a water bottle whose label she could peel too—anything to distract her from the cavernous discomfort sprawling between them. But she powered through.

"Every morning when I wake up the first thing I think about is you. It used to be in a lovesick puppy kind of way. The butterflies were more powerful than a strong morning coffee—I just wanted to get out of bed and rush to see you, to feel your presence. Being with you was—and still is—so much better than not being with you. I mean, it must be serious if I'm willing to sacrifice sleep for you." She chuckled and chanced a peek across at Sam. His eyes were closed. If he'd been frozen before, he seemed to be thawing out now.

She forced herself to continue. "But now, there are no butterflies. Every morning I wake up and there's this pit in my stomach, because I know that somehow, at some point, I messed things up between us. I don't know how, why, or when, or whether it goes all the way back to that night in the park in Bangkok when you tried to kiss me for the first time and I pulled away. I hate myself for that, by the way. I wish every day that I could go back in time and kiss you back, and never stop kissing you.

"What would have been different if I had, Sam? Would we be together by now? Would you never have slept with Bling? Would . . ." Kayla gulped, trying to banish the lump in her throat. A breeze tickled the hairs on her arms. "Would I never have kissed Oliver? Things have changed—your feelings have changed, I can see that—

and it's horrible. It makes me feel sick to think of how things used to be. How amazing it felt. All I want is to go back to that."

Sam looked like a man whose brain, body, and heart were at civil war with each other. "We can't, Kayla. We just can't." His brain was obviously winning.

"But *why*?" She dropped her hands into her lap. She felt like a petulant child. "I don't get it. I love you, Sam. You're making me wish I didn't, but I do."

There was a rich silence that stretched out far in front of them, bouncing off the mountains and rippling over the lake. A quiet uncertainty; a moment in time in which anything could happen.

Then it was shattered. Sam stood up, pushing his weight off the ground with his damaged hand, and grimaced.

He looked out over the lake and said the last words Kayla would ever heard him say. "I'm sorry."

Then, for the last time, he walked away.

"No. No!"

Russia was in outrage. She, Bling, and Dave had passed Sam walking back to the villa as they were all making their way to the lake for a sunset dip, and as soon as she spotted Kayla and her solemn, tearstained face, she demanded to know what happened. Kayla brought her up to speed.

"I'm going to bloody kill him, I'm so angry," Russia said. "Oh my God, I will actually kill him." Kayla could have sworn there was actual, literal steam wafting out of her Russian friend's ears. Nope, false alarm. She'd just lit a cigarette. She offered the pack to Kayla, who happily obliged. "Let's smoke these and calm down. Then . . ." Russia tapped cigarette ash onto the dry mud. "Then I have something to tell you."

The two of them sat shoulder-to-shoulder on the banks of the lake, smoking their cigarettes in silence. This was not the hopeful, tense silence of five minutes earlier, but rather a pensive, resigned blanket of quiet. Not too far away, Bling and Dave were splashing each other with water from the middle of the lake. Kayla heard Dave challenging Bling to a swimming race, demanding he have a head start due to his disability. In true, ruthless Bling style, she refused him the sympathy he was fishing for and set off toward the other side of the lake with an elegant breast stroke, leaving him spluttering and flailing in a bid to catch up with her. Kayla couldn't help but smile. She had amazing friends.

Russia finished smoking her first cigarette and instantly lit another. "Do you remember the night Oliver grabbed you on a night out and Sam responded by grabbing him by the throat?" she asked.

Kayla nodded. It was difficult to forget. Russia delicately blew smoke rings through the O shape in her lips. Kayla knew that to an outsider, her friend would look pretty yet vacant. If only they knew how sharp she was.

"Okay. Well, he made me swear I wouldn't tell you this. Sam, that is, not Oliver. I saw him storming toward the end of the road—the opposite direction from the bus stop. I assumed that meant he was planning on walking home, which, as you know, is a bit of a hike, and not exactly through the best area. I was worried, so I ran after him.

"Then I realized he was on the phone, so I hung back a little bit. You know me, I'm unbelievably nosy. And he kept saying stuff like, 'Please, stop,' then he hung up abruptly. I kind of thought he might have been talking to Oliver, so I ran up behind him and jumped on his back. I mean, he must have heard me coming—it's not like I snuck up on him—but he looked like I'd given him a heart attack. Really on edge. I thought he was going to yell at me, but he just started crying."

"Crying? Sam?" Kayla asked incredulously.

"Yup. It shocked me too. I didn't know what to do, so I just kind of hugged him and asked what was wrong. He was talking into my shoulder so his voice was kind of muffled, and he just kept saying that he didn't know what to do."

"About what?"

"I'm not sure, entirely. I asked if it was about you, 'cos, you know. I've seen the way you look at each other. It doesn't take a genius to work out that the pair of you are madly in love." The revelation shocked Kayla. She barely knew what to make of her own feelings, and hadn't been aware that others were analyzing them too. "And he said yeah, it was about you, partly."

"Really? What else did he say?"

"He said, and I quote, 'I love her, Russia. But we can never be together. And that kills me.' I asked him what he meant by that, why you couldn't be together, but he just started walking away and begged me not to follow him. So I didn't."

Kayla tried to let what Russia had said sink in, but she couldn't. Her brain was spinning too quickly. She sighed. "I wish you had gone after him."

Russia shrugged and took hold of her hand. "I could say the same thing about you."

KAYLA KNEW WHAT she had to do.

She took her time walking from the lake back to the bungalow, Russia's words ringing in her ears the whole way. *I love her, Russia. But we can never be together. And that kills me.* What did he mean by that?

He did love her. She knew it. She knew she wasn't crazy.

Padding across the bungalow's tiled floor, she crept down the corridor toward Sam's room. She had no idea what she was going to say, how she was going to tell him she knew he felt the same without implicating Russia. How she could possibly put into words what she was feeling right now. Maybe she'd just kiss him with everything she had and hope he kissed her back.

She went to knock on his door, but paused just before her knuckles made contact with the wood. That's strange, she thought.

The door was ajar.

Chapter 35

June 17, Thailand

THERE WAS ONLY *one other time in my life I'd seen this much blood.*

Or, at least, this breed of blood—not the poppy red hue of a shaving cut swirling into bathwater or the stale maroon of a drying scab begging to be scratched. This was angry. A deep crimson syrup whose quantity betrayed its origins. This blood was a consequence of pain.

My mind whirled, stuck on a waltzer of panic.

The worst part was knowing who the blood belonged to. It belonged to the man I cared about most in the world.

Why was it always the ones I loved the most?

My stomach lurched. This couldn't be happening. Not again. Someone had to be playing some sort of practical joke, albeit a sensationally cruel one. He was gone. How could he be gone? How could there possibly be this much blood? I'd only seen him thirty minutes earlier, when I'd told him exactly how I felt. When he gazed at me through his sad brown eyes and uttered the last words I'd ever hear him say: "I'm sorry."

I stepped back from the crimson pools. The bedroom started spinning. My thoughts were bleeding into each other. Splotches of red seeped into my vision.

Think, Kayla. Focus. This cannot really be happening. Not again.

There were no indicators of foul play. No smashed windows, no screaming, no sirens wailing in the distance to tend to the crime scene. Just blood. Lots and lots of blood.

But somewhere deep within my gut, I knew the truth. My body knew. My knees buckled. I fell to the floor, causing a ripple in the red lagoon rapidly forming on the tiled floor. Sam's blood. The sticky air was difficult to inhale, and I could feel myself losing consciousness. Good. Maybe I'd wake up and realize none of this had ever happened.

But it had happened.

Sam was gone. And somehow, it was all my fault.

Chapter 36

August 2, England

THE ACCOUNT WAS created at this address.

What the hell does that mean? Did Gabe send those messages to himself?

She couldn't think clearly. She felt drunk, disorientated, still disconcerted by the mysterious figure on the rope swing. Her skin was crawling, as if the revelation about the origins of the IP address meant she could no longer trust her own house. The bricks and mortar had eyes, the wallpaper had ears, the very foundations were built on dark secrets and cruel intentions.

She left a voice mail for Sadie. Of all the times she needed to speak to the detective, this was the most urgent.

She reopened her laptop and logged into Facebook, typing hastily into the search bar. Daniel Burns: one mutual friend. Daniel Burns, who joined Facebook in February this year. Daniel

Burns, who drove her brother to suicide. Daniel Burns: a fictional character who was born in the building she used to call her home.

Hang on a second.

Daniel Burns joined Facebook in February. That couldn't be right.

There was only one person living at Berry Hill in February. And that would mean . . .

Kayla froze.

Oh dear God, no . . .

Chapter 37

August 2, England

THE STUDY IN Berry Hill House had a unique smell that transported Kayla back to her childhood.

It was a vast room with high ceilings, an ornate fireplace, and three very expensive—yet exceedingly uncomfortable—sofas. Every wall was lined with deep mahogany bookcases, which formed a series of enclaves, much like a library. They were stacked with shelf upon shelf of classic old books in traditional burgundy and forest green leather covers. *Great Expectations, Wuthering Heights, Pride and Prejudice.* Kayla had a vivid memory of perching on the rope swing at the ripe old age of seven, a heavy, leather-bound Mark Twain book sitting in her lap as she struggled over each and every word, loving every second of it. Her mother had found her, bent her over her bony knee and smacked her three times on the bottom. Hard. Those books were not for reading. They had cost a fortune, didn't you know?

Fake. The whole thing was fake. The books were never read, the glorious shelves never scoured for the next captivating story, *Encyclopaedia Britannica* never opened and pored over like it deserved to be. The books had been bought in bulk as a decorative display, not painstakingly built over a long career of collecting and cherishing each title.

But no, those books were not for reading. They were all part of the act.

Kayla shuddered as she opened the door to the empty study and was hit by a waft of musty air; the odor of expensive mahogany and unloved books. It triggered a twitch of resentment buried somewhere deep inside her. She wondered how long that had been suppressed.

She walked over to the desk at the back of the room, facing intimidatingly outward like the one in her old headmaster's office, and lowered herself into the chair behind it. She switched on the computer—which was rarely ever used—and tried to steady her shallow, rapid breathing as the machine croaked slowly into action. As the browser history loaded. She tapped her foot impatiently on the wooden floor. *Come on, come on, come—*

"Kayla." A warm voice, laced with a glimmer of unease, from somewhere near the door. Kayla leapt out of her skin. She hadn't heard anyone follow her in. "What a surprise. I haven't seen you in the study since you were little."

Mark Finch was leaning against the door frame with a too-big smile plastered on his face. The bags underneath his eyes bulged angrily, and his jaw was covered in thick, steel-gray stubble. His pale lilac shirt, unbuttoned at the collar, accentuated the sickly tinge to his pale face. Growing up, all of Kayla's school friends had a crush on her dad; he was rich, attractive, and powerful. She wondered whether they'd still fancy him now. Haggard and balding, with the dull, lifeless eyes of a man very much in the depths of a dark and prolonged depression.

He walked slowly toward the desk. "What are you doing in here, sweetheart?"

Kayla searched her brain frantically for an explanation. "I—I . . . my laptop isn't working. I just wanted to . . . ch-check this one too, to see if it's a problem with the Internet server or just my own computer." She could feel her cheeks burning furiously. *Subtle, Kayla. Really subtle.*

Mark looked at her strangely. "Why didn't you just reboot the router? It's in the kitchen, not the study. You know that."

"I . . . erm—yeah. I mean, I could have done that. I should have. Sorry, I'll go and do that now."

Kayla stood up shakily and started to walk, as confidently as she could, toward the door. Her dad edged to the left, blocking her path. He grabbed her arm, his eyes boring into her pupils, scaring her. She'd never been scared of him before. He spoke in a stony, measured tone. "I don't like it when you lie to me, Kayla."

"Wh-What? I'm not. What?"

"What were you doing on my computer?"

She tried to shake her arm free but his grip was too tight. She felt like a trapped animal. "I just told you."

He took a step closer to her, so his face was inches from her own. She could smell strong coffee on his breath. "And I just told you I don't like it when you lie to me. Why were you on my computer?"

Kayla gulped. "I found out something strange today. I was just investigating. That's all."

His grubby nails dug even deeper into her arm. She wanted to yelp in pain, but her pride wouldn't allow her to. "What did you find out that was strange?"

There was no point in trying to lie. Kayla sensed, instinctively, that he already knew the answer. "The Facebook account that sent Gabe those messages was created in this house. According to the dates, I was away skiing, Gabe was at boarding school and Mum was in rehab. There was only one person that could have created that account, Dad. Please tell me it wasn't you."

Mark held her gaze for a moment, then collapsed to the floor as though every bone in his body was made of cotton wool. "Shit, Kayla. Shit. How . . . h-how did you—"

"How did I find out?" Kayla's voice was shaking more than her knees. Which was a lot. "Guy I went to school with tracked the IP for me. I checked the dates. Please tell me I'm putting two and two together and getting five?"

Silence. Mark's head was lulling in circles. His neck looked dangerously close to snapping.

"Dad? What the—" She tried to sidestep around her father's crumpled figure, but his hand snatched her ankle.

"You can't leave, Kayla. I'm sorry. It's not safe. I'm so, so sorry."

"Dad, you better tell me what the *hell* is going on. Now." Kayla didn't know whether she felt angry, scared, or utterly baffled. Probably a mixture of all three. "And let go of my leg!" She jerked her ankle free.

Mark clambered to his feet with the trepidation of a baby taking its first steps. He seemed to recover, then grabbed Kayla by the wrist and dragged her toward the desk chair, thrusting her into the seat. Her coccyx collided with the arm, and the pain took her breath away for a millisecond.

Mark walked around to the front of the desk and started pacing across the wooden floorboards. His hands were planted on his head as he patrolled his territory like a frantic police officer. "I can't believe this is happening."

"*You* can't believe it?"

"I know. I *know*. This was never supposed to happen. Never. Nobody was ever supposed to find out . . ."

"Find out what? Dad, I swear to God, if you don't start telling me what's going on . . ."

Mark continued to pace as Kayla sat in silence, trying and failing to understand what was happening. Eventually, he stopped abruptly and turned to face his daughter. His voice was calmer now, more measured. His tone, however, was still strangled, almost manic. "This was never supposed to happen."

"So you said," Kayla replied coolly.

"It all seemed so simple, so easy. Nothing could possibly go wrong. We had it all worked out; it was a simple solution. But you know what they say about things that seem too good to be true."

"They usually are?"

"Yep. I sure learned that the hard way." Mark ran his hands through his thinning air and gazed skyward. As he lifted his arms, the dark purple sweat patches spread even farther down his shirt. "Fuck. *Fuck*."

"Dad," Kayla whispered. "Tell me. Please."

His voice quivered. "I tried so hard to keep you from finding out. So hard. You have no idea . . ." His eyes were wide, popping out of his skull. "Knowledge isn't power, Kayla. Knowledge kills."

She could have sworn the temperature had dropped ten degrees. Goose bumps tickled her arms and a cold sweat trickled down her spine. The dusty smell of old books was half nostalgic, half suffocating. "What are you talking about?"

Tears started to stream down Mark's face. His mouth remained open, threatening to howl like a wounded wolf. Kayla couldn't help but cringe—nothing made her shudder quite like the sight of her father crying.

For a while it looked like he might throw up. Then his pacing resumed.

This time when he spoke, his voice was quiet. Distant, like he was sleep-talking. "I guess there's no harm in telling you now. You'd figure it out for yourself, anyway, soon enough. Soon enough. Oh, Mark. Mark, Mark, Mark. You always knew this would happen." He stopped walking and sat on the edge of the desk, facing away from Kayla, rocking steadily with his eyes closed. He looked deranged.

"Kayla . . . you know how important the family business is to me. It's my life, and it was your grandfather's life too. He built Finch Marketing from the ground up, then he left it all to me, right after we joined hands with Greyhawk Financial."

"Wait. All this is about *business*?" Kayla asked furiously.

Mark's eyes shot open. "Are you going to let me explain or not?" Kayla said nothing, terrified she'd broken the trancelike state in which he seemed ready to finally explain. His rocking movement continued. "All I've ever wanted was to do right by him. Your grandfather was a great man. I wish you could have gotten to know him better, Kayla. He would have loved you. He was so wise, so generous, so loyal. So unlike me. I was never cut out for the business world. Not in the way he was. I've always been weak-minded. Easily influenced.

"So when Greyfinch started struggling shortly after my dad died, and Eric Walsh—the CEO of Greyhawk Financial—came to me with a solution . . . I crumbled. I knew it was far from ideal, and it was incredibly dodgy, but I was weak. Overwhelmed by grief, my own young family, and a badly bruised ego. I should have said no—hindsight is a fine thing, I guess—but I didn't. Not a day goes by that I don't regret that decision. Not one day."

Kayla could hardly breathe. "What did you do, Dad?"

Mark swallowed hard. His throat was dry and raspy. "Think about it, Kayla. We had control over every single camera in the United Kingdom. The only people who could access the footage were regional police chiefs. Good guys. That was always the intention—we wanted to provide a pure, functional system that benefitted everyone, and could also turn over a profit. That's it. We never wanted more than that. We knew such a system was open for bribes and blackmail, of course we did. But we trusted our police chiefs and we trusted ourselves. I thought that was enough. I was wrong." Mark thumped his forehead three times with the heel of his hand. "My God, was I wrong."

Although it could only have lasted thirty seconds or so, the silence that followed seemed to last an eternity. "Th-The running costs,": he finally went on, "they were much higher than we anticipated, Kayla. We barely made a penny. O-Our marketing staff was overwhelmed by the pressure, the strain, so we had to keep hiring more and more to deal with the sheer quantity of reports we were being hired to produce. But the extra staff . . . they ate into profit margins, and the money for most jobs didn't come in straight away. We had to have a whole department dedicated to chasing debt. We were being swallowed under, but it wasn't just about us any more . . . it was about our country. Our *country*, Kayla. So when . . . when we were in our most desperate hour, and an offer came in that could solve all of our financial problems . . . you can see why we faltered."

"What was the offer?" Kayla was still struggling to keep up.

Mark paused, again for a gaping stretch of time that was so silent it felt like a vacuum.

"Dad?"

Mark lowered his voice, as though saying it quietly would somehow dull the impact of his words. "It was an anonymous data request from someone outside the police force. We get them a lot. Husbands determined to catch their cheating wives, bosses checking whether their employees really were off sick and not just away on holiday, that kind of thing. We always ignore them. But this one was different. It was an e-mail, sent directly to the request account. It simply said: 'I need last night's footage from camera number C1029K to be doctored. I'll pay one million pounds.' Obviously, we looked to see what was on that footage. It was basically nothing, an empty back alley mostly. The only thing of note was a man in a stained yellow hoodie running past the camera at five past eleven. You couldn't even see his face that clearly."

Kayla felt sick. "So you took the money."

Mark closed his eyes. "Yes. We altered the footage so there was never a man running down the street, and the million was transferred into our account. I paid our head accountant to keep it under the radar, make it look legitimate, and we got away with it. For a while our problems eased off. We had cash-flow again."

"Did you ever find out why the person wanted it changed? Was it another cheating husband scenario?"

"That's where it started to get messy. A week later, I was checking the news Web sites and happened to notice a small news story in the regional section, about a missing-person-turned-murder case. The body was found on the next street from the alleyway whose CCTV footage we doctored. I'm willing to bet the murderer didn't want to be implicated. We never did find out who it was, exactly, but they must have had serious cash lying round to be able to cough up that amount of money just to keep themselves out of jail. Either that or it was an investment by a very smart man. It turned out to be the latter."

Kayla frowned. There was a lot to take in, and none of it seemed to be making any sense. "What do you mean?"

"My heart sank as soon as I read that news story. We'd been bribed, and we'd taken it. As a result, we'd set ourselves up for a massive blackmail opportunity."

"I still don't get it."

Mark sighed. "Think about it. We'd allowed ourselves to be bribed, and the murderer had evidence of this happening. He could have exploited us at any moment. Told the police or the press. We'd all have been arrested. Jailed. It was *treason*. But instead, he used his knowledge as a bargaining chip. Sure enough, a month after the story had broken, the demands started pouring in. First, he wanted his money back, or he'd leak his story. He'd tell the world that the most powerful surveillance system in the world was corrupt. So we obliged. Then he wanted another million. Then . . . then he wanted information."

"What kind of info—"

"Private information. Information about . . . about the movements of certain influential figures. Foreign consulates. MPs. The governor of—"

"The governor of the Bank of England?" Kayla finished.

Silence.

She blinked in disbelief. Her stomach dropped. The terrorist attacks. Waterloo. Heathrow. Kings Cross.

People dead. People missing. Blood, tragedy, fear.

Her dad.

Words frothed from her mouth. "You're a terrorist. A *terrorist*. How can you even look at yourself in the mirror having facilitated that? There's blood on your hands, Dad. You're fucking *drenched* in it, you—"

"I *know*. Jesus, don't you think I know? I hated myself—I still do. But there was absolutely nothing I could do to stop it, you can see that, right?"

Kayla said coldly, "No. You could have told the police. You could have owned up. After the first attack at Heathrow, didn't you . . . ? How could you? How could you not stop this?"

Mark recoiled as if he'd been slapped, pushing himself up off the desk and twirling around to face Kayla. "Don't you understand? I didn't have a choice, I—"

"Will you stop acting liking a victim and insisting you didn't have a choice? Every single thing you've just described to me was a choice. Every single thing. Stop trying to shift the blame. You're the bad gu—" Mid-rant, a chilling thought hit Kayla. "Wait a minute . . . what does this have to do with Gabe? Or with the Facebook account? Did the guy from behind the camera send those messages? Did things get that personal?"

Mark shook his head slowly. "No. No."

"So how is it all connected?"

"Gabe was a smart kid. There was an attack about six months ago. Smaller. The first time we were blackmailed. An important City broker murdered in a black cab. Do you remember that? Footage was posted on a jihadist Web site. Gabe . . . he'd been interning at Greyfinch for a few days and worked it all out, even though I'd never uttered one word about it to him. I have no idea how he found out—I still don't—but the fact is, he did. And we couldn't risk him going to the police, or worse, the press, to confess the truth."

Kayla's blood turned to ice. "Y-You . . . you *killed* him? Just to keep your own fucked up secret safe?"

Please say no. Please say you didn't kill Gabe.

"No! God, no. How could you even think that? I would never kill my own son. I'd rather kill myself! And believe me, that thought did cross my mind. I'm not proud, but . . ." Mark's eyes clouded over. The fog of depression still clung to him. "I just begged Gabe not to go public with it—I knew the kind of people I worked with—and I even sent him away to boarding school to try and keep him out of harm's way. I knew Walsh wasn't as . . . emotionally attached as I was. He would have no qualms over eliminating a threat like that. I tried to keep Walsh from finding out that Gabe knew, but somehow he did. I assume he's the one who sent the messages, though I have no idea how he did it from this computer."

"So did Gabe actually commit suicide? Or was he murdered?"

Mark's cheeks were lined with wrinkles and splotches of red. "I truly don't know. I asked Walsh, of course I did. I demanded that he tell me what happened to my son . . ." He wiped his forehead with the back of his hand. There was a sheen of sweat on his jowly face. He sniffed. "But he wouldn't. He always was a cold, heartless man."

"Wonder what that's like," Kayla muttered. She was overwhelmed by what Mark had told her, shaking violently, drenched in cold sweat. *Terrorism. Treason. So much blood.* "Can you tell me one more thing?"

"I don't see why not," Mark said, and laughed sourly. "What does secrecy matter now?"

"Is what happened to Sam in any way linked to all of this? Or was it just a freakish coincidence?"

Mark sat back on the desk, this time angled slightly toward her. Gently, he said, "I'm so, so sorry Kayla. You were never meant to fall in love with him."

The bottom fell out of Kayla's stomach, and her heart swiftly followed. The color drained from her face. She couldn't speak. Mark fumbled to find more words to fill the void. "I knew Walsh was sending people over there to keep tabs on you. I'm willing to bet there are some here in England too, knowing Walsh. I know he ordered them to give your pal Sadie Winters a shock, anyway." *Sadie? Sadie knew too?* Kayla couldn't keep up with the endless list of betrayal.

Mark continued, "But while most of them kept their distance in Thailand, he sent one extra person on the same trip as you, and paid them generously to befriend you and report back on whether you were behaving as expected. You know, acting the way a girl who didn't know that her father was a corrupt bastard would. But one night—the night before Sam disappeared—I overheard Walsh on the phone. From what I gather, he was concerned that the spy had become *too* close to you, and that the prerogative was no longer to protect Greyfinch. And obviously, he couldn't let the spy walk free and do as they pleased—if their loyalties really had been compromised, they were almost guaranteed to go to the police. So Walsh ordered the others out there to eliminate the threat. Which, in this case, I assume was Sam. The next day, we got your phone call about what happened. I'm so sorry, Kayla, I really am. After everything you'd already been through."

Kayla didn't know whether every fiber of her being ached more because Sam was definitely dead or because he was never who he said he was.

Even through the excruciating pain, self-preservation kicked in. "Wait a minute. If both Gabe and Sam were killed to keep this quiet . . . what's going to happen to me?"

The grandfather clock behind her ticked loudly. Somewhere in the house, a floorboard creaked. "I don't know," Mark said slowly, something resembling fear creeping into his voice. He still couldn't look her in the eye. "At this point, nobody but me knows that you've heard the whole story. So we could carry on as normal, but . . . I don't know. I don't trust Walsh. It wouldn't surprise me if he had this house bugged. We have to get you somewhere safe— somewhere they . . . th-they can't get to you. I've already lost one kid, and I'll be damned if they try to harm you too."

"Is there even anywhere safe left?" Kayla asked.

She would never hear her dad's reply, because at that moment her nan walked through the door.

Hang on. Isn't she supposed to be in Oban?

Kayla was about to warn her to leave, to run away from this crooked family and never look back. But there was something strange about the look on Nan's face, about the twisted smile and the narrowed eyes. Something that told Kayla her nan already knew.

Chapter 38

August 2, England

EVEN IF YOU struggle to know what's real when you're dreaming, you can always identify reality when you're awake. And this nightmare was very, very real indeed.

"Mum?" Mark seemed as shocked as Kayla. "What are you doing here?"

"I always knew you weren't up to it, Mark."

"What the . . . What are you talking about? Up to what?"

"Your failure to fulfill your father's wishes, to continue building his empire with honor and integrity. That's what I'm talking about, Mark. He'd turn in his grave if he knew what you'd done."

Kayla had never heard her nan's voice so strong, so assured. Her head spun viciously, whooshing and swirling like she was drunk.

"How did you . . . how did you know?" Mark asked.

"How did I *know*? Please. I know more than you ever will. I was there with your father from the very beginning. People think I was just some trophy wife who attended functions, wore red lipstick, and smiled politely while the men were taking care of business. But the whole time I was calculating threats, seeking opportunities, building contacts. Your father had the vision, the initial idea, and the unstoppable ambition, but I had the brains. I could see through the sales talk, know when we were being played, and know how to play our enemies right back. But while I did it for the good of the company, I always kept my morals. Never lost sight of what was right and what was wrong. It's just a shame the same can't be said for you. I'm still respected within that company, Mark, more so than you ever will be. I've known about the blackmail since day one. Known my own son was . . . was a traitor."

Mark slid off the desk and fell to the floor, his head falling into his hands. "I'm sorry. I've failed everyone. I've . . . I-Innocent lives have been lost. I'm sorry. So sorry. If I could change it all—"

"Yes, you are a failure. But there's no point being emotional. We have to clean up this mess, Mark. Think of what would happen if this got out. We'd all be arrested for countless offenses: perverting the course of justice, murder, treason. Aiding and abetting terrorists. The country would fall apart, knowing that the surveillance system was so corrupt. All of those who argue about the panopticon, the Orwellian monitoring, the ruthless breaches of privacy, the Big Brother state . . . they'd be right. It'd be disastrous, there would be outrage, riots. Not only would the Finch name be in tatters, but the United Kingdom would be too."

"Kayla won't utter a word, Mum. She knows how deadly this secret is. Stop talking like a Bond villain." He laughed nervously.

"This is hardly funny, Mark. Everything our family has worked for over the last half a century is hanging in the balance, and all you can do is make jokes?" Iris shook her head in disgust.

"So what are you going to do, Nan? Kill me to protect your name?" Kayla demanded, only half joking.

Iris spun around to look at Kayla. There was a wildness in her eyes that Kayla had never seen before. "Why not? I already killed your brother."

All of the air was sucked out of the room. Everything was still for a moment, frozen in light of the revelation. Kayla's heart stopped.

Mark screamed, "You WHAT? You killed my son? Your GRANDSON? All in the name of some twisted ideologies? You sick old bitch! What the hell is wrong with you?"

Kayla screamed even louder than her dad. "YOU KILLED MY BROTHER? It was *you* who sent those Facebook messages? You drove him to suicide—"

"No, I didn't. I tried to." Iris's voice wobbled. "Don't get me wrong—I tried to talk him down first, to convince him not to go public, but he wouldn't back down. Didn't want to be complicit in our heinous acts. Then I tried to threaten him online, on social media, but it was too little, too late. He knew too much, and he was determined to bring us down. I . . . I didn't see another option. Time was running out, and I panicked. So I waited until everyone was out, went into his room and saw he was taking a nap. I handcuffed him before he could wake up and overpower me, then I slit his wrists, so it'd look like he'd done it himself. I stayed with him until I could be sure he was dead. You think that was *easy* for me? To watch my grandson die a slow and painful death? To hear him spend his last waking minutes begging me to help him? Well, it wasn't. It . . . it still haunts me every day. But that's the difference between you and I, Mark. I can see the bigger picture. I can prioritize the greater good."

Kayla felt like she'd been punched repeatedly in her torso. This could not be happening. Her nan could not have just confessed to the murder of her brother. She glanced at her father. He was broken. Shattered.

Tears pricked behind Kayla's eyes, but she blinked them back. There was one prevalent image through the pain and grief: Sam. In spite of everything, she still loved him. And he had died because he had loved her too much to betray her trust and report back to Greyfinch – he put her safety above his own. Her life above his. That had to be worth something. His sacrifice meant she had to fight for herself.

Think, Kayla. Keep her talking. Keep her talking while you think your way out of this mess. "Do you really think I'd go to the police about this? Do you really think my sense of justice is so strong I'd bring shame to my own family? Gabe's morals were stronger than mine. I wouldn't tell a soul." The words were spilling from her mouth, and they tasted dirty.

"I'm sorry, Kayla," Iris said, walking toward her. Her voice softened. "But I know you. I know you couldn't live with yourself if you kept that secret. It would rot inside you, like it has your father."

"Living with the secret, with the lies . . . that's better than not living at all. Even I know that," Kayla said, with a lot more assurance than she truly felt.

Iris wavered. Kayla saw it. And as she wavered, something flashed in the corner of Kayla's eyes. Lights.

Both women turned to look out of the window. It was evening

now, and the sky alight with blue and red flashing lights. Police cars. Coming up the driveway.

"How? I . . . how?" Iris stuttered, staring at Mark accusingly.

He looked as confused and terrified as she did.

Footsteps pounded down the hallway.

Chapter 39

August 2, England

THE POLICE STATION in north Northumberland was worlds away from the one in Phuket where Kayla had fallen apart less than two months ago.

It was clean, clinical, devoid of personality. The floors were covered in plain linoleum, the walls painted an unassuming shade of builder's white. The officers were professional, formal, and most sympathetic toward Kayla. That was the key difference: Kayla was no longer being treated as a suspect. Everyone was finally behaving like she was a victim, which, in more ways than one, she was.

She hadn't yet had time to process how the police knew what was happening at Berry Hill. It wasn't high on the list of agonizing facts to work through.

Like the fact that Gabe had known. He knew everything.

Her stomach cramped painfully.

Had he ever tried to tell her? Protect her from this dark, dark secret?

The night in Dad's study. When he sat there, paralyzed, and I asked if I could help. And he said no. He told me to leave.

He had never tried to protect her.

A tall, lanky junior officer with a weak chin and pale face peppered with angry pink pimples approached Kayla. She was in a small room off to the side of the interrogation room where Iris was being held. This room too was strangely empty. There was a handful of the kind of fabric-covered metal seats you'd find in a village hall, a small plastic table holding a coffee machine and a rather pathetic-looking potted plant, and the lingering smell of new paint that stung her nostrils. A geriatric TV set bolted to the top corner of the white walls blinked and flickered on mute.

The young man looked uncomfortable. Kayla assumed he was new to the job, though even the most experienced officer was bound to find this tangled web of interfamily homicide deeply disturbing. "Miss Finch, hi. My name is Paul Mecklenburgh. How are you doing?"

"Oh, you know. I just found out that my nan killed my brother and my dad facilitated the whole thing. Oh, and they're behind several domestic terrorist attacks over the last few months. So I'm doing good, thanks."

Paul didn't seem to register the thick sarcasm. "Well, I'm glad to hear that. Can I get you anything? A tea or coffee?"

What is this? A hairdressing salon? "N-No, thank you. I'm fine."

"All right, well let me know if that changes. We might be here awhile—we'll need to take your statement, but I'm not sure when that'll be. You have reliable evidence to support you, though, in the form of the CCTV recordings, so it shouldn't be too much trouble."

The CCTV recordings. Of course. "Okay, thanks." Paul turned to leave the room, but before he approached the door, Kayla blurted out, "Actually, there is one thing."

"Yes, Miss Finch?"

"Can I go and talk to my nan?" Kayla swallowed. "I know that's not really standard procedure. I just . . . I really want to ask her a few things. Now that she isn't threatening to kill me, and all."

Paul looked uncertain. "Well . . ."

"Please?" Kayla adopted a voice as weak and watery as the tea in Thailand, playing up the poor victim act.

Paul chewed his lip. "Let me see what I can do."

IRIS FINCH LOOKED older than she ever had. Her shoulders slumped and her skin had developed an ashen tinge.

Kayla had expected to walk into the room, sit down in front of her grandmother and ask her, matter-of-factly, everything she wanted to know. How she'd fooled them all for so long, was she ever really the kindhearted woman Kayla had grown up to know, whether she regretted any of it. Whether justice and shame was a powerful enough threat that she'd consider permanently silencing her own granddaughter.

Instead, Kayla sat down in the hard plastic chair, took one look at the broken woman in front of her, and burst into tears. And not calm, elegant drops rolling down her cheeks. Her gasps and gulps were frantic, uncontrollable. A horrendous six months finally surfacing.

"Kayla . . ." Iris said, her chin wobbling.

"How could you do this? What kind of person does it take to murder anyone, let alone a blood relative? An innocent blood relative? Sweet, lovely Gabe . . . you slit his wrists, for fuck's sake! How could you do that? How could you see the pain in his eyes, the fear, and keep slicing through his skin, his veins? You're a monster—"

"Kayla—"

"No! Don't you dare speak to me. You killed my brother, you killed the man I loved, and you were about to kill me too—"

"What did you—?"

"How could you do that? I genuinely can't wrap my head around it, how anyone could be so evil—".

"KAYLA!" The sharp tone of Iris's voice stopped Kayla in mid-rant.

"What? What could you possibly have to say to me? Other than an apology that will never make any of this okay?"

Iris frowned. "Did you say the man you fell in love with?"

"Yes. Sam. The man you sent to spy on me, the man I accidentally fell in love with, and the man you killed as a result. Ring any bells?"

Iris shook her head slowly. "No. Not really. The person I sent to spy on you, to join the Escaping Grey group . . . she was a girl."

Not for the first time that day, Kayla's heart stopped. "A girl?"

"Yes. Ai Ling something."

Chapter 40

KAYLA'S HEART WAS RACING.

Bling was the traitor? Not Sam? What does this mean?

She was back in the small room with the plant and the coffee machine, fumbling with a sachet of mocha.

But Bling is still alive—she texted me back a few weeks ago. Did they kill the wrong person?

She stirred in a packet of sugar, then another, and took a massive gulp. It was so bitter it made her cringe, and it burned her taste buds and the back of her throat, but she didn't feel it.

So where is Bling now?

Kayla sat down, her legs not strong enough to bear her weight, and turned the volume up on the TV. She found a rolling news station and, sure enough, there was a breaking news story flash-

ing across the screen: SURVEILLANCE MOGUL GREYFINCH INTER-
NATIONAL IMPLICATED IN TERRORIST ATTACKS.

A statement had already been released.

How is this happening? How is this real?

Kayla's erratic thoughts were interrupted by a tap on the door. Sadie. A very red-faced Sadie.

The detective looked breathless as she rushed over to her. "Kayla! How are you?" She didn't wait for a response. "I came as soon as I heard. Well, that's not strictly true . . . I got locked in my boss's office—my own fault, I was snooping around looking for information about this case, actually—and as I was sorting through old footage from Berry Hill, I noticed the live feed in the corner of the screen. I knew something wasn't right as soon as I saw it."

"My dad's study?" Kayla guessed.

"Your dad's study. It looked off. It was a strange setup—you sitting in the chair like you were trapped, your dad pacing the floor like a madman. The look of terror and disgust on your face. So . . . I enabled sound. I listened in. And the first thing I heard you say was, 'What did you do, Dad?' And by the fear in your voice, I knew something was wrong. I listened for another thirty seconds and sent the police cars before he even finished answering."

Kayla sat in stunned silence. Sadie had been spying on them, but it had saved her life. How was she supposed to feel?

Sadie cleared her throat. "When your nan walked in and started with all that talk about the family name and the greater good . . . I thought I'd been too late. I didn't think . . . I didn't think they'd get there in time." Her voice caught on her words. She stared into her cupped hands. "Anyway, I think they'll let me off with snooping around in my boss's office, considering what's just come to light. Another thing I should tell you . . . My boss was complicit. He knew about the whole thing. Mason Shepherd. He erased all the footage from Berry Hill that night—the footage that would have shown Iris walking into Gabe's bedroom around the time he lost his life. That's why he was so off with you, and why he wanted me to bury the Sam case as soon as possible. So I wouldn't go rooting around in this mess. So I wouldn't figure out it was all connected. So I wouldn't implicate him in the process. As it turns out, your nan did all the implicating we need to prosecute."

The revelation should have shocked Kayla, but it slotted into the betrayal perfectly. Besides, she was all out of shock for one night. She felt drained now that the initial adrenaline had worn off. Barely whispering, she said, "Did you hear the truth about the spy in Thailand?"

Sadie sighed and closed her eyes, taking a seat next to Kayla on the rigid chairs. "Yes, I did. I'm so sorry, Kayla. I know how much he meant to you—"

"It wasn't him," Kayla interrupted. "It wasn't Sam. It was Bling."

Sadie's eyes shot open. "What? How do you—"

"My nan just told me. It wasn't Sam." The words felt good. Tears prickled at her eyes, but she wiped them away on the back of her sleeve. "It wasn't Sam."

"Wow. That, erm . . . that still raises a lot of questions." Sadie's writing hand twitched. Kayla could tell she was dying to take notes. *So where is Sam? Is he dead? Where is Bling? Why? How? Who?* "How are you feeling about it all?"

Kayla didn't know where to start. The questions were racing through her tired head too. "I, erm . . . I'm okay. As okay as I can be, I guess." One of the questions burned hotter than the others. "Where have you been?"

"I just told you, I was stuck in the off—"

"No," Kayla interrupted, trying to keep the resentment from her voice. "I mean these last few weeks. Why have you been ignoring me?"

Sadie shuffled uncomfortably. "Time to face the music. I didn't want to have to tell you this, Kayla . . . but after our last meeting I was . . . followed. Attacked. Threatened."

Oh God. Will the hideous truths never stop flowing? "What! By who? Why?"

"I can't be sure who, but I assume they were working for someone at Greyfinch. Or Shepherd. Maybe even your grandmother. They got a bit friendly with a knife and told me to stop looking into Sam's case, or they'd pay me another . . . visit. So I did stop, with the exception of a few conversations with Dr. Myers, who was worried about you." Sadie couldn't meet Kayla's eyes. "I must admit, I was too. But still, I stayed away. Until tonight, when you called. I listened to your voice mail. Then I started digging again."

"Jesus Christ, Sadie. I'm sorry you had to go through that." Kayla suddenly remembered something: the sounds of a struggle, pounding footsteps, and a white van flying past the car park. "Shit. I—I think I heard you being abducted. Oh my God, I should have come after you, I should have—"

Kayla was cut short by her phone vibrating in her pocket. As she fished it out, she thought it'd be her mum—she must have heard the news.

But it wasn't Martha. It was an unknown number.

Kayla answered. "Hello?"

A hoarse voice replied. It was a gentle voice. One she thought she'd never hear again.

"Kayla? It's me. It's Sam."

Chapter 41

August 3, England

It was four o'clock in the morning, and Kayla was sitting on a creaking swing in a spookily dark play park opposite the police station where a large proportion of her family were under arrest. She should have been terrified, but she'd never felt safer in her life.

Because Sam was on the swing next to her.

The tension crackled between them like electricity. Kayla wanted nothing more than to kiss him, to confess her love for him once again, to allow the day's ridiculous events melt away and feel his body became one with hers. To tell him that her bubbling happiness that he was alive was more powerful than the devastation of her family's betrayal.

But she couldn't. Not yet. Not until she understood.

"I don't know where to start," said Sam. He'd come to meet her as soon as he saw the story on the news. He'd been doubtful that he would be able to make it to Northumberland from London before dawn on the creaky night bus, but Kayla told him to get a taxi. It had cost three hundred quid, but she didn't think her dad would have much use for his credit card in prison.

Sam looked different. The last time Kayla had seen him, his face was contorted in anger and fear. That had since evaporated, but there was a tiredness, a world-weariness, left in its place. One thing hadn't changed, though: the delicious tingling that pulsed through her body whenever she was within ten feet of him.

"Um, how about you tell me where the hell you've been for the last six weeks?"

"You're not going to believe me." Sam laughed. Kayla shivered—she still couldn't believe she was hearing that laugh for real, instead of the simulated version that haunted her daydreams.

"Trust me. Nothing can shock me after my nan pointed a metaphorical gun at my head."

"Fair point. Okay . . . well, you know when we visited the Daen Maha Mongkol Meditation Center, and there were all those residents who lived there all year round?" Kayla nodded. "Well, I thought, 'What better place to hide than a place where there was no TV, no news, no social media?' And I was right. Nobody questioned my presence—they had no idea I had been reported missing. As far as they knew, I was just some handsome stranger who'd grown tired of Western civilization and wanted to join them on their journey of meditation and discovery."

"You joined the Meditation Center?" Kayla couldn't help but laugh. Sam was one of the least spiritual people she knew.

"I'll have you know that I became a very valuable member of their community, actually. And I don't appreciate your tone," he chuckled, slapping her upper arm playfully. Kayla winced It didn't hurt—it was a reflex from the adrenaline-fueled evening she'd just endured. Sam looked instantly panicked. "Shit Kayla, I'm so sorry. Did that hurt? God, I'm so—"

"No it's fine, honestly. Just a reflex." *And it's overwhelming to have you touch me again.*

"Are you sure?" He got up off his swing and stood in front of hers. He wrapped arms around her back, hugging her face into his abdomen and kissing her head. Her chest ached. "I really am sorry, Kayla. For everything you've been through. For everything I put you through."

"It's okay. Well, it's not." Kayla leaned back, and Sam took her hands in his.

He sat down cross-legged on the tarmac in front her. "I know it's not. But I didn't have a choice, I hope you know that. I would never leave you out of choice."

"I'm getting tired of hearing about people having no choice, but to hurt me." Kayla smiled sadly. "Can you please just start from the beginning? *Why* have you lived in a meditation center for the last six weeks?"

"Okay . . ." Sam paused, as if gearing himself up to share a painful truth. "Remember when I slept with Bling?"

"Well, yeah. It's fairly imprinted on my memory." *But I forgive you. I forgive you everything.*

"I'm sorry, Kayla. Again. Well, a few days before that, she and I were at a cash point getting some money on a night out. I happened to look at her balance—come on, we all do it, it's human nature—and it was a lot. I mean *a lot.* Not just an I-have-rich-parents-and-daddy-spoils-me amount. We're talking six figures. I thought it was strange, but didn't mention it to her, of course. In fact, I forgot about it until that morning I woke up in bed next to her. Her phone rang, and honestly, I've never seen anyone leap out of their skin quite like that. She sprinted out into the corridor to answer it, and came back looking really flustered. I thought that was odd too, especially when I asked her if she was okay and she snapped and ran away to the toilet. But she left her phone on the pillow.

"So when an e-mail came through and flashed on the iPhone screen, and I saw it was from a woman called Iris Finch, naturally I freaked out a little bit. I'd heard you talking about your nan, and wondered why the hell she'd be e-mailing Bling. So I read the e-mail. I'm not proud of it, and I wish I hadn't, but I did."

"What did it say?"

"Something along the lines of Bling's payment being stopped if she didn't stop messing around. I flicked back through the earlier conversations they'd had, and I swear to God, I was nearly sick. Bling had been sending your nan reports on your activity, mainly to the tune of you not seeming suspicious, the secret still was safe, that kind of thing. The reports had become more infrequent as time passed, which I assume was why your nan was getting pissed off. I didn't know what the hell it all meant, but Bling came back from the toilet, so I couldn't do any more snooping."

Kayla blew air out from between her lips. "Wow. Where is Bling now? I thought Greyfinch ordered the spy to be eliminated. That's what I thought had happened to you. Why I thought you were almost certainly dead."

"You thought I was the spy?"

"Well, what would you have thought?" Kayla shrugged. "You were missing."

"I suppose it was the logical conclusion. Though I can't believe you'd ever doubt my intentions," he said, grinning despite the situation. "I actually have no idea where Bling is. I kind of hope she's okay, and that she got away safely. Is that weird? Yeah, it's weird. The massive amount of blood I lost must have messed with my head. But we'll get to that.

"So anyway, over the course of the next few weeks, I started doing some investigating. I went to Internet cafés and read up on your dad's company, all the controversy surrounding it . . . and your brother's death. I figured it *had* to somehow be related to the fact your own family had sent somebody to spy on you, just to make sure you didn't figure out a secret of theirs. I just couldn't work out exactly what. I desperately wanted to fill you in on everything I'd learned and see whether you had any idea what it could all mean."

"So why didn't you?" Kayla stroked his hands with her thumbs.

"Because one day it hit me: telling you could put you in danger. It seemed an outlandish theory, but I started thinking, 'What if Gabe was killed because he found out this awful secret?' It seemed completely ridiculous, but the more I thought about it, and the more I monitored Bling's behavior, it made sense. For a brief time I also thought Oliver might have been paid to follow us to Phuket too—that's why I freaked out on him so aggressively. In hindsight, though, I think he's just a creep.

"Then I noticed I was also being followed. I kept seeing the same two guys everywhere we went. Bling must have reported back that I was acting strangely and that I might have started to figure it all out. After they almost knew for certain that I had, I saw them just before we went swimming with sharks—"

"Is that why you didn't feel well out in the water? And we had to go back to shore?"

Sam nodded. "Yes. That, and I'm shit-scared of sharks."

Kayla laughed, a girlish giggle that made her sound like a love-struck teenager. Which was exactly how she felt. "So how did you eventually work it out?"

"I couldn't. I drove myself crazy, dreaming up these fantas-tical theories that I'd never be able to prove. I thought it might have something to do with Greyfinch, as a business like that, by its very nature, was just waiting to succumb to corruption. And what other secret would be more worth killing for than one that proved your family guilty of treason? So in the end I took a risk. I set up a new e-mail account almost identical to Bling's address. I started sending progress reports on your activity, in exactly the same format as the ones I'd read on Bling's phone. It worked, and your nan never noticed the difference. Then, after about a week of fake reports, I sent an e-mail saying I didn't feel like I could accurately report on whether you had figured out their secret, when I myself had no idea what the secret was. It was a massive risk—what if they'd already told Bling and they realized I was a fake? But they hadn't. Your nan confessed everything about the blackmail to me without realizing. I filled in the blanks about Gabe."

"Holy shit. Nice one, Sherlock." At the mention of Gabe's name, a fish hook pierced her heart. *Gabe. I love you. I love you for trying to put a stop to this. I'm sorry. I'm so sorry for what our family did to you.* Kayla could hardly breathe. She wondered if she'd ever be able to think about her brother without crippling pain again.

Sam rubbed his face, hard, like he was trying to scrub the memory away. "But I wished so much that I'd never found out. You can't unlearn that kind of knowledge. A girl you're rather fond of's family played a part in some of the biggest domestic ter-rorist attacks in years? I put myself in massive danger, and even worse, I put you in danger as a result. I knew I couldn't tell you, or

God forbid you'd meet the same fate as Gabe. But I couldn't spend every day with you and not tell you either. I'd be betraying you every single second, and I just couldn't do that."

"So why didn't you just fly home, escape the whole mess and forget you'd ever met me?"

"Because Greyfinch found out that my e-mail account was a fake. Bling must have sent something that contradicted what I said, because I woke up one morning to an e-mail demanding to know who was behind the account. That night, when you came into my room, was when the threatening phone calls started."

"Wow."

"Yeah." Sam looked away bashfully. "Kayla . . . the day you chose to sit with me by the lake and tell me how you felt about me, it killed me that I couldn't tell you that I felt the same. That I'd never thought it possible to love someone as much as I loved you. But I knew it was only a matter of time before Greyfinch shut me up permanently, and I couldn't complicate things any further."

"So, logically, you faked your own death and disappeared to Daen Maha Mongkol."

"Yup. I planted all the drugs so the cops would think that was an appropriate explanation, sent those messages to my phone, where even the most moronic detective would find them—"

"Wait, how did you plant messages on your phone?" Kayla asked.

"Really? That's what you wanna know? Well, I actually did contact the dealers to buy the drugs to plant—most terrifying thing I've ever done in my life, by the way. They aren't the friendliest people!—then I just used this app that lets you fake iPhone messages. And I called my mother to ask to borrow some money, so that when the drugs theory came to light, she'd believe it.

Knowing it would kill her—that hurt more than . . . you know. The blood. I left a drastic enough amount in the villa for them to assume me to be dead. Though I very nearly messed it up and *actually* killed myself. I cut a little too deep—I'm obviously not the greatest med student in the world. Luckily there was a medic at Daen Maha Mongkol. He was about a thousand years old, but handy with a needle and thread." Sam rolled up the sleeve of his navy hoodie, revealing an angry scar running across his wrist.

Kayla shuddered, tracing her finger over the length of the cut. It looked so deliberate. "Didn't it hurt?"

"Of course it bloody hurt. Have you met me before? I'm a complete wimp. I nearly bailed after the first millimeter."

Kayla planted several soft kisses along the scar. "I'm sorry, Sam. I'm sorry you had to do this to yourself because of my messed up family. I'm sorry you did this for me."

"I'm not that much of a hero! I did it to save myself too. And my family. I'm actually not a hero at all, when you think about it."

A lump formed in Kayla's throat. "I—I thought . . . I thought you were dead, Sam. I thought I'd lost you."

Sam got to his feet, stepped forward and wrapped his arms around Kayla, stroking her hair softly. The air was warm and still. "I know."

A hiccupy sob. Kayla's. "I'm glad you're not. Dead, that is."

Sam chuckled quietly. "Me too."

A thought dawned on Kayla. Sniffing tears away, she looked up at him. "Hang on. Does your mum know you're alive and, for the most part, well?"

Something flashed across Sam's face but disappeared too quickly for Kayla to work out what it was. "Yeah. I called her from Thailand a few weeks ago, once everything died down a little, on the condition that she didn't tell a soul. I thought she might expire with happiness. She asked me to come home, of course, but I think she understood why I couldn't."

The penny dropped in Kayla's mind. "That explains why she stopped talking to me!"

Sam cocked his head. "Hang on, you and my mother had been *talking*?"

"Sam, after everything that's happened, are you really still going to freak out about me meeting your parents?" Kayla laughed.

"My *parents*? Plural? Kayla. I mean, I think you're cool and everything, but this is all moving a bit fast—"

"Oh be quiet!" She pulled out of the hug and slapped his uns-carred arm. "So why did you come back from Daen Maha Mong-kol? You couldn't have known it was safe to return?"

"I knew the story had died down, and nobody was really on the lookout for me anymore. But I had no way of gauging the situation from over there. I desperately wanted to come back home to see my mum, to show her I really was fine, but I didn't want to put her—or myself—in any danger. I've been hiding out in a dingy little hostel in London, keeping my head down, trying to work out my next move. Then I saw the story on the news—that the secret we were all running from had been made public—and nearly cried. Because of the pain you'd be in, and because it was finally over."

"And you came to see me before your mum?"

Sam squeezed Kayla's hands. "I knew you'd need me more. She already knows I'm okay—I called her in the taxi on the way up." He swallowed and bit his lip. "And . . . I never told you I love you. So I needed to do that."

He stood then, took Kayla's hands and pulled her up from the swing to stand in front of him. He cupped her face in his hands and in the softest voice Kayla had ever heard him use, said, "I love you too, Kayla."

Then he kissed her, with the passion of a man who'd spent the last six weeks in a Thai monastery dreaming of this very moment.

Chapter 42

September 14, Turkey

"So, how many people have died doing this?"

Sam's knee bounced up and down; an old nervous habit.

Ali, their new Turkish friend, sat in front of them. His eyes darted frantically as he tapped the last of his cigarette ash out of the bus window. "Here? Four or five. Something like that." With one last puff, he flicked away the glowing remains and reached into the pocket of his khaki trousers for another.

"Re-Really? That many?" Sam choked back his horror and tried to gaze nonchalantly out of the window. The falling temperature sent a shiver down Kayla's bare forearms. The violent lurching of the twenty-year-old minibus careering over boulders and potholes rendered any attempts to relax futile. In any case, the three-thousand-foot cliff edge beginning half a meter left of the semiflat tires was enough to twist even the steeliest of stomachs.

Ali nodded gravely. "One guy had a heart attack halfway through. Very sad. Very, very sad. Cigarette?" Sam shook his head. He'd never been a smoker, ironically preferring to err on the side of caution for the majority of his life. Kayla accepted the offer.

Ali inhaled deeply on the white stick dangling out of his mouth. Kayla was sitting with her back to the driver, and Ali was sitting opposite. His eyes looked like lumps of charcoal set within his cappuccino skin and had too much white surrounding the pupils, giving the impression that he was constantly a combination of surprised and manic. When he smiled, his blindingly bright teeth and obscenely wide grin made him look more like a cartoon villain than a middle-aged Turk who Kayla and Sam had entrusted with their mortality.

Erkut, the grey-haired mountain of a man next to him, decided to elaborate. "Another was impaled on a tree." His eyes remained firmly shut behind his thickly framed glasses. He did not smoke, instead opting to gently hum an improvised tune and tap his index finger against his bicep in time with the repetitive rhythm. "Gruesome."

Sam's knee began to bounce with increased velocity. Despite the cool mountain air and the goose bumps speckling every inch of her exposed skin, beads of cold sweat started to trickle down the back of Kayla's neck. What had previously felt like flutters of excitement in her stomach had now evolved into intense cramping, similar to the sensation she usually experienced after one too many cups of coffee. The dense cloud of tobacco smoke clinging to her nostrils and lungs did little to alleviate her panic, instead adding to the sensation of being smothered by a lethal combination of ash and fear. They were only fifteen minutes away. She kept smoking.

Ali suddenly erupted into raucous laughter. It was a chesty cackle, evidence of his three-packs-a-day habit, and caused Kayla to leap out of her seat in shock. "Why the sad faces?" he roared. "It's only life. So what if you die? We all do someday." He delved into his backpack and emerged with a camera, attached to the end of a metal pole with peeling duct tape. "SMILE!"

Kayla wasn't sure what she thought the build-up to running off a 6,500-foot mountain, supported by a single parachute, would feel like. Perhaps she had never truly believed they'd go through with it. In fact, she still wasn't sure. Ascending this mountain in a minibus whose last MOT couldn't have been more recent than 1992, accompanied by four mentally unstable Turkish strangers with no insurance whatsoever, was slightly out of her comfort zone.

After Kayla's father and nan had been arrested, Sam suggested they get away from England for a while. Not on another epic adventure. Not yet anyway.

They'd invited Dave and Russia to join them in Turkey, but since the happy couple was currently traveling through India— exploring Dave's heritage, he in a wheelchair, until he couldn't explore anymore—they were preoccupied. Bling was somewhere overseas too, though neither Sam nor Kayla had any idea where. Shortly after the Greyfinch scandal leaked into international news, Kayla had received a text message from her.

Kayla, there aren't enough words in the English language to explain how sorry I am. I had no idea what I was agreeing to—if I had, I never would have done it. I really hope you're okay. I would love to meet you in person to apologize properly, but for now it's not safe for me to return to England. I truly hope you can forgive me, even though I wouldn't. Lots of love, B x

Kayla had replied maturely, much to Sam's utter amazement, with genuine gratitude for Bling's apology and well-wishes for the future. Maybe Cassandra wasn't such a bad shrink after all.

One day she and Sam would return to the university to pursue careers of their own. Sam? To take another stab at med school, yes, but ultimately to dedicate his life to finding a cure for ALS. Her? Crime scene investigation and forensic science. Joint honors.

But for now it was all about the present. About love, and about adventure.

THEY HAD SPENT the first three days of their holiday in Olü Deniz sipping lukewarm beer by the pool and admiring the paragliders overhead as they descended onto the pebble beach a hundred meters away; silhouettes of fearless fliers strapped onto the bottom of brightly colored parachutes, gracefully weaving their way down through the gusts of wind that kept them airborne. From the ground it had looked almost peaceful.

Much to Sam's horror, Kayla introduced the possibility of doing it themselves. He came up with thousands of reasons not to: it was too expensive, too hot, they were too hungover from last night's abuse of the all-inclusive bar. It was a bit cloudy that day. Kayla was much more proactive. As usual.

Polishing off the last of her postbreakfast vodka, she stood up from her sun lounger and wrapped her stripy beach towel around her midriff.

"Right. Let's go and find out how much it costs with one of

those street vendors on the beachfront." She deftly twisted her thick, Bourneville chocolate-colored hair around in her fingers and tied it up out of her face.

"But if we go with them, we won't have insurance. At least with Thomsons, we know we're covered if something goes wrong."

"Yeah, and they charge over a hundred quid for the privilege. Realistically, if something goes wrong at six-and-a-half-thousand feet, we're dead anyway. Don't really need insurance for a mild case of death, do we?"

"I s'pose not. How do we know if the guys on the street are legitimate?" Sam sat up on his sun lounger, took a gulp of beer and put down the dog-eared crime thriller he'd been reading.

"Well, that guy we met in bar last night seemed nice, if a little odd, and he's a paraglider. Let's go and find him."

"Do we even remember what he was called?"

"Andy or Ali or something. I don't know. Shall we go?"

"What, now?" Sam hastily threw his feet into his battered, sand-dusted flip-flops and readjusted his faux Ray-Bans, which regularly slid down his heavily sunscreened nose.

"Well, why not?" Her logic was flawless.

"Because I don't have any trainers. And we'll miss lunch. And it's cloudy."

"So? We just had breakfast."

"You have to wear trainers. I don't have any."

"It'll be fine. I bet Dave wishes he could do something like this. Let's go."

Bloody Dave. Sam sighed. "Okay. Just let me nip to the toilet first."

Ali had pointed at them and shrieked as they walked through the shop front, presumably in the place where the door should have been, and announced that they'd like to go paragliding with him. "NO WAY! Are you serious? Shut your face. I saw you drinking last night. You're not serious!"

But unfortunately they were serious. And forty-five minutes, fifty pounds, and some alarmingly casual paperwork later, they were clambering into their rusty white minibus armed with some parachutes, borrowed trainers and a hipflask of Raki. The bus smelled like sweaty socks and laundry that had accidentally been left in the washing machine overnight.

"Does anybody ever get to the top then change their minds?" Kayla asked.

"No, never. Because the ride back down the mountain in this old thing would be ten times worse than running off the top. You'll see."

He wasn't wrong. The dirt track that led up to the summit barely seemed wide enough for a Mini Cooper, let alone a rickety old bus full of equipment and people. With every rock the bus hit, the wheels lurched to the side, and at one point Kayla was certain they tilted over the edge. She made a mental note never to allow her future self to indulge in the luxury of fear again. Rather like when you have the flu and would trade anything for normality and fully functioning sinuses, she really missed being at sea level, and swore she'd never underappreciate being at a sensible height again.

They were nearly at the top. Sun and warmth had given way to compacted snow and clouds that engulfed the bus and reduced visibility to a mere few feet. The knot in her stomach tightened. Ali was ranting about Brits, Americans, and their apparent obsession with health and safety.

Sam was staring out of the window in terror. "So who will I be flying with?" he asked.

Ali gestured toward the well-built man sitting in the passenger seat at the front of the bus, who was hanging out of the window with his video camera and, inevitably, smoking a cigarette. "You're with me. Kayla will be flying with Erkut, he will keep her safe," Ali explained, winking at Kayla before taking a gigantic slurp out of the hip flask swaying steadily in his right hand. Erkut peeled open one eye and, by means of confirmation, allowed one corner of his mouth to curl upward in a semismile. He sniffed and readjusted himself in his seat, zipping his fleece all the way up to his chin and tucking his hands into the deep front pockets before closing his eyes once again.

Kayla couldn't figure out whether she desperately wanted to arrive at the summit to escape the smoky and dingy atmosphere inside the bus, or whether she never wanted to move again. *It's quite frankly incredible that after everything that's happened over the past couple of months, I'm still capable of such crippling fear.* Sam appeared frozen to his seat, his fingers tightly gripping the sides, and the air felt thick and furry around them. *Give me Mek the Bengal tiger over this, any day of the week.*

Too soon, the ancient brakes screeched abruptly to a halt. They had reached the top.

Even though they hadn't passed a single car or bus on the way up, the large paved area was full of people. It followed the natural shape of the mountain peak, with very little flat surface and plenty of slopes to run off. All over the widest point, paragliders were sprawled on the ground surrounded by their rucksacks and parachutes, absorbing the incredible views before they flew down to the ground like exotic birds. Some had brought picnics, others hip flasks, and everyone looked relaxed and happy. Kayla overheard one couple talk about the various locations they'd visited for this very reason.

"If it was that traumatic they wouldn't do it twice, right? Just like childbirth. If it was that horrific, nobody would have more than one kid," Kayla whispered. "I mean, Ali does this every day."

"Yes. But Ali is bloody mental." Sam shivered. It was extraordinarily cold, considering they were wearing shorts and T-shirts. Not the kind of numbing cold that stings the skin like a whip burn, but rather the shiver-inducing temperature usually present toward the end of British autumn. The regulars stared at the newcomers with a certain level of bemusement from behind the comfort of their windbreakers, hiking trousers and fleece jackets. Luckily, Sam and Kayla were soon provided with canvas flight suits to protect them from the mountain chill.

From twenty feet away Ali's notorious guffaw ripped through the air. Kayla and Sam walked hand in hand back to the minibus, the supposedly safe place in which their easily torn parachutes were slung carelessly over the back of the moldy chairs, and stared in disbelief.

A mountain goat had broken in and perched right on the seat that held the equipment. Its huge brown eyes gazed dopily back at them, seemingly amused by their utter bewilderment. Ali was clutching his sides, doubled over with laughter, as Erkut tried to shoo the docile creature away before it could do any serious damage to the gear. It hopped out of the bus obligingly and trotted away back down the dirt track. Kayla began to wonder whether she was hallucinating. *Am I really about to run off a cliff strapped to a total stranger? Did a mountain goat really just break into our bus? Will my mother murder me for running off said cliff without insurance? Probably.*

And then the wind changed, and all hell broke loose. Apparently, the relaxed people hadn't been chilling out at all—they'd been waiting for the gusts of air to switch to the right direction for their flight path. Clusters of pilots began gathering their belongings and loading up their backpacks in a bid to beat the rush, and the smiles and chitchat made way for looks of intense concentration and focus. Some held up flags in order to analyze the exact wind direction, while others ensured that all of the appropriate straps of their parachutes were securely fastened.

From behind her, Kayla heard the stomping of heavy boots picking up speed, and turned around just in time to see a flier take off. The wind caught in the fabric of his bright green parachute, lifting the black boots clean off the rubble they'd been running over. Instead of leaving the mountain face and starting to descend immediately, the lime green mass rose in the air and glided away toward the coast. For a moment nobody spoke. It was like staring into a log fire and becoming utterly entranced by the movement of the flames. They couldn't tear their eyes away.

The silence didn't last. The aggressive Turkish commands rang in Kayla's ears as two pairs of hands grabbed her by the waist and hoisted her into the suit with the speed and precision of a Formula One pit stop. They then began strapping her to a fluorescent orange parachute that had last been seen beneath a goat's backside.

"Okay. You'll go now. Start here, please."

"Wait, I thought Sam was going first?"

The instructor attached himself to the back of Kayla's suit and gripped the ropes with both hands.

"There was a problem with Sam's chute, you go now."

"A problem? With his *chute?*"

"Go!"

"Now?"

"Now!"

"But wait, what do I do? Help! Oh my God! Wait!"

"Start running and don't stop. If you stop, if you sit down, you will die. DON'T STOP."

"But my shoelace is untied and my sunglasses are steamed up. I can't see! What if I trip?"

"You will die. GO!"

So Kayla started running, because she knew if she didn't shut down her thoughts and go, she never would. The last thing she saw before her three-sizes-too-big trainers began to pound the rubble was Sam, suffering from what appeared to be a violent panic attack.

And then she was flying.

About the Author

LAURA SALTERS IS a twenty-something magazine journalist from the northernmost town in England. *Run Away* is her first novel.

www.laurasalters.com

Discover great authors, exclusive offers, and more at hc.com.